# Death of a Psycho

# by

# Alexandria May Ausman

Book cover illustration by Alexandria May Ausman
Editor: Jon M. Ausman

Library of Congress Control Number: 2025919868

ISBN: 978-1-963335-55-2 (ebook)
ISBN: 978-1-963335-54-5 (paperback)


Published By:
Ausman & Cousins LLC
1700 North Monroe Street
Suite 11, Box 284
Tallahassee, Florida 32303-0501

For author interviews: ausman@embarqmail.com

# Das Kaiser Haus Series

The Rise of the Priceless (Chapters 1 to 10)
Metal Illness (Chapters 11 to 19)
Jonas the Vampire (Chapters 20 to 29)
Prince of the Elders (Chapters 30 to 40)
Leo's Lamb (Chapters 41 to 50)
Mastermind Malfred (Chapters 51 to 58)
Priceless Lost (Chapters 59 to 67)
Broken Silver (Chapters 68 to 74)

# The Collar King Series

Return to Das Kaiser Haus (Chapters 1 to 7)
Felicity's Child (Chapters 8 to 14)
Tears of the Violin (Chapters 15 to 22)
The Golden Collar (Chapters 23 to 30)
Rise of the Mortar King (Chapters 31 to 38)
Prisoner of the Stone Palace (Chapters 39 to 46)
Mortar Transformation (Chapters 47 to 54)
Taube Returns (Chapters 55 to 62)
Chocolate Dreams (Chapters 63 to 70)
Pocket Soup (Chapters 71 to 78)
Lucus's Revenge (Chapters 79 to 86)
Night of the Stasi (Chapter 87 to 94)
Revenge of the Mortar King (Chapter 95 to 102)

# The Most Brutal Man in Europe Series

Claus's Revelations (Chapters 1 to 8)
Priceless Changes (Chapters 9 to 17)
Silver Well (Chapters 18 to 25)
Book Four (Coming soon)

# The Psycho Series

Cemetery Kid Redux (Chapters 1 to 20)
Stop Calling Me Psycho (Chapters 21 to 33)
Motor-Psycho (Chapters 34 to 44)
Delusion of the Collar and the Key (Chapters 45 to 53)
Brutality's Prisoner (Chapters 54 to 64)
Aesthetic Akathisia (Chapters 65 to 74)
Metallic Burden (Chapters 75 to 83)

# 27 Masters Series

Anita the Benevolent (Chapters 1 to 7)
The Beast and the Witch (Chapters 8 to 16)
High Priestess of Schizophrenia (Chapters 17 to 24)
The Professional Dominatrix (Chapters 25 to 33)
Triangle of Trust (Chapters 34 to 41)

# Stand Alone Books

The Grannybat's Weird Tales & Gothic Stories Volume 1

# Book Ten Characters: Death of a Psycho

Baker, Doctor:  a clinical psychiatrist
Barbara:  a former Master
Bastard:  a shard of Boyd
Billy Strong:  a pothead
Boyd:  a deputy sheriff, a secret Master
Calvin;  Boyd's biological father
Candy:  Dot's mother
Carla:  spouse of Dennis
Cathy:  a deputy sheriff, dispatcher
Charlie:  a law officer in next county over
Cheryl Rutgers:  a county manager of DCFS
Christian Axel:  secret husband of Psycho/Rachel, trainer and original Master
Circe:  a previous Master
Coussins, Doctor:  a veterinarian
Debbie:  Psycho's psychopathic and sadistic mother
Delleh:  Queen of the Green Rings, deceased
Dennis:  the county sheriff
Dirk:  a drug addict child kidnapper
Dot:  a three-year old raped child
Dude:  a command hallucination, an aggressive anger shard of Psycho
Fax:  a shard of Psycho
Gothic Barbie:  a vengeful, sexually sadist Dominant shard
Gray, Missus:  a DCFS caseworker
Hannah:  a shard of Psycho

Harold:  a DCFS supervisor
Hawks, Doctor:  a Wells Regional hospital doctor
Health:  a court bailiff
Holcomb, Doctor:  a Ph.D. in Sociology
Jane:  DCFS employee under Sheryl
Jennie:  Dirk's drug addict girlfriend
Jim:  a Vocational Rehabilitation Counselor
John:  a law officer
Jon Ausman:  the current Keyholder
Judy:  a nurse
Julia:  a friend of Sheryl and ex-foster mother
Karrie:  a kidnapped child
Katheryn:  a local attorney, a former Master
Kayla:  Doctor Holcomb's receptionist
Keith:  a deputy sheriff, a jailer
Kenny:  a child rapist, Dot's father
Linda:  a deputy sheriff
Looper:  a disembodied voice, Psycho's narrative hallucination
Maggie:  Dot's grandmother
Marcy:  a DCFS secretary
Mary:  a Maiden who takes care of Psycho's children
Matthew:  a deceased submissive
McKenzie:  a mental health patient
Morgan:  an abused and raped small child
Nelly:  Boyd's biological mother
Niemand:  Master Boyd's new name for Psycho
Nora:  a DHS employee
Patty Strong:  a pothead

Paula:  a county DCFS employee
PC:  a shard of Psycho
Psycho:  a schizophrenic trying to survive
Psycho Tron:  a shard of Psycho
Rachel:  Psycho's birth name, Simon is Rachel
Randell:  a deputy sheriff, a bull
Randy:  a state employee rapist at the Snake Pit
Ronnie:  Maiden Mary's live in partner
Rufus:  a state prison inmate
Samuel:  a psychopathic teenager
Scruffy:  the original fire dog
Seine:  a fire dog
Sheila:  a Secretary at DCFS
Sheryl:  a DCFS manager, the 17th Master
Simon Brag:  a command hallucination shard of Psycho, her lost inner self
Stephanie:  a nosy high school classmate
Stephen:  son of Patty Strong
Straight, Judge:  a judge
Susan:  Doctor Holcomb's scheduler
The Chose One:  a shard of Psycho
Timmy:  Psycho's spouse
Tom Turnbol:  a therapeutic foster parent
Upchurch:  foster parents

# Preface

Our wild ride came to a crashing end. We were sure all was as lost as Master Boyd's black car. To our surprise, this would mark the beginning of something most unexpected and the end of something that had always brought us comfort.

Our world was evolving rapidly filled with both promise and hope for a better life. We were burying our past and attempting to fulfill our childish desires for the future. It had been a long hard road to redemption. We were ready to receive our reward for all that suffering.

Then came Master Boyd.

'They' had gotten the demented Dominant/submissive pair. Separated and scared, the two would dream only of their delusional home in the woods. The Dominant is taken prisoner while the submissive slips through the cracks of the system. Luckily, the collar is always loyal. In an act of equal service for equal service a kindness will be repaid.

Sheryl has been suffering without her prized investigator. She has chemo in her unit and power on her brain. It is time for the holidays to end. The vicious Interim Master has decided to fight for her collar. She didn't toss it. It was stolen from her. The Interim will come calling for what she thinks is hers while the Dominant Master is being subdued by 'they.' His submissive was unable to recognize the threat. The shattered will start to crumble.

Ah, do you hear that? It is the thunder from a spring storm. Don't be afraid. It is of course going to destroy the realm we created, but that is okay. Our delusions of being normal could never hold anyway. It was never real. So, if you all want to get back on this trip to nowhere, then grab that shitty Medicare card and the handcuff skeleton key off your nightstand. Oh, don't forget the electrical tape. We are really going to need that very soon. Ready, steady, run, run, run.

## Chapter 74: Take These Shackles Off My Heart
## The Fall of Psycho & Rise of Neimand
## Master Boyd

*"I think you are overreacting Niemand. Your worry is not that uncommon. A lot of people fear they are going nuts, but they rarely are. It is very simple, if you are still working then your symptoms can't be that bad. Look make an appointment with Susan. I think I am booked for the next three months. Take a day or two off. You are just stressed is all, but fearing you have schizophrenia? Nah, you couldn't have that. There is no way you could have worked this long if you did. Whoever told you that is the one who needs reality testing."*
**--Doctor Holcomb to Niemand when she attempted to get help for increasing severity of psychotic symptoms, April 1999.**

I opened my eyes. The glare of the light made my head hurt. My mouth was so dry and it felt as if someone filled it with cotton. I moaned and tried to sit up. My unit was held down. Shit, I was restrained to the bed.

I looked around as my sight adjusted. A heart monitor made a steady beeping noise. A bag of fluids hung above my head. The white door was closed. Ah, the hospital, I am in the hospital. I listened and heard nurse's shoes squeaking on the scrubbed smooth hallway floors outside my room.

Closing my eyes tightly, I tried to focus. I needed to recall how I had ended up in the hospital this time. Nothing was coming to mind. Something had to have happened. Did I get into an accident? Was it another catatonic fit? Had I tried to commit suicide? I sighed when all I could get was the sound of my whirling cogs slipping. I couldn't remember anything.

"Ah, you are awake. How are you feeling?" I opened my eyes startled by the voice.

I groaned out realizing I must have fallen asleep. Damn, was I tired for some reason. I looked at the person speaking to me. A young woman with short brown hair wearing blue scrubs was smiling at me kindly.

"Where the fuck am I and why am I here," I rasped out.

The nurse frowned. "You don't remember?"

I glared at her. "If I fucking did would I be asking you? Christ why doesn't anyone just answer my God damned questions when I ask them? Do you people get off on psychological torture or what? Where is the fucking doctor? I want to speak to my lawyer. And for the record, I didn't do whatever the fuck you think I did. Now where the fuck am I and why am I here," I yelled out angrily trying to push on my restraints.

The nurses face fell. "Oh my, uhm, okay, I am not at liberty to speak about this with you Ma'am. I think you should ask your doctor these questions. Uhm, okay I need to take your vitals and I will see if I can get him to come speak to you." She started to come at me with a thermometer.

I growled. "Keep your motherfucking paws off me bitch. Go get that prick who says he is my doctor. I will not put up with this shit. I know this drill. You say you will get the asshole then next week maybe someone will come by. This ain't my first rode, baby. So fuck you. You tell me why I am here or kiss my ass." I turned my head so she couldn't get the instrument into my mouth.

The nurse stood there sighing. "Look sweetie, I am just trying to do my job. If you give them trouble, they will sedate you again. Let me do my job and I promise I will get the doctor to come as soon as he gets a minute…" I interrupted her.

"Or I can get someone here pretty fucking quick. Help, someone help. The nurse is killing me Call the police. No, no please help me. Anyone, help." I started screaming, cussing, yelling, and struggling in my restraints.

The nurse ran from the room to get that asshole doctor. I knew exactly how to get attention from these fucktards. I was very seasoned at this game. If I had allowed her to fill me full of that poppycock it would be maybe the next day before anyone told me shit. Those doctors think they are Gods and they don't give two fucking shits if you are scared not knowing what is going on.

**NOTE:** *You see it is your unit, your life, and you are the client. You pay them, but they act like your boss. So, they withhold information about your situation until they stop gossiping or bullshitting with some asshole about their ingrown toenail. Maybe they will come later that day,*

5

*maybe not. That fucking nurse knew why I was there, and how I got there but she won't tell me because that would step on the Gods' toes. It would of course calm me down, but who cares about my terror? This is all about them. (Okay, uhm, do I rant much? Geez Niemand, take a fucking sedative, will you? Shit, prodromal much?) On with the story, I think? Sheesh, what the fuck was that about?*

Within only moments a middle-aged portly man with brown hair wearing a white coat came running into my room. He had the nurse with him who was carrying a syringe full of 'sleepy time' medication.

The second I saw him I smiled calming down immediately. "That won't be necessary Miss. I am fine. Now if you would be so kind as to tell me what is going on Doctor, there won't be any more trouble."

He looked at me in surprise. "Oh, you are coherent? Do you know your name? Where you are and what day it is?" He put out his hand gesturing the nurse to hold the shot for a moment.

I rolled my eyes. "Okay doctor, this is a trick. Of course, I don't know anything but my name. If I did, I would likely not be here. Last, I remember it was around Christmas but I would think some time has passed so it is January 1999. The date and day, well how long have you had me doped up? I assume I am in a hospital. I am thinking probably Wheatly Regional but that is just a guess. Now I showed you mine, let's see yours handsome." I smiled wickedly at the doctor.

He cleared his throat appearing a bit disturbed that I was indeed rational. "Uhm, well yes, it is January 9th, 1999. It is Saturday. You are at Wheatly Regional and I am Doctor Baum. You were brought here by ambulance in a severely psychotic state three days ago. We have been treating you for dehydration, contusions, concussion, infected wounds, pneumonia, exposure, and schizophrenia. You were one very sick lady. How are you feeling now?" He looked at my heart monitor results while spouting out my various bullshit problems without even looking back at me.

I snorted. "Oh, is that all that is wrong? Shit, that is my usual weekend doctor. So, can you let me out of these restraints so I can take a piss on my own like a big girl? I feel fine. I am not going to go murder half the staff with a machete and I don't want to die. In fact you could just sign those papers and send me on my happy way. Sorry to take up your weekend with my happy horseshit. Hey, honey, release the straps will you? My nose itches." I giggled while looking at the stunned nurse.

Doctor Baum looked into my eyes with his light. "Well, I am shocked at your rapid bounce back. However, I can't deny you do seem lucid and your numbers are looking better on the labs. That Thorazine is pretty potent stuff. If you keep on improving, we can have you out of here by tomorrow. I want you to talk to Doctor Baker first though. If he clears you, then we will be happy to release you. We can always use the vacant bed. We will leave the straps on till Doctor Baker says it is okay to let you out. I hope you understand it is hospital policy, but I imagine you'll be out shortly." He smiled while I smiled back knowingly.

He nodded to the nurse and the two started to head out the door. "Too bad your fiancé has not improved as fast. He is likely to be with us for a while. See you in the morning Missus Voss." They walked out leaving me stunned.

I laid there suddenly recalling Master Boyd. I could hear him wailing and yelling my name, the blood, the, oh shit, they. We were captured. I remembered all of it with suddenness that made me gasp. My Master was here at this hospital too. They were holding him prisoner tied to his bed somewhere close no doubt. He told me to bust him out, it was a directive.

I looked around the room for some cameras. Noticing this was a regular hospital room I began working the straps to escape my restraints. I had been held like this so many times in my violent psychotic history I had learned a thing or two about getting out of tight spots. In fact, I had become almost a regular Houdini.

It only took me about thirty minutes to work my right wrist out of the leather wrist bond. Quickly I released my left arm then my ankles. I needed to figure out how to get out of that bed without setting off the heart monitor. I got out of the bed and pulled the power plug killing the noise of the machines. Thank Goth. I hate those things.

I then ripped out the IV and used the bed blanket to stop the bleeding. I felt very dizzy but clear headed enough to realize I had to pee like a drunkard. I grabbed the bedpan and took care of business while I thought about how to bust my beloved Master from the hospital. I looked at the hospital gown. This would never do. I would need to get back to our house and get him clothing, and me too. I decided to go home first, then come back for him once I had everything we would need to get back to our hiding spot.

I peeked out the door and waited till the coast was clear. I walked right out of the patients wing without anyone saying a word. No one was looking for me to be causing trouble. After all, the loon was restrained in her room, right? I went to the waiting area in the front and bummed a dime from one of the awaiting family members of some poor patient. I used the pay phone and called the only cab company in that shitty town.

Within less than twenty minutes I had blown that pop stand. The cab driver raised an eyebrow at my hospital gown but said nothing. I gave him the address, he took off rushing home to the A-frame house Master Boyd and I called home.

When I got to the house, I went inside and collected the cash to pay the cabbie. He rushed off while I ran inside to ditch the gown for more appropriate attire. I raided Master Boyd's closet packing up his clothing and extra boots sure that they had taken his clothing too. My mind was whirling wondering if they had discovered my escape yet. I worried I would be recognized. I looked at my disheveled appearance in the mirror.

The doctors had granted me the dignity of allowing me to keep my wig, but it was in bad shape. I took it off and got the black one Master Boyd had bought for me. I applied heavy make up to hide my bruised and cut up face but was careful not to appear too ghoulish. I didn't want to attract too much attention.

I smiled at the metamorphosis from sickly psychotic to 'normal' as I applied my red lipstick. No one would be wise that this was the same Psycho who had evaded them only one hour before. I grabbed the bag of clothing and car keys then headed out back toward the hospital in the Taurus.

I giggled uncontrollably realizing if I hurried, me and Master Boyd could be back at the tent before dinner time. Wait, did I put that turkey back into the fridge?

I was deep in my disorganized thoughts about that fucking turkey when I almost missed the turn into the hospital parking lot. I slammed on the brakes almost spinning sideways as I wildly pulled in the drive. Some of the pedestrians looked up at me curiously, wondering if perhaps I was carrying an expectant mother or bleeding child. I could hear them thinking that through the radio waves.

I parked and grabbed the bag trying to remind myself not to appear anxious. They would sense my fear and panic. I took deep breaths while I walked slowly into the hospital trying to appear as if I were just there for a visit.

I went to the information desk and asked what room Boyd Simmons was being held hostage, errr, recovering in. The lady looked at me strangely and said he was on the third floor.

I smiled. "Okay, but what room?"

"He is not permitted visitors Miss. I am sorry. You can speak to his family if you want to know more about his condition. We are not allowed to discuss patients with non-family members." The secretary said seeming just a tad irritable that I had bothered her.

I nodded. "Oh okay. I apologize Ma'am. I didn't know. Thank you for the help." I smiled to myself as I walked off headed for the elevator.

I had been on the third floor many times. There were only three beds there. Finding my Master was going to be a breeze. Getting past the nurse's station a no brainer. This hospital was simply not equipped to deal with one of our kind. They only wanted the wealthy worried well. Their psych wing was a joke without any kind of security. The doctor's idea of keeping a schizophrenic from harming themselves or others was not even as significant as the white cell. Master Boyd would likely be in a regular room. I had no doubt they had tied him to his bed. He would be sleeping off the heavy sedatives they used to keep us quiet up there, so we don't disturb the 'real' patients of that place.

The doors opened. I stepped out onto the third floor shuddering. I did hate the smell of that place. Alcohol and gauze with a hint of bleach, barf. I looked down the hall and as predicted, no one was around to stop me. I walked back to the area where the three rooms were located. To my thrill I found Master Boyd in the very first one I investigated.

I stood at the door shocked into silence. His forehead was swollen and stitched like a Frankenstein monster. His beard was gone but it had been hiding numerous cuts, bruises and very sunken cheeks from starvation. His wrists and hands were wrapped in bandages from his many injuries, not unlike my own. His purple blackened eyelids were closed, and his breathing was that of a deep sleep.

They had strapped him to the gurney and restrained him with the cuffs. He had apparently been giving them quite a fight to double bind him like that. I smiled with satisfaction that my Master was no pussy. He made them work for it. Good for him.

I closed the door behind me and approached my unconscious lover. I bent down kissing his mouth deeply. His eyes opened slowly. He looked at me appearing unable to recognize me at first. I kissed him again and he began to kiss back as his memory of our love flooded back to him.

"Niemand, I thought I would never see you again. Is this real," he rasped out then coughed with a dreamy look in his eyes.

I smiled while gazing at him. "Yes Master, it is real. I have come to take you out of here. I brought your clothes. Let me undo your straps, hold on." I began the process of releasing him from bondage hell.

He sat up rubbing his wrists almost falling back from the dizziness. "Whoa, the room is spinning. What the fuck?" He reached up and rubbed his eyes wincing.

I shrugged. "The sedatives, the medication poison, the head injury, could be anything causing that Master. Please hurry. They will be looking for me and could come check on you. We need to get out of here."

Master Boyd nodded. "Yeah, okay. I am going to need help. I am so weak. What have they done to me?" he coughed again.

I grabbed his shirt from the bag while he tried to get his gown off forgetting the IV in his arm. He was fighting the lead unable to understand the problem. I reached over and ripped the needle out then told him to use his gown to apply pressure till it stopped bleeding. He nodded then did as I told him while I started putting on his pants, socks and boots. When I had finished, I looked up to see my Master had fallen asleep while sitting up.

I rousted him then aided him in putting on his shirt while he laid his chin on my shoulder barely able to keep his consciousness for more than a few moments at a time. They had doped him to the gills.

"Can you walk Master," I asked him while his head bobbed and rocked in a trace.

He nodded. "Yeah, but I think you have to drive. I am not feeling well. Did we get back from California in time?"

I giggled. "Yes, now we are going back to live there forever. I never liked this stupid town anyway." I helped him stand up.

He looked around wildly.. "Dennis was here He said we were sick Niemand. Were we sick?"

13

"No. He is lying. Let's go." I helped my Master start walking to the door when it opened, and Dennis walked in with Carla.

Dennis's eyes went wide while Carla grabbed her chest in shock. "Carla honey, go get the nurse. I got this. Go now," he said while pushing her back out of the room.

I glared at Dennis. "Move out of our way now. I am not kidding. I really don't want to hurt you but if you make me I will Dennis," I growled out angrily.

Carla took off down the hall as Dennis stood there blocking the door. "Niemand, Boyd is very sick. He needs help. Let the doctors help him. If you love him, you will leave him here until he is better. Then you two can go home and it will be like it was before," he said softly but refusing to move from my escape route.

Master Boyd looked at Dennis glassy eyed. "Get out of our way Dennis. You plan to take her from me. I know what is going on. I want to be with Niemand. Leave us alone. We are going to California where you and everyone else won't be bothered with us anymore," he slurred slightly from his heavy sedative tongue.

Dennis shook his head. "No, no Boyd. I am not going to say another word about you and Niemand. You two can get married, live together, whatever you want, but only if you get back in bed and let the doctors make you well. Do we have a deal?"

14

Master Boyd looked at me then back at Dennis. "And if I say no?"

Dennis hitched up his pants. "Then I will make sure to send Niemand to the Snake Pit and you too when you are well enough to be moved. Or you can lay back down and let the doctors do their job, you stay here till you are well, then you go home and be with your fiancé. That is my offer. Take it or leave it. Boyd, don't piss with me on this."

Master Boyd groaned. "How long are they keeping me here?"

Dennis growled. "Forever if you don't get back into that God damned bed Boyd. Niemand, put him back. Stop acting a fool."

My Master looked at me with sadness. "Okay Dennis, I will stay if you promise to leave us alone the minute they let me out." I looked at him shaking my head terrified I would have to leave him there for the monsters to fuck up his mind.

Dennis smiled. "That is a promise Boyd. No more interference with the two of you love birds. Now back to bed before you fall down and break something else, damn it."

Master Boyd moaned. "Okay baby, help me back to bed. We will take Dennis's deal."

I shook my head wildly. "He lies, no. He lies." I tried to pull him forward.

He looked at me fiercely. "Put me back to bed now. You know better. Do what Dennis says and don't test me." I could see that he wanted to say and that is a directive. But luckily he stayed his urge.

I shuddered. "Whatever you want. I will mind what you say but please hurry home." I helped him back to the bed and kissed him while he stroked my cheek lovingly.

"Don't worry Niemand. I will be home soon. You can come and visit until then. She can come see me, right?" He looked at Dennis.

Dennis nodded. "As soon as you are stable Boyd. Now, Niemand, let the nurses come back in here and get him set up on his medicine again please. Come with me and let them do their job." He motioned for me to follow him out of the room.

I kissed my Master once more while we said we loved each other then followed Dennis out into the hallway. Two strong looking nurses rushed into the room causing me to narrow my eyes suspiciously. They were going to restrain him again. That pissed me off, but my Master told me to let it go. I had to obey him.

Carla stood down at the nurse's station while Dennis asked me to follow him down to talk outside where no one would hear our conversation. Like a stupid fool I assumed he wanted to tell me when I could see my Master.

Instead, the second he and I were out of the hospital doors, I was greeted by my old buddy Linda. Dennis and my Goddess worked together planting my face in the pavement, then cuffed and stuffed me into the waiting squad car. I sat in the back of the rolling cage cursing Dennis while the two police officers hauled my loony ass to jail. I was to be treated an all-expense paid vacation in the white cell for trying to break my Master out of the hospital. Who knew that was a crime?

Turned out they were not charging me with anything. Dennis just wanted to make sure I was where he could keep an eye on his ward's very disturbed fiancé. My little stunt had caused him alarm that I may impede the doctor's attempts to bring Master Boyd back from his trip to Mars. (Oh ye of little faith, Dennis). The white cell was the one place he could be sure I would not escape to cause any further troubles.

**NOTE:** *Now, many of you are likely saying to yourself, wait, Niemand is also seriously psychotic. So, why is she not in a bed on the third floor too? Ah, well you see, my Guardian (you know the one who makes sure I am treated fairly by unscrupulous, uncaring physicians and psychiatric staff) was not available to fight to get me any kind of aid for my own very serious problems (more serious, in fact but no one realized it yet). Without anyone to give a shit and crappy insurance (Medicare is useless by the way) the doctors were in a huge hurry to clear my insurance poor ass the fuck out of their bed.*

*Dennis was aware I was significantly psychotic. The reason he didn't step in is he feared Master Boyd's wrath if he had me assessed and sent to the only place that would take a hard case like me, the Snake Pit.*

*The Wheatly hospital only had three beds. With Master Boyd in one and the other two occupied, well I was just shit out of luck. It didn't matter that I was one sick motherfucker. Sicker than Master Boyd to be honest about it.*

*As usual, I slipped right through the cracks, or should I say continued to crack, while those with lesser issues took up the other two psych ward beds (an anxiety disorder and a neurotic known in the psychiatric world as the worried well were the other patients on the third floor).*

*They allowed a dangerous psychotic to run free. The doctors assumed because of my frail size and female status I couldn't do much harm. In error, they only subdued the biggest and scariest of the two they had to treat. I mean me grabbing a weapon to equalize me against normals could never be a possibility, right?*

*Oh well, it sucks to be me, and them. This mistake would come around to bite everyone in the ass in time. For now, I was locked in the white cell to keep me separated from Master Boyd just as he told me they would do. Maybe he wasn't as delusional as you all thought he was.*

I fumed and kicked as Dennis and my Goddess hauled my loony ass to the padded jail room. They promptly restrained me to the cot using straps that even I couldn't escape. I was told if I didn't settle down, they would call in for a sedative to calm my crazy shit down. Like it or not, I was to be their guest for a few days. I demanded to speak to my lawyer. Dennis chuckled while he told me they were taking an emergency twenty-four-hour hold. A lawyer would do me no good. He then sat down in a chair next to me and took out one of the missing bottles of medication I thought they had stolen. Dennis pulled out the proper amount then told me to open my mouth and take them or I could be assured of a trip the Pit the second he could get me loaded into the back of the squad car.

I did as I was told but glared at him hatefully while he gave me water to wash the nasty shit down. He smiled then leaned back in his chair.

"Niemand, Boyd certainly does love you an awful lot. It is both beautiful and scary to see that boy come out of his shell like he has with you at his side. I should have been paying more attention when the two of you said the medication wasn't working. I assumed he was getting so bad because of your distracting him. Now, it is clear he was the one sick, and you, well you are just being your usual self. The doctor said it was just his time. That disease the two of you have is one hellish thing. I have watched you suffer with it since you were just a youngster, and Boyd too. I admit I am not always aware of what kind of a nightmare it must be to be touched, but it seems to cause you both a great deal of pain. That said, I do love Boyd as my own and only want the best for him. For whatever reason he got smitten with you the very first time he laid eyes on you. I am sure he has told you that. I am verifying it is case he has done nothing but pine over you for years with old cupid making a hit square in his heart." Dennis rubbed his moustache looking at me with what seemed to be pity.

"Is there a point to this Dennis? I know Boyd loves me and I love him. Are we done here? This script is running long." I growled out trying to test my restraints by flexing my arms and legs.

Dennis sighed. "Well, what I am trying to tell you Niemand, is that Boyd is sicker than he led you to believe. He has obsessions you know. You are one of them."

I rolled my eyes. "Yeah Dennis, he is schizophrenic. The nut balls always have obsessions. Get to the fucking point will you and release me from this God damned bed. I am not going to cause any more trouble. Shit, if you wanted to hang out, we could have done this friendly like, you know. No need for you to pull out all the stops for little old me."

He nodded. "Oh, I think it was necessary. I need you to listen and you tend to be hardheaded. I also don't know how you are going to take what I am about to say. I am being cautious. I mean I did just have to chase the two of you for two weeks around hell and back. Boyd's car is at the junk yard and the buzzards are eating well out of the ditch in front of his house thanks to that insanity the two of you just pulled. I am not taking either of you lightly ever again," he said matter of factly.

I snorted. "Fair enough. Say what you need to say, then leave me in peace. I have had enough company for today. I just got back from California. I still feel a bit of lag from the trip. I could use a nap."

Dennis chuckled. "No one can talk shit like you can Psycho, errr, Niemand. Anyway, I need to ask you to do me a favor for Boyd's sake."

I looked at him wide eyed feeling fear grip me. "I am not going to stop seeing him Dennis. Forget it if that is what you are wanting as a favor. I really do love Boyd. Get used to it."

Dennis crossed his arms nodding his head. "I am a lot of things, but I am not a damned fool. I would not bother to waste my time trying to talk sense into either of you. You and Boyd have a lot of brains, but sense, well that is one line you both seemed to miss when God handed out abilities. No, what I want is for you to stay married to the Voss boy."

I gasped in shock. "Huh? Wait, you told me to divorce him. Did I hear you right? You want me to stay married? What? Why?" I narrowed my eyes at him suspiciously.

The old bull took a deep breath. "Likely Boyd told you Carla and I are his legal guardians. Now you can see he needs that kind of thing just like you do. Well, if he marries you Niemand, then you are his guardian and he is yours. God help us all if either of you had to be responsible for the other one. The two of you couldn't even find God damned food when you're off your medication. Your both plumb near starved to toothpicks and got fucking pneumonia to boot. You can't take care of yourself. That is why you wear that collar thing, right? How the fuck you going to take care of Boyd? Do you really think you can do what is best for him?"

I looked at the ceiling feeling I may cry over the truth he was speaking. "No, you are right Dennis. That is why I wear a collar. I need help because I am a loser." Tears did well into my eyes as I realized Master Boyd was my guardian and he shouldn't be, or my Master either.

Dennis saw my rain clouds forming. "Look sweetheart, I am not trying to hurt you or Boyd. I mean it when I say I love you both. I didn't mean to upset him or you by trying to get you to understand you can't be married. You can't be a pair. You are both too sick for it. You will eventually hurt each other with symptoms you can't control. You'll never know how much it pains me to see Boyd and you unfit to have anyone to call your very own. It must be very lonely. It kills me to watch it but I told you I am not a fool. It is not only likely to stay that way, but also the only way the two of you will survive long. There is never going to be a cure, and if there was it would be too late for either of you now anyway." He sighed.

I looked at Dennis as I now began to cry. "That is not true Dennis. We can love so that means someone could love us back, not to judge us but to accept us as we are. It is possible. You are wrong. I won't say you are wrong about Boyd and I being wrong for each other. What you are saying sounds about right. But we are going to try. If that doesn't work, a normal could love us. They could. They could cure the fucking thing, they might," I said with a lot of hurt in my voice.

He shook his head then looked at me hard. "If either of you think someone without your sickness is going to just overlook the schizophrenia and love you no matter what the disease makes either of you do, well you are in for a world of hurt missy. You should already suspect it more than that pigheaded boy of mine. So, I am asking you; don't divorce the Voss boy. Boyd can't fuck up his life if he can't marry you because you are already married. You cannot be his Guardian. Ain't no other girl in this town going to be stupid enough to marry a schizophrenic either. Without a wife to take control, Boyd will stay under my and Carla's protection for the rest of our lives. After that, well if he lives that long hopefully he will be too old to cause much hurt for anyone with that nasty temper of his and that fucked up mind to add to the troubles."

I closed my eyes. "And what if I refuse to listen to your request for a favor Dennis? What will you do then? I could divorce Timmy tomorrow if I wanted to. I could marry Boyd and prove you are all wrong about us. Why should I listen to you? If you had it your way, Boyd and I would be denied everything in life. Haven't we given up enough already? Tell me Dennis, how many times have you been tied to a bed? Been locked in a cell for months, even years when you didn't commit a crime? Had a needle stuck in your ass? Been shocked till you have so many seizures you can't remember your own fucking name? Been ignored when you beg for help because someone is hurting you, but no one believes you because you don't matter? Been alone because no one wants to deal with the pain you feel, not them." I moaned out feeling great despair.

## DENNIS TELLS THE STORY
## OF HIS RELATIONSHIP TO MASTER BOYD

Dennis teared up a bit as he started his story. "Yeah sweetheart, I hear you. I have always heard you, and now that you know about Boyd you can finally know I was always telling you the truth. I can't pretend to know what it is like to be you or him. I can tell you it does hurt the ones around you who do stand strong to care. No one hears us either Niemand. Do you think it is easy for Carla and me?

Did he tell you that I have known him since he was born? Did he tell you Carla was his babysitter when he was just a little tadpole? I bet you didn't know he and I used to go hunting together when he was just a young kid before the sickness took him from us. Boyd was someone else before he got sick Niemand.

He was outgoing, popular, loved to play sports and was damned good at basketball. Ah, the girls loved old Boyd, but he was a gentleman and kept his eyes on his books. He told me there was plenty of time to worry about courting for a wife. He wanted to go to college and get his doctorate first. You see he wanted to be a professor in mathematics one day. Boyd would work on equations for hours. The boy has always loved his numbers.

Then when puberty came, he changed into someone none of us recognized anymore. He took to keeping to himself. He shut us all out, got secretive, quiet and temperamental. His momma took him to the doctors, but no one could figure it out. Till God started talking to him.

I was just a young bull myself when the call came in that Boyd was walking down the middle of the road into traffic.

I caught him and took him to the State Mental Hospital myself. The boy was rambling, out of his mind. He didn't even recognize me. He was trying to kill himself by running into traffic. God told him he was a sinner and death was his only way out of hell.

Only you can understand the heartbreak it caused me and Carla when the doctors told us he was schizophrenic. It was then that his momma turned her back on him for good, not that she was ever there for him in the first place.

Nelly, his mother, God rest her, was angry because the doctors had told her she had this disease, but she didn't believe it. His mother would go around preaching to everyone that doctors were devils in disguise, and she refused to take medication to calm her psychotic shit down a bit. No one could stand that nasty woman. Hell, everyone felt sorry for her husband and for Boyd. That woman was a shrew if I ever met one.

Now, his father, Calvin, God rest him, was a nice fellow. He was the quiet, calm, easygoing sort. Boyd took after him. Boyd even got Calvin's blue eyes. Old Calvin was everybody's friend. From what I knew of Nelly, I can tell you the man was a saint. Only someone with one fine heart could have tolerated that woman. You know, I see his daddy in Boyd more and more each year that passes, but then I also see that demonic momma in him too. Especially when he cycles.

Boyd had always clung to me and Carla because of Nelly's nasty and bitter attitude toward him. She was so religious, and not that loving God is a bad thing mind you, that everything was a sin. Poor old Boyd would hide at our house to avoid her constant nagging that he was offending God with every move he made. I admit we probably took to him so easily because Carla never could give me but one child. She really wanted to give me a son. In Boyd we found the compromise. He needed us, and we sure were happy to have him too.

Boyd had only just been diagnosed with his sickness when he got the googly eyes for that hill girl. Carla and I didn't even know a thing about it. He was so withdrawn by then, we barely saw him at all. He took to hiding out in the woods, talking to God and Bastard. It was then we started to notice his obsession with numbers and making lists that were full of nonsense. Then that girl he was chasing after, she took her life. Boyd came apart again and tried to join her on the other side. We had to take him back to the Snake Pit. They did everything possible to fix his broken heart, but when they sent him home he wasn't any better. His behavior was out of control. Town folk saw him mumbling and talking to no one. They started to view him as a loony.

So, it was damned easy for the State police to pin that rape on the poor insane kid. He was so sick he didn't know if he was coming or going. They even convinced him and his mother he did the crime. Carla and I testified he could not have done it because he was with us when they said it happened, but with Boyd flipped out and Nelly claiming she knew he did it, well the rest is history. Boyd did time for another man's crime. When he got out, I helped him get a job at the department to offer him a future despite all his setbacks. Otherwise, he was sure to be lost, maybe out there living in Darlin with you kiddo.

Anyway, it was not what Boyd had wanted out of life. He was devastated by the loss of all his dreams. Life in the Boy's Home had been harsh for him. The Boyd that came out of that kid's prison was even more mixed up then the one they put in there. Carla and I took him in to help him readjust to life outside a little cell. Randell took the day shift and I took the night so that I could keep Boyd close to me and make sure he got as good a start as possible.

After only one week of being out, I noticed Boyd was acting strangely. I discovered a letter of apology he had written to the hill girl. In them, he was discussing ending his life. I went to Nelly and Calvin asking them to intervein and do something before Boyd ended up committing suicide. Neither of them took me seriously.

Then the very next day after I spoke to his parents, we got called out to a runaway from the schoolhouse. He and I went out on the call and found a pretty little blue-eyed teenaged girl trapped in a barbed wire fence.

As it happened, the girl was reported to have schizophrenia, like Boyd does. From that moment on, Boyd suddenly had purpose again. I saw the boy begin to come back from the dead almost immediately. He studied hard to become a great cop, and when his parents were killed, God rest their souls, he moved back into their house living independently, and until last month, he had only been showing mild signs of his illness.

Everyone knew Boyd was sweet on you from the moment he saw you that day. Carla and I never expected he'd be stupid enough to try to make a go of it. I had warned him for years to keep his distance. I always made sure to keep you two as far away from each other as possible. I knew if you two ever started to see each other, well what happened would happen. Now you lay here listening to the gossip from an old bull cop, while my officer lays in a bed strapped down, full of dope with his head half bashed in. Niemand, what do you do to my officers?" He sighed while staring at me in confusion.

I chuckled bitterly. "The same thing Boyd did to Carla and you, Dennis. Endure my nightmare so another's dreams can come true. After all Dennis, we are schizophrenics, fantasy is our forte."

He nodded suddenly realizing there was validity to my statement.

"I will stay married to Timmy and never marry Boyd, but only with conditions Dennis. Nothing is free in this world, my friend. If I am to give up the only possible empathetic marriage I could ever have and condemn my lover to a lifetime of guardianship, I should get us both something in return for it." I said sniffing back my tears as I fiercely looked at the old bull.

Dennis rubbed his moustache. "I'm listening."

I nodded. "I want your promise on your mother's grave that you will never put Boyd in the Snake Pit again, or me either for that matter. I demand that you never say another word to Boyd about marrying me, breaking up with me, or otherwise interfering with this relationship until it either succeeds or fails, baring criminal behaviors. You know what I mean. I also want this to stay between us, never to be uttered even under the pain of torture. Lastly, I want you to grant me the right to see Boyd when he is inpatient without having to sneak in wearing disguises. Either promise me all that or take a hike and I will marry him the second he gets out of stir." I put my cards on the table.

Dennis sighed. "Deal and fair enough. I can tell you I don't expect you and Boyd to survive as a couple either. Or am I reading more into your words than I should be?"

I felt despair wash over me once more. "Dennis, I am no more a fool than you are old friend. I am aware of my disability. I read in Boyd's records that he was an independent functioning schizophrenic but one thing I do recall from Boyd's recent discussions with me is that somehow that is a misprint. You have just verified that he is like me in his disabled functioning by telling me you are indeed his legal guardian. That means Boyd and I have the same problem. We cannot care for ourselves without a normal around. With that in mind, we sure as shit can't care for each other. That means together we are doomed as a pair. But stranger things have happened in my life. So, I intend to give our life as lovers a chance. We will survive or fail like any normal couple does. Either way, Boyd can never say 'if only.' I am myself, tired of uttering those words Dennis. Boyd was willing to die for me the night you arrested us. He would have done it just to keep you and the others from sending me to the Pit where they hurt me. No one has ever loved me that much. So, I owe him this chance to be happy. If nothing else, he will never have to cry while saying 'if only.' As it is, I will do that almost every fucking night. I hope you can understand and forgive me for it."

Dennis smiled as he nodded. "You may be the craziest person I have ever met Niemand, but you may also be the wisest too. I have never seen anyone able to look so closely at anything and just call it what it is like you do. I have always been in awe of it, and you have always had my respect. Not many could take what you have and still lay there and say what you just did about Boyd, or anyone. You have my blessing sweetheart and my silence. This conversation never happened."

I chuckled. "Oh you know me Dennis. I hear voices all the time. You can never trust a fucking thing I hear, say, or see. They don't call me Psycho for nothing you know."

He frowned. "Around this station they had better not call you that ever again. Niemand is a beautiful name and perfect for such a beautiful soul. I will get Linda to come and let you out of the restraints if you promise to behave. However, you are staying with us until they let Boyd out. I am told they will keep him three more days. So, relax and enjoy your rest. See you on Sunday for supper." He grinned, hitched his pants then let Keith know he was ready to leave.

Linda checked with the Wheatly hospital to see if they would like to have their missing psychotic back. They were told, amazingly, that I was free to go. No reason to keep me any longer just check back with my psychiatrist when convenient because all was well. Huh?

She came into the white cell to let me go of my bonds just as Dennis promised me he would. My Goddess walked in looking sad. I smiled at her, but she said nothing as she loosened then unhitched my buckles.

"Okay Goddess, enough of the silent treatment. Are you angry about something," I said as I sat up rubbing my arms to get the circulation back.

She backed up looking at the floor appearing ashamed. "Well, not angry. I am embarrassed Mother. I didn't know Boyd had schizophrenia. I said those awful things to you about him. You had to sit there saying nothing. I can only imagine what you thought about what. I say that about you. I should never have said that about him. Oh Mother, I feel awful, just awful. I am just so sorry."

I shook my head chuckling. "Think nothing of it Goddess. I knew it was all salt and pepper. It is true Boyd and I are more alike than I would like to admit, but you didn't know. It is okay. I know you love me and I love you. I forgave you the moment you said it."

She looked up and smiled. "Oh thank the Goddess above. When Dennis told me the secret, Mother I almost died of shock. Boyd, well, no one ever cut him any slack you know? We all just assumed he was creepy or evil. He never spoke much and always was slinking around. Hell, I would too if I were afraid everyone would find out I was a fruit loop. Oh shit, I am doing it again. Linda open mouth and insert your foot here. Geez." She covered her mouth with her hand.

I laughed. "Oh it is okay. Boyd is a fruit loop." I winked at her.

She giggled. "Mother, I am not sure I could be so cool about it after all that has happened. Hey, I just have to know. You two were gone more than two weeks. We looked everywhere. Where the fuck did you go?"

I looked at the floor. "We went to California, Linda. Boyd was worried that Carla would be pissed he left the turkey out too long. We bolted in psychotic fright. He is delusional you know. Crazy bastard thought he was a truck driver or some shit. We would have been back sooner, but he kept falling asleep at every damned rest stop all the way back. The man drives like a maniac. We got lost because the nutjob ate the map."

Linda looked at me appearing startled. "California? Over a turkey? He ate the map? Wow, he was off his deck for sure. Well, I was there, Boyd was gone. Hell, I have only seen you that bad once or twice. He was really messed up. Nothing you tell me he did surprises me. Were you scared? I mean I would have been."

I shook my head. "Of Boyd? Never. He loves me too much to hurt me. I just went along with his bullshit. You know they say you should never get a crazy person upset by fucking with their delusions. It was just best I went with the program. The scrip ran a bit longer than it should and no doubt we got a virus from the affair but all in all it's nothing that a little rest and electrical tape can't fix." I smiled at her feeling sure that would indeed fix the issue.

Linda looked at me a bit confused. "Mother, sometimes you speak in riddles that much I know. One day I hope to really understand everything you try to tell me before I get bit in the ass by it. I had heard about the pneumonia, and that you were not as sick as him, but the electrical tape analogy has me lost. I admit it. Unless you are actually talking about the restraints?"

I narrowed my eyes suspiciously at her. "I don't need those. Why are you bothering me about this shit? Please tell Keith to stop playing that radio so fucking loud. He may enjoy that kind of music, but it is getting old. I am told I will be stuck here for three days. I need to call Sheryl and tell her I will be late to work. This is bullshit by the way. We are fine. We feel great. There is nothing wrong with us. We do not have any problems."

She gasped. "Uhm, okay, sure Mother. I will see about that phone call and I will tell Keith to cut out the radio." She left the cell in a hurry.

I laid back on the cot watching the ceiling light up with the coding. I knew all I had to do was solve those fucking codes and everything would be just fine. Master Boyd and I were now safe from Dennis's interference, so I could go back to fucking work. I had enough of this vacation business. It seemed like a waste of time and energy. Well, except the sex. That was pretty nice.

I fell asleep listening to the band the police were looping on Keith's radio, cursing him for not heeding Linda's warning. I was awakened by a familiar voice.

"Well, well, so this is where you have been hiding?" I opened my eyes to see Sheryl standing above me looking down.

"How the hell did you get in here," I blurted out shocked to see the failed Master in the white cell.

She laughed bitterly. "Shit I was about to ask you the same fucking thing, Psycho. What are you doing in jail? I had started to assume I would need to fire you if you didn't show up for work soon. Then I get this call from the Sheriff telling me they found you and that nut ball Boyd. I hear they have him on the psych floor. But you, my beauty, are here in jail. I guess you were right that you are not crazy. But that asshole sure as hell is."

I glared at Sheryl. "You drove all this way to insult Boyd? Could have done that by phone, cupcake. I will ask you again. How the hell did you get in here? Let me add, why the fuck are you here?"

Sheryl backed up while I sat forward in the cot. "I came to try to bail you out, Psycho. They said they have you on some bullshit emergency hold. I need your ass back at work. The relief worker has quit. None of the case workers want your job. Honey, I can't give your position away even with a paycheck attached."

I snorted. "I wouldn't take it either. Well, they have me here for another three fucking days. Nothing I can do about it. Let me tell you what. Don't leave the God damned turkey out. Shit, they get awful pissed around here about stupid stuff like that."

Sheryl crossed her arms. "You are still talking about a fucking turkey. Damn Psycho, no wonder they locked you up. Well I don't care if you are around the bend, I need you back in the field. Can you get that shit box brain of yours back together pronto please? I think we can handle another three days, but after that. Psycho, you have to get back to work or you are fired honey. I can't keep waiting for you to get your head out of your turkey," she growled.

I nodded. "I hear you. Look I would go back right fucking now if they would let me out. I am ready to go back to work. Unless you can slip me past the guard in your purse my ass is grounded another three days. I have enough trouble out of these flat foots. I don't need more."

Sheryl chuckled. "Okay, okay, three more days. I brought you a new pager. This one is even better than the last one. It can record several numbers at once. Oh and here is a cell phone too. I managed to get the State to give you one. I don't want Boyd having that phone number, you hear me? Oh, so he is in the hospital. Guess you have no Master huh? Picked a winner there didn't you sweetheart? Bet you regret cutting off my collar now."

I glared at her. "Oh fuck you, Sheryl. I didn't see you trying to save me when he was hauling my ass all over the fucking country on some fucked up delusion. In fact, you gave me the year off I seem to recall. Good job there Master Sheryl. Got me hijacked off to some fucked up vacation to California with a fucking schizophrenic. Really appreciated the pneumonia though. Every time I cough, I think of you. It is the gift that keeps on giving you know, and one I intend to return immediately." I coughed deeply without covering my mouth.

Sheryl stepped back appearing upset. "You devil. You know I am on chemotherapy. Pneumonia could kill me."

I smiled diabolically. "Yeah and so can sixteen days without food or water bitch. Just give me the fucking pager and phone. I will see you in three days slave driver."

She snorted. "I thought you had a turkey out there in California, smart ass. I ought to cane you within an inch of your miserable life for running off with the fucking psychotic boyfriend of yours and leaving me to have to cover your workload," she said as she handed me the pager and the phone.

I laughed out loud. "What's that? You missed me. Awe, are you sure baby? Nah you didn't. Your direct hit melts my cold black heart. I feel the burn. Great aim you got there. You think you can beat me with your cane? Oh Lordy, Lordy, please don't beat me no more Master. I will get to picking that cotton in three more days. Tell that old man overseer I will be coming right back, Master. I don't want any more trouble now, Master. I will be really good for you, Master. I know my place at the Master's pretty feet." I dramatically cowered while speaking in an old dialect which pissed her off to no end.

"Cut the shit Psycho. I swear you try my patience with your nasty attitude. Why the fuck do I keep putting up with it," she yelled out angrily.

I chuckled while coughing deeply, "I am only what you make me, Master. You put up with yourself and no one else is that stupid."

She nodded at that. "Yeah stupid is the right word. You are not psychotic, you are dumb. Okay enjoy the rest, sweetie pie. Come Tuesday, the fun is over. Back to work you go. No excuses. I would kiss you, but you have that fucking bug."

I laughed while making an obscene gesture at her with my mouth. "Come on over here Master and I can make it worth dying for foxy momma. I will show you paradise, then send you right to hell where you belong." I winked as I began to giggle wildly.

"Fucking nutball," she said under her breath as she knocked on the door to have Keith let her out of my cell.

Linda came running into my cell only moments after Sheryl left appearing shocked. "Oh my Goddess, is that your Master? That woman is a mega bitch Mother," she breathed out.

I nodded. "Uhm yeah, most of them are. Something I can do you for? What is with all the fucking company lately?" I shook my head in disbelief at the amount of traffic they allowed to bother the already disturbed these days.

She looked at me appearing anxious. "Dennis said Boyd is super pissed that you are in jail and not getting to come see him. So, uhm, he says to release you. You are to go visit Boyd right away to calm him down."

I laughed long and loud. "Ah gotcha. Well there you go. Freedom at last. Not a second to soon either. I was going to brain fuck Keith over that God damned radio." I got off the cot headed for the door thrilled to be leaving.

"Mother, Keith doesn't have a radio. In fact there isn't one anywhere in the cell area. They are forbidden," said Linda looking at the floor appearing concerned.

"No radio? Humm, okay whatever. We will just have to agree that he doesn't. I wouldn't want to get my old buddy in trouble by telling on him and his contraband radio. I won't tell if you don't darling." I put my finger up to my lips making a hush motion.

Keith opened the door and I was let out of the white cell. Linda gave me a ride back to the hospital so I could visit my Master and pick up my Taurus. I decided to call Sheryl after letting her stew in her juices for the rest of the day. I was ready to get back to work. No need to wait the three days anymore. After all, there wasn't anything wrong with me. I was fine. I didn't have problems. No psychosis here.

I smiled as I rode the elevator back up to the third floor. I giggled realizing it had only been three days since being classified as an endangered missing person for sixteen days. I had been involved in a psychotic car chase, hospitalized for pneumonia with other serious physical and mental health issues, left the hospital AMA (leaving without permission), and trying to break my Master out of the psychiatric ward, I had been released back to the streets deemed healthy. Wow! Brilliant move. Bravo. I stand up and bow to the Gods of Morons.

I walked to the first room and barged through the door not even knocking. My Master was awake staring at the ceiling without company. He also was not restrained. He saw me and immediately smiled.

"Niemand, you are here. I didn't think you were coming." He was much more coherent than he had been that morning.

"Of course I am here, Master. You are feeling better I take it?" I pointed at the now discarded straps.

He chuckled then pulled me down for a deep kiss. "I told them if they took those off, I would behave myself."

I laughed hard. "And they believed You? Shit. That never works for me. Come on Master. Be honest, you promised to fuck the nurse if she let you out of the buckles, didn't you?"

Master Boyd grinned. "If you think that would work, tell her to get her ass in here and I can go home with you right now."

I narrowed my eyes pushing him in the chest playfully. "You only get to fuck me, Master. You promised monogamy like a damned fool. I don't think you want to see what service for service looks like when you betray the collar." I smiled evilly.

He winced. "I have got one hell of a headache, baby. Did you smuggle in any Ibuprofen?" He rubbed his stitched forehead.

I went and closed the door. "Nope, but I bet I can make you forget about the pain in that head by attending the other one." I watched his face light up in delight as I came over to provide oral special services in our 'private room.'

He was a bit disappointed when despite all my best efforts his drives were not responding to my adoration of him. His urges were strong, but ability was blocked. This confused and angered him immensely. After a full fifteen minutes of attempted stimulation he grabbed my head telling me to stop.

"What the fuck is the deal," he said looking very upset by his lack of performance.

I shrugged. "The medication Master. It happens. You will likely be grounded for the next year. I suppose you were off it too long. You will now have to wait for the side effects to calm down. That's okay. It is part of the disease. It sucks to be us. I do apologize though. I hope you are still willing to keep my collar now that I am of little value to you." I kissed his cheek.

He looked stunned. "What do you mean little value?"

I looked at the floor. "Well you will no longer desire special services of the collar. You could hire a fucking maid and a cook. I'm not much use to you now."

Master Boyd grabbed my arm harshly making me yell out. "Niemand, you ever say that again you will not like the punishment. You are not just a piece of ass to me. I love you. Now you fucking take that back, now." He was squeezing my arm to the point of agony.

"I beg mercy Master. I take it back, You love me. Please I apologize," I yelped out.

He pulled me to his face forcing a deep tongue kiss while groping my breasts roughly. "We will just have to try harder. We will beat this shit. I will not give up sex for medication for a fucking disease I do not have," he growled while kissing my neck roughly pulling me onto him on his bed.

"Master, the nurses will come in and throw me out if they catch this," I warned him.

"Fuck them. I pay for this God damned room." He started tearing at my clothing panting and moaning but to his dismay his unit was not responding to his internal desires.

Master Boyd's inability to become intimate with me was setting off him vicious temper. Before I could fight him off he flipped me to my back on his bed nearly ripping out his IV as he pushed himself between my legs while swearing with fury at his nothingness. He pushed up my shirt exposing my breasts while I whimpered that we were going to get into trouble if he didn't stop his useless attempts to engage in carnal congress with me.

My pleas that he end his bid for such an act only made him more enraged at his impotence. He then tore at my unit more violently. Master Boyd's wild scratching and clawing was quite painful, but I couldn't yell out or it would alert the staff about our elicit, and likely forbidden, actions.

I closed my eyes and gritted my teeth against the agony of his harsh courtship. I was hoping he would not shortly resort to backhands or worse given the dangerous level of intensity his frustration had risen to. I knew my Master well and while brutality at home or in private was permissible, in this potentially public forum I was terrified I would be in jail or he would be if he continued to behave like the schizophrenic he is.

"Please Master, you will be out of here in three days. We are going to get caught. They will use the ECT if they think you are dangerous. Please it can wait. The Thorazine is causing this. You can't beat the medication's side effects. This is what happens to everyone when they take it. It is okay. I love you no matter what," I begged.

Master Boyd finally seemed to hear what I was saying. "Oh shit, I did it again. I lost it. What the fuck is going on? I couldn't stop myself again. You say the medication is doing this? The Thorazine? It was the medication all along, wasn't it? It is making me mean, making me hurt you." His voice trailed off as he leaned down onto my still prone unit to give another wanton kiss.

It was just then that the nurse came in to check on her psychotic patient. She saw my Master on top of me in his bed, my clothing askew and his hands up my shirt. She let out a yell and took off down the hallway to get assistance. Oops.

# Chapter 75: Breathlessly Running Down a Dream
## The Fall of Psycho & Rise of Neimand
## Master Boyd and Sheryl the Absent Interim

You have all seen madness in its purest form in these many chapters of this seemingly never-ending story. Our latest Acute cycle would be classified as the worst in our history to this date (with the only exception being our onset). We have banged our head, looked for short circuits, taken a wild vacation to nowhere, and still no one has put that fucking turkey back into the fridge. Somehow, the real have missed our profoundly serious break from reality.

It was to be expected. The normals were overwhelmed to discover not only one but two bats were in the belfry. They were not accustomed to all that chaos. Unable to expand their minds and grasp the true powers of schizophrenia they mistakenly stereotyped the chronic one and focused on the newly discovered one instead. This mistake of missing the actual danger, would have long range and catastrophic results for the true Psycho. As with all infections, it is not the superficial but the one layers deep that could kill you.

Ready to go? Ah, feel that? That is the pulse of insanity. Come with me and drop your boundaries. Allow the elementals to fill your pores as you become transparent. Surf the Grid with us. Do not be afraid. We may get lost but oh my Goth, what a ride. Capture that wave of electricity. Forget about what was, could have been and never will be. We are on our way to the center of the Earth to be deposited with all that pain we have dumped over the many years of torture. This time we have found Hell for real. Just remember, once you go you can never come back. Abandon all hope ye who enter here and fall right to the fucking bottom this time.

*"I have already fucking told you. I own your electricity fucker. It answers to me. If you piss me off, I will set this fucking place on fire with my powers. Now get the fuck out of my way. Where the hell did I park the God damned car. Jane, hey Jane, get over here. Tell this asshole I am the Chosen One. I need him to move the fuck out of my way. I'd hate to have to kill him but I will and you too because I never fucking liked you anyway. Simon, start the God damned car. We are out of here. These motherfuckers are insane."*

**--The Chosen One's threats to Jane & ER doctor during emergency mental health assessment, Well's Regional Hospital, May 2nd, 1999**

Master Boyd jumped off my unit. I rushed out of his bed adjusting my ruffled clothing trying to look less molested before the nurse could return with the doctor. My Master laid back in his bed while I quickly pulled up his blankets trying not to giggle at getting caught heavy petting with him by the psychiatric nurse.

We had barely gotten the near sex scene cleaned up before the psychiatrist came pushing angrily through the door. To his surprise he found me sitting in the visitor chair and my Master pleasantly chatting with me. Nope, no X-rated bullshit here Master Boyd and I looked at him appearing surprised.

45

"What's up doc," chirped my Master which made both of us giggle wildly.

Doctor Baker stared at him and I narrowing his eyes. "My nurse just came to tell me she caught you two practically engaged in intercourse in the hospital bed. That is not permitted in this hospital. We do not tolerate that kind of tomfoolery here. This is a respectable place and Mister Simmon's you are far too ill to be even considering such a strenuous act in the first place."

Master Boyd looked at Doctor Baker appearing surprised. "What? Intercourse? That is bullshit doctor. Your nurse is the psychotic one. She came in while I was visiting with my fiancé and she took off like a loon. Maybe you should do some reality testing on her. Geez."

Doctor Baker looked at me angrily. "Missus Voss, I am most unhappy about your leaving AMA this morning. I came down to do the bed check and found your bed empty. How did you escape those restraints? Now, I find you up here. This is irregular and I don't like it. The two of you should be down at State. This hospital is not equipped to handle problematic and complex cases such as yours." He pointed at my Master and me.

"Well we are not at State. So lump it, Doc. Are we done here? It is time for you to go take your medicine I am sure. Tell the wife and kids we said hello but don't eat the turkey. It was left out too long." I smiled not even recognizing the blathering statement that just came out of my mouth.

Master Boyd raised an eyebrow at me. "Uhm, what Niemand is trying to say is we are not breaking any hospital rules. You need to move the hell on unless you have come to release me," he said to Doctor Baker still looking at me appearing confused.

Doctor Baker stared at me hard. "Missus Voss, I would like you to check yourself back into this hospital. You have pneumonia, and your still demonstrating significant symptoms of cognitive slippage. You are risking your physical and mental health by not receiving proper treatment…"

I raised my hand while snorting to interrupt the doctor. "Save it pal. I am done with this bullshit conversation. I am due at work in the morning. I came by to see my fiancé, not to get into a psychology discussion with the likes of you. I am not your fucking patient, but you are wearing mine down quickly. You may leave now; the lines have been cleared." I coughed deeply covering my mouth trying to stifle an annoying giggle.

Master Boyd now looked worried. "Niemand, I think the doctor is right. You sound awful. Maybe you should go down to the ER and see if they can re-admit you."

Doctor Baker snorted. "Yes Missus Voss, go to the ER and I will tell them you are coming down. I will arrange for the ambulance and call State to get you all set up."

Master Boyd and I looked up in terror. "State? What," yelled out my Master while I began to panic.

Doctor Baker frowned. "Missus Voss's reality testing shows she needs long term treatment. Her disease is not responding to her medication, Mister Simmons. She has other problems with her brain chemistry I am sure you are aware. They are just not able to help her much here. Plus there are no beds available at this time. The State Hospital is the best place for her to be. That is what I am going to recommend. Okay Missus Voss, just come with me and we will get you all fixed up in no time." He smiled at me.

Master Boyd looked at me his eyes wide. "Baby? Jesus, they are wanting to send you to the Snake Pit."

I looked back at him nodding. "Uhm, got to Boyd. See you when you get home lover." Without a second hesitation I jumped from my chair ran past the surprised doctor into the hallway nearly tripping and busting my ass.

I flew past the elevator and headed full speed for the fire exit. I ripped open the door and descended the steps nearly falling several times. My knees felt wobbly from the fear that filled my unit. I was having trouble taking deep breaths which only intensified my panic. Despite my failing lung capacity I pushed my unit with all my strength to escape Doctor Baker's promise to send me for a long rest in the Snake Pit.

**QUICK NOTE:** *I needed help so why was I freaked out? The Snake Pit was not a place anyone would have enjoyed. You have read about its horrors several times in these many chapters. Hell, I had been there more times than I liked to recall. I had spent almost five months there,* *including my 16th birthday, during the onset of my disease (you may remember I took over a classroom and bashed my head into a locker?). Another six months during Master Julie's reign in a Hebephrenic fit (who could forget Snake Pit employee Randy's rape and my 17th birthday there) and then the seven months in the criminally insane unit due to my kicking in a church door as the prophet there during Kazan's reign. That is just to name a few of my incarcerations. There had been others just as bad already.*

I knocked over a couple when I bashed through the door out of the stairwell on the ground floor. I didn't bother to offer apology to the stunned man and woman but continued my frantic race to the parking lot. I made it to the Taurus without being grabbed by anyone. I was certain they were coming to haul me away to the Pit.

I jumped into my car, speeding from the parking lot like a madwoman. I didn't even check for oncoming traffic. I could have been very easily killed right there if anyone had been rolling by at that moment. I tore down that road headed for the DCFS building in Cumberland already forgetting what I was running from. For some reason, I believed I was merely headed to work. My mad dash from the evil Doctor Baker and my visit with my Master were already gone from my shattered memory.

I pulled into the DCFS parking lot just as my Brother the Sun went to bed. I yawned then stretched coughing hard, feeling short of breath as I got out of the Taurus. It seemed like I was forgetting something, but I couldn't recall it for the life of me. I unlocked the door and headed for Jane's office to see PC and Fax.

I flipped on PC's switch. He whirled to life appearing surprised to see me.

"Psycho Tron, wow, it has been a real long time. Where the hell did you go," he said with a look of shock on his electrical face.

I shook my head. "Unknown PC. This data seems to have been erased from our hard drive. The map is no longer available. That program has been corrupted. Please update my systems. Thank you, have a nice day," I said in a monotone voice.

PC narrowed his electronic eyes. "Something is wrong Psycho Tron. You have a virus. Oh shit, you are infected with the Trojan Worm. You're going to lose all your data and the spinning ball of death is coming. Shit, just shit. Get to a technician immediately. Oh God, did you back your hard drive?" He began to whine loudly hurting my ears.

"Shut up, shut up everyone. Shut up, no more noise, God damn it," I yelled out, coughing hard while covering my ears against the offensive sounds.

"Psycho, Psycho, listen to me. PC is right. Get to the doctor now. We are sick, something is wrong with our lungs," Simon said as he pushed into the office coughing and sweating heavily.

I turned to look at him. "Shut up. All lines are busy. Please hold. We thank you for holding. An assistant will be with you shortly." I got up and began to pace while mumbling and grinding the palms of my hands into my ears.

I felt very dizzy and could not stop my dry hacking. It felt like my chest had a tight band around it slowly smothering me. This was confusing. I removed my shirt and bra assuming they were too tight. It seemed to offer no relief. PC and Simon watched my anxiety driven antics with worry on their faces.

"Malfunction. Malfunction. PC, we have a malfunction. Please advise," I yelled out monotone without affect as I put my bra and shirt back on shivering from the chills.

PC looked at Simon who nodded. "Technician, go to Cumberland hospital and get a technician. This virus is going to end the program and destroy the hard drive," said PC sounding very frightened.

I nodded. "Yes, Cumberland Hospital. There is no technician named Baker there. I cannot function. The script is running long." I grabbed my purse and headed for the car but forgot before I got inside where I was supposed to be going.

I sat behind the wheel unsure where to go or what to do. My exposure driven pneumonia was growing in strength. The weakness from poor oxygen intake was making me drowsy. I closed my eyes hoping to just nap for a moment but fell into a fever driven deep sleep.

Tap, tap, tap, tap, tap. The noise filled my head. I could feel it hitting my force shield like a hammer. I opened my eyes to total confusion. A woman was standing behind glass looking at me. She was using her hands to make that horrid sound. I glared at her while she knocked on the glass again.

"Psycho, Psycho, wake up. Aren't you freezing out here," said the woman with large black glasses and tightly curled red hair.

"Go away freak," I growled while trying to close my eyes again for another tryst with my lover the Sandman.

"Hey, your page is going off in the office, Psycho. Aren't you supposed to be working? Where have you been? You left the computer on," yelled the woman as she banged harder on the car window.

I woke up with a start. "Oh, my job. Fuck me, I overslept." I shook off the grogginess.

Jane looked at me appearing mildly concerned. "You okay Psycho? Hey, what are you doing sleeping in the car? Long night? Did you come back to work last night or something?"

I open the door and used the vehicle to steady myself while the dizziness passed. "Uhm, yeah, I guess I did. You said the pager is going off in the office?"

Jane nodded. "Yeah, and you left your computer on. You know that is how you get hacked or get viruses you know."

I coughed deeply almost going to my knees. "Virus? Yeah I think I was dreaming about getting one in PC. Okay, let me grab that pager." I felt the chills running down my arms and legs like electricity while I followed Jane into the DCFS building.

The pager was vibrating so loud I covered my ears from the annoying sound. I didn't even have to look to know it was Sheryl. She must have found out I had been released from jail. I reset the pager quickly to shut it up then dialed Sheryl's number in her office more than a hundred miles away.

I coughed. "Yeah? What do you want Sheryl? I haven't even had my coffee yet you know."

Sheryl snorted. "Well I was going to chew you out. I called the jail to check on you but was told you were released. Then to my shock I get your call from the Cumberland office. I see you did the right thing and went right to work like you are supposed to do. Bravo. Now get over to Julia's place and get your fucking coffee. After that, check on Samuel's readjustment with the Turnbols, and I will fax over the case load for today. Good to have you back on the job, not a moment too soon either."

I coughed again. "Julia? Are you fucking serious? I have a shit ton of stuff to catch up on Sheryl. Tell that heifer to take a number." I was feeling short of breath again.

Sheryl growled. "Don't fuck with me Psycho. You are skating on thin ice here. I have barely been able to keep from having to terminate you. Is that what you want? I can make that happen you know."

I rolled my eyes. "Yeah boss, I hear you loud and clear. Color me gone to the Stubbs house. Want me to give her a wet sloppy kiss for you?" I giggled at the thought of sharing my germs and ending Julia once and for all.

Sheryl snorted. "Get going you screwy bitch. Enough chit chat." She hung up on me.

I winced at the sound of the ringtone which seemed to reach into my ears and loop around inside my head. "Love you too baby," I said out loud.

Jane snorted. "Sheryl has been in one foul mood, Psycho. You shouldn't mess with her like that. She has been really fighting that cancer. Don't you have any empathy at all? Damn you are maybe the coldest hearted person I know."

I sneered at her. "Shut up and eat your paper towel, Jane. Don't you even know how to cook? I swear some people. Never mind. I have no time to fool with the likes of you. Why are you here on Sunday by the way?" I lowered my eyes in suspiciousness at her.

Jane looked startled. "Sunday? Psycho, this is Monday morning."

I looked at the floor trying to figure out what happened to Sunday. Saturday I was at the Wheatly hospital with Master Boyd. I came to Cumberland that night. What the fuck happened to Sunday?

"You are a fucking liar, Jane. Today can't be Monday. There is a Sunday every week, right?" I shook my head in anger at her trying to mess with my head.

Jane chuckled nervously. "Uhm, yeah there is. Sunday was yesterday Psycho. Today is Monday. Do you think I would come to this shitty place on a weekend? Hell no."

I looked at my fingers. "Monday, Tuesday, Wednesday, uhm, Saturday, fuck. Okay, so it is Monday. Whatever, I must get going. Is Fax on?" I got up to check my co-worker for my case list.

Jane nodded. "The fax is always on numbskull. Hey, who was that guy you were with the other day? The day Sheryl got all pissed off?"

I grabbed the sheet as Fax spit it out at me moaning at the number of cases, locations and types listed. "You mean Simon? You know Simon,, Jan …stop acting stupid. My God he has worked here for as long as I have. I am tired of your silly attempts to play head games with me. See you around." I flipped PC's switch and took off leaving a very worried looking Jane sitting at her desk.

I was almost to Julia's house when the cell phone Master Boyd gave me started to ring. I groaned assuming it was my Master calling to take a chunk out of my ass too. Everyone seemed to be lining up to kick the Psycho that morning.

"Yeah, make it quick, I am almost at a client's house." I growled into the phone.

"Uhm, Niemand? It's Dennis. Are you doing okay?"

I snorted "Define okay, Dennis. Since when did you start fucking calling to check on my inner feelings of peace and happiness?"

He cleared his throat appearing unsure what to say. "Well since you went missing yet again. Where have you been girly? Boyd said you ran off Saturday during a visit upset as hell. No one has heard or seen you since. Did you say a client's house? Are you at work?"

I started ranting angrily. "Yeah Dennis, I am working. Look I am sorry I didn't think to check in with all of you to get approval to do my God damned job. I will try to keep that in mind the next time I decide to, you know, earn a living, be a responsible citizen and all that crazy shit. This is out of control. If you feel the need to keep up with my every move then call the motherfucking judge and get an ankle bracelet, or maybe a tracking device shoved up my ass. I didn't realize I was now subject to seeing a probation officer once a month and calling my daddy Dennis to let them know I needed to take a piss so no one worries about where I went every fucking second of the God damned day. *(I suddenly calmed down and lowered my voice while sounding friendly)* Oh hey, Dennis, could you tell Carla thanks for the left-over turkey from dinner last night? Remind Boyd to put it into the fridge so it doesn't ruin. Thanks Dennis. You're a Prince among men. See you Sunday. Don't work too hard, man." I hung up the cellphone as I pulled into Julia's driveway.

I leaned my aching head forward onto the steering wheel feeling horrid. My unit was tight and weak. It seemed I was forgetting something, but I could get my broken thoughts to work in a line. It felt like everything was too loud, too bright and too chaotic all around me. The transmissions were pluming in greens and yellows like geysers from the Yellowstone Park.

Thunder was rolling in the distance while the ground seemed to be shaking. I shivered while a series of chills ran through my limbs with their little clawed feet. I stared at Julia's house feeling hypnotized by the rhythms of the electrical grid flowing just above my head. I swayed unblinking, unable to get out of the car, stuck in my trance.

I watched her door open and saw Julia step out with her arms crossed glaring. I still could not break free of my catatonic spell. She walked over never taking her eyes off me. Julia had a look of caution on her face as she approached. She banged on my window. The sound smacked me in the side of the head like a baseball bat. I fell over to my side wailing in agony.

"Ah! For Christ's sake, shut the fuck up. Shut it up. Ah," I screamed while trying to rip my ears off my head.

Julia let out as yell then opened the door clawing at me trying to drag me out of the seat. "Oh my God. Stop that. You're going to hurt yourself. Oh God, oh God," she yelled while finally hauling me to the ground.

I fell to the earth with a thud which knocked me out of my episode. "Oh shit, what the fuck are you doing, you crazy bitch," I yelled while coughing till I thought I would faint right there in her yard.

"Psycho, oh fuck. Hey, get up. You were freaking out. Oh shit, what do I do?" She squatted down next to me while I laid on my side still coughing and gagging.

"Don't (cough) don't touch me. Don't (cough) touch," I wheezed out.

Julia stood up and moved back as I got up on all fours still hacking.

"Jesus, Psycho. That sounds really bad. Are you sick? You're really pale. That black hair maybe? I don't know. That cough, you may need to get that checked out," she said while keeping her distance.

I turned my head sneering at her. "What the fuck do you care Julia? I just need coffee is all. Stay out of my business. I believe we have had this conversation before. Nosey bitch." I used the car to pull myself to my feet while I waited for the dizziness to pass.

Julia looked my unit up and down. "Seriously, you look horrible. What is with all the bandages? Where the hell have you been? Someone kidnap and beat the shit out of you or what?" She stepped back another pace.

"Coffee, I need fucking coffee," I yelled out angrily.

Her eyes went wide. "Uhm, okay, sure. I have it ready at the table." I nodded then staggered slowly to her kitchen.

I sat down wincing while trying to take a deep breath. "Do you have some Ibuprofen? My head is killing me I groaned out while wiping my eyes trying to clear my vision of the flashing blue and red lights that kept exploding in my visual field."

Julia got up quickly then returned with the requested over the counter medication. I took the pills from her hand.

I swallowed washing them down with my coffee as I smiled at her. "Thanks Julia. I am sure that will help a lot. I just a woke up on the wrong side of the coffin, you know?" I giggled at that.

Julia sat back down still appearing a bit pensive. "Yeah, seems so. You sure you're feeling okay? I have seen healthier corpses you know."

I chuckled at that. "Oh? When? So, how have things been? Feeling any better?" I grinned at her calm and friendly.

She raised an eyebrow. "Uhm, yeah I have been feeling great. Been missing our coffee chats though. Sheryl said you went on vacation but she told me you'd be back New Year's Day. That was a couple weeks ago." She took a drink of her coffee.

I looked at the table feeling irritation rising. "Can't a person go to California without getting the fucking third degree? I mean first the fucking cops, now you. Look, you don't own me. I can do what I want. I never had a mom when

I needed one. It is a bit too late now, isn't it? Get off my ass." I glared at her.

Julia jumped back appearing scared. "Hey, I was just saying is all. You are right. You can do what you want. I am not your mom. So, California? Lucky. How was the trip? Did you get to see any of the sights? What part did you visit?" She took another drink of her coffee.

I rolled my eyes chuckling, suddenly changing my mood from agitated to friendly again. "Oh you know the middle part. I was with this truck-driver. Nice fellow. Kind of scruffy looking though. Anyway, I went dancing a bit. The food sucked. Hey, do you have anything to eat? I haven't had a fucking thing since the pancakes in Vegas yesterday. I would kill for some pancakes." I got up and walked to her refrigerator and rudely began to search through it for food.

**NOTE:** *you may not have noticed but I have never said a thing about anyone feeding me at the hospital, to the jail, to now. Truth is I had not eaten anything but grass and paper towels since the Boswell dinner over sixteen days before. The three days in the hospital I had been heavily sedated. I was given fluids but no food. No one had thought to offer me a meal or remind me to eat since my capture with Master Boyd the night we wrecked his car. I was now dangerously thin and developing a urinary tract infection thanks to pressure on my system from pneumonia. I was so psychotic I didn't notice I was now pissing blood and tissue as the infection began to spread throughout my unit. Within only a few more days the signs of sepsis will begin to show as my battered immune responders will throw even* *the kitchen sink into the battle against my bacterial invaders. I was about to get closer to taking the dirt nap than I had since trying to take my life and the poisoning that had led to this situation in the first place. The lack of anyone stepping in to aid me in my darkest hours is beyond pathetic. Do understand the only persons who would have helped were either in the hospital himself (Master Boyd) or unaware of even my whereabouts (Maiden Mary). These other fucktards, well what did they care about a stupid schizophrenic's failing health. Sad but true.*

I found some cold mashed potatoes in a bowl covered with plastic wrap. Without even the common decency of asking permission I ripped off the plastic took the food from the fridge sat down in the floor and began to eat it ravenously with my bare hands.

Julia sat in her chair too stunned by the odd sight watching me eat like the starving person I was. The fridge started to beep to alert the owner that the door had been open too long. This caused me to drop the bowl and cower startled beyond reason. While the sound was only mild to a normal, for my psychotic senses it sounded like a fire truck siren in my ears.

"Christ, make it stop. Mae it stop. Shut up. Shut up," I screamed out trying to cover my ears while looking about wildly for the emergency vehicle sure to bearing down on me any second.

Julia, who had appeared to be in a trance of disbelief at the weird scene she had been watching unfold was finally shocked out of her daze. "It is the refrigerator alarm, sorry Psycho." She got up and closed the door ending the noise immediately.

I pulled my hands down from my ears still looking around confused. "Shit. Where the fuck am I? Have you seen Simon? We are going to be late. We are supposed to be headed to Julia's place. Sheryl is gonna be pissed. I will get fired you know."

Julia sat down in a chair looking at me appearing interested in my responses. "You don't know where you are?"

I shook my head starting to tear up with fright that I could not recall but knew I should know. "No, I have forgotten. Please help me. Where am I? I have lost my location…do I know you? Do you know me?" I felt the terror inside rising. Why couldn't I remember anything?

Julia shook her head. "I am Julia Stubbs. You are Psycho. You are at my house. Look, I think maybe you had better stay here for a bit. I will fix you something to eat. Or at least let me warm those potatoes. You are very thin. I think maybe you have not been eating. Will you eat something for me please?"

I looked at her frightened out of my mind. "Should I? Is that the right thing to do? Christ, why can't I remember?" I began to wail, upset at my lack of understanding about anything anymore.

Julia got up and left the room while I cried and rolled into a fetal position in the floor. The terror inside had taken me hostage. I was now its bitch as the cognitive slip raged on causing complete sensory overload. She returned with a blanket and very gently put it over my entire unit immediately causing darkness. The sudden loss of perception and a feeling of security began to calm my inner demons almost immediately.

Julia then turned on her radio to a station that played soft rock songs without interruption. She turned the radio up very loud while gathering her bowel of half-eaten potatoes off of the floor. While I laid there recovering from my trip to Mars, she put the food into her microwave warming it up then placed it on the table with a fresh cup of coffee. Julia then sat down in her chair quietly watching to see if the tools to calm a psychotic fit would have any effect.

The music blotted out the thousands of sounds, voices and noise from my head allowing me to focus on something that had meaning and direction. Slowly, my cognitive wheels began to turn in the proper direction as I laid on the floor under the heavy quilt shivering in terror trying to recall my location, identification and memory.

Twenty minutes later I suddenly recalled my purpose and function. I felt the undertow inside let me go so I could resurface in the world of the real for air once more. I pulled down the blanket to look at Julia who was still sitting quietly in her chair watching me.

"You with me again, Psycho," Julia said in her unusually husky voice.

I nodded. "Yeah, I am not sure what happened there. I apologize for that. I have been sick with pneumonia. I guess I should have taken more time off work. I am not sure I am well enough yet." I got off the floor and started folding the quilt while Julia went and turned down her stereo but did not turn it off completely.

"Seems to me you might be right. Sit down and eat something. That pneumonia did a number on your figure sweetheart. If you turned sideways by a fence post no one would find you." She pointed at the mashed potatoes and silverware on the table.

I sat down and devoured the meal feeling a bit better after that and two more cups of coffee. The fatigue was overtaking my unit again while I struggled for almost every breath. Julia watched me appearing humored at my appetite.

"You took starve a fever and feed a cold a bit far didn't you, Psycho?" She chuckled as I finished the food.

I shrugged. "I don't know what you mean, Julia. Do I owe you anything for the meal? Thank you for that by the way. I was going to eat the turkey, but someone left it out too long. I had to throw it out."

Julia snorted. "No, you don't owe me shit, Psycho. It was my pleasure. Never seen anyone eat so fast. Damn, you must have been starving. Hey, speaking of turkey let me fix you a couple of sandwiches for the road. You should try to get some weight back on you. You look better with meat on those bones. Personally, I think you should tell Sheryl to take a fucking chill pill. You need to be at home resting, not running around working. You are not well, not by a long shot. I will call her today and give her a piece of my mind. I mean you can't visit anymore if you are dead. You know pneumonia can kill you. In fact, if I had the power to do it, your ass would be at the fucking ER right now. Hell, it is affecting your mind. That is fucked up." She got up digging in her fridge for items to make a lunch for me.

I looked at her suddenly very confused. "ER? I am supposed to do something there but I can't remember what. Did I by any chance tell you that I had a case waiting for me at one?"

Julia chuckled as she put the sandwich items together. "Uhm, not that I can remember. You know what Psycho. You are quite a trip. Since we started hanging together, I can never complain it has been boring. You did say something about a Simon. You have said that name several times since coming here. Is that your husband or fiancé maybe?"

I started laughing wildly, which caused a very startled Julia to laugh along with me. "No. Simon is not my husband or fiancé? Now that is fucking funny." I howled out.

She nodded while laughing along with me nervously. "It is, why?"

I snort laughed. "Because he is an old, toothless, drunkard railroad man, Julia. Simon is my best friend silly."

Julia stopped laughing. "Huh? What? Oh my God. Why would you hang out with someone like that?"

I suddenly stopped laughing too, filling with sudden despair. "I don't have a choice Julia. I ate the oatmeal. I should have noticed it tasted like metal but I didn't notice. I believed her. You know what? Keep the sandwiches. I have changed my mind. No more food. That is how they get you. I know your game lady. I know all about all of you sonofabitches. Forget it. I know what you are trying to do. You are not my friend. Simon can see through you. I have to get out of here. Oh God, I almost ate your oatmeal. Fuck." I got up and fled to the Taurus.

I spun tires as I raced out of her driveway leaving a stunned Julia standing in her doorway. There was no doubt she was confused at my odd paranoid behavior. I sped down the road till I was sure I was far enough away to outrun her if she tried to follow. I pulled over got on my knees and forced myself to vomit up the potatoes. I could distinctly taste metal.

"Shit, she was trying to kill me. Did you see that," I yelled out to Simon who watched me from the passenger's seat.

Simon nodded. "I warned you not to go back. Like those little bastards that ate that witch's candy house. They got caught. That witch was going to eat them. Julia is that witch, Psycho. She is setting us up. Watch out, beware."

I groaned from my upset stomach while coughing hard. "Simon it was Hansel and Gretel you are talking about. Fuck,

66

can you read a grown-up book occasionally? Look my stomach is killing me and I can't breathe. You sit there useless as the tits on a boar hog talking shit about fairy tales when we have lost the God damned map and there is no electrical tape anywhere. I need to stop this hunger. It is not safe to eat. Grab those napkins from the back." He reached into the backseat then handed me a handful left over from happy meals bought for frightened children being hauled to foster care.

I took the paper and tore it into tiny bites. I ate all five of the napkins slowly. Simon watched me with his eyes wide. "You know we can't hold out long doing that. This is bad Psycho. Remember if you do that too long we can die."

I nodded. "Yeah, I know Simon, but I have to kill the hunger. It will hold for a day now. I promise I will try to find food that is not tainted. Now who is first on the list? It is time to get to work my friend," I said smiling at him feeling very weak but less agitated for a change.

**QUICK NOTE:** I *had learned during the many years of forced starvation at the hands of my mother Debbie that toilet paper, napkins and paper towels could be consumed to kill hunger pains. I have eaten a ton of paper, and other horrible things you don't even want to know about, in my life in sheer desperation to fill my stomach due to hunger. Hopefully, most will never know such hunger nor know what one is willing to eat to survive.*

*You would be surprised what hunger can drive you to do actually. I may write about the years with Debbie sometime in the future and you can get an idea or just take my word for it. Paper products offer no calories, but they are safe to consume and will pass without blockage if you don't overdo it.*

*When and if you see someone eating napkins you have one of three things: one, a schizophrenic with a delusion they are being poisoned; two, an anorexic trying to kill her hunger so she doesn't eat; or three, a near death starving, desperate person. Okay let's just get honest, anyone you see doing this is actually number three no matter what drove them to it.*

I drove to my first case and assessed the situation. The report appeared to be unfounded. I couldn't see any evidence of the reported abuse of this child. She appeared happy, healthy and not a single sign of violence was discovered. I hacked and gasped through the entire investigation.

When I finally finished up I had to lay my head on the steering wheel for some time before I could even get the strength to start the car to head to my next report.

I groaned as I looked at the address on my list. Shit, Wells again. I would have to drive through Wheatly to get to that mountain town. Only one way in and one way out. I tried to take a deep breath and winced while the sharp pains ripped through my chest. Man, did I ever feel horrible.

I took off down the road flying like a bat out of hell. It seemed if I rushed through Wheatly no one would even notice me coming through. I looked at my brother the sun. That was weird, he was very low in the sky. I shook my head in surprise that it had taken me all morning and afternoon just to do one fucking case, and an unfounded one at that.

Damn, I was slowed down. I grimaced while looking at the discarded pager and cell phones in the passenger seat. I could see all three were lit up with green lights. Fuck everyone was trying to contact me. They were all likely pissed too.

I sighed while trying to decide who to deal with first. I picked up Master Boyd's cell phone and saw his house number appeared in the missed call list many times. I almost drove right off the road when I saw to my horror that his numerous calls spanned from Tuesday to Friday. Wait, how the fuck could it be Friday. It was Monday. The phone was claiming it was Friday, January 15th. That could not be correct.

I pulled over to the side of the road feeling dizzy and confused as I dialed my Master's number to return the call. Surely, the phone was just in error. Deep inside the terror started to rise from the realization I may have just lost an entire five days of time.

"Niemand, is that you baby? Please say it is you," yelled out my very upset Master.

"Yes, it is me Master," I said barely able to breath well enough to force out the words.

"Oh my God. Where are you baby? Please tell me. I have been so scared. Where are you," Master Boyd said excitedly sounding as if he was about to cry.

I shook my head. "What day is it Master? I have been at work. Are you out of the hospital yet?"

Master Boyd sniffed. "I have been out for days baby. Why did you run away like that? Where have you been? Dennis said you hung up on him. Even Sheryl couldn't find you. Baby listen, come home. Come home to me right now, okay? Stay on the phone with me till you get here," he said trying to sound calm.

I began to tremble. "Master, what day is it?" I closed my eyes terrified to hear the answer.

He coughed. "It is Friday baby. Come home. Stay on the phone with me. I think you are very sick. Please stay with me. Where are you?"

I looked around suddenly realizing I didn't know where I was. I gasped as terror spread through me.

"Oh my God Master, I am not sure. I am lost Master. Don't let them take me to the Snake Pit. I can't come home. Doctor Baker will send me. He said so. You heard him." I started crying in a complete breakdown.

Master Boyd sounded confused. "Niemand, Doctor Baker has not spoken to me since your last appointment with him in December. Baby, when did you hear him threaten to send you to the Snake Pit? Did you call him recently?"

I shook my head. "Stop messing with me Master. You heard him. In your room. That stupid nurse told on us. I told you we would get into trouble for fooling around. Now

70

Doctor Baker will take me away to the Pit," I blubbered into the phone.

Master Boyd gasped. "Niemand, Doctor Baker did not come to my room. He is not my doctor baby, he is yours. Think. The nurse told us to cut it out or she would have me sent out of the hospital. You freaked out and took off running. No one has seen you since honey. Everyone has been looking for you. You are in the car, right? Let me help you find your way home. Stay on the phone. Look around, do you see any road signs," he said trying to sound calm.

I strained my eyes seeing nothing but fields and forest down the lonely two laned road. "No signs Master. I am on a road that I should know this road, but I can't remember it." I started to wail getting very agitated.

He began to hush me. "Calm down baby. It is going to be okay. Alright, are you driving or parked?"

"Parked in a ditch Master," I sobbed.

Master Boyd spoke very slowly using simple words, "Start the car. Get on the road. Stay on this phone and talk to me. Tell me what you see. Do it now baby, that is a directive," he said keeping his voice soft.

I nodded while I followed his orders. I began to drive down the two laned highway telling him what I could see around me. He was patient with me often telling me that I was to ignore the green and yellow transmissions and focus on parts of the real world such as buildings, road signs and the natural landscape.

"Okay, it sounds like you are on highway 80 heading to Wheatly. If you can drive keep going till you get to town. I want you to park the car on the side of the road as soon as you see Stevenson's red barn. Park and wait. I will come and get you from there. We can be together again. I will take care of you and make this stop okay? Repeat what I told you, that is a directive," he said appearing to sound relieved.

"Uhm, you want me to drive to Wheatly and park next to the Stevenson's red barn and wait for you? Did I get that right, Master," I said still feeling unsure I had recalled all his instructions.

He chuckled softly. "You did perfect, baby. Okay, I must call for a car so I must hang up for a minute. I will call right back. Drive slowly, I will call back. Answer my phone when I do that is a directive. Do you understand me?"

I nodded. "Yes Master, I understand." He hung up and I dropped the phone onto the passenger's seat crying like a baby feeling very sick and unable to breath.

The pager began to vibrate wildly and Sheryl's cell phone started to ring off the hook. The noises startled my already agitated psyche. I screamed out for everyone to shut up while irritation filled me to the breaking point. I whipped wildly to the side of the road. Then I rolled down my window and threw all the electronic devices out the window into the ditch demanding silence. I had no concept that I had just thrown out Master Boyd's phone along with the offending items.

I took off like a shot back onto the road driving right past the Stevenson's red barn speeding for Wells to attend to the case on my list. I didn't recall I was supposed to be waiting for Master Boyd, nor did I recall that I had lost over five days of time. I had already forgotten the whole conversation.

I was weaving all over the road feeling lightheaded and struggling to breath when the blue lights lit up my rearview mirror. I groaned. "Fuck,, a ticket. I don't need this shit." I pulled over to the side of the road while trying to find my license and registration.

Two police officers got out of the car with their guns already pulled. I heard one yell out, "Out of the car nice and slow. Put your hands on your head. Do it now."

I gasped my brain whirling in panic. What the fuck? I was getting arrested over a road infraction. Really?

I looked in the rearview mirror to see the two officers standing behind their doors using them as a shield. I groaned again. "Fuck, they are going to shoot me. Could this day get any worse." I opened my door slowly.

I stepped out of the car and fell to the ground unable to stand. The world was spinning as my heart pounded in my chest demanding to be let out of its bony cage. I rolled on the pavement fighting to breath while my lungs sputtered. I couldn't get up if I had wanted to. My pneumonia and UTI had laid me low at last. The police would just have to put me out of my misery or they could just wait a minute. I wasn't too far from taking the Reaper as a lover. I was already swooning to his romantic song.

"Niemand? Honey can you hear me?" I looked up trying to focus my blurry vision on the mustached police officer standing over my fading unit.

I smiled still unsure if I was seeing Dennis or wishful thinking it. "Hey Dennis, am I late for dinner? I am sorry. It wasn't Boyd's fault. You know women, we, uhm." I trailed off coughing and spasming.

"Just be still sweetheart. Linda, tell Cathy to call for an ambulance. We have a situation here. Hurry up. Niemand, honey, stay with me." I felt the void closing in around me pulling me deep inside myself.

I realized I was falling but for some reason I was not afraid. I wondered briefly if Master Boyd had managed somehow to reach the mountain. We must have driven off the edge. I tried to flap my arms as a shred of fear hit me, but it didn't slow my decent.

I strained my eyes in the blackness. Everything was so dark. I could hear the whirling electricity through the grids, and the sounds of a siren. There was ragged breathing, like that of someone in the throes of death. A gentle thumping sound kept tempo with a long-forgotten song. I was so cold. I hate to be cold. There was the sensation of ants crawling up my arms. Someone was speaking to someone/ I couldn't understand the words.

Out of the darkness hands grabbed me around my throat. They squeezed till I couldn't catch my air. I panicked and tried to scream but my arms and legs wouldn't move. I opened my mouth but nothing came out as my killer tightened their grip around my neck. I was dying, helpless and unable to fight it anymore. I felt the tears roll down my cheeks as I finally gave up my battle. The void of nothingness washed over me and I was gone.

I woke up to the sound of a heart monitor. An oxygen mask was over my face. I was restrained to the bed. I tried to understand how this had happened but my thoughts were scattered. Someone was speaking to me. I couldn't understand their words. I felt panicked at my situation. I began to try to fight the person as they shined lights into my eyes. The strange fellow was wearing a mask like mine. The fellow had blue hair. What?

I tried to scream but something was in my throat blocking my sounds. Terror struck as the stranger shook his head and stuck a needle into a plastic wire above me, darkness again.

Once again I awoke. This time, nothing was on my face or in my throat. I gasped feeling my mouth full of sores and my insides burned like they were on fire. I moaned out in agony. Someone said something. I turned toward the voice trying to clear my vision while focused on this noise.

Master Boyd stood there looking afraid. I smiled at him feeling very tired and confused. He smiled back while taking my hand. He said something but I couldn't understand his words. I looked at the ceiling trying to recall where I was, and how I had gotten there.

"Niemand? Can you hear me baby? Are you awake," said Master Boyd, his words finally making sense.

I tried to speak but nothing came out other than loud rushing air. I began to cough up foul tasting sputum in a painful series of hacking fits. My throat was ripped apart and bleeding into the lung discharge.

Master Boyd grabbed a tissue and held it over my mouth telling me to spit the bloody discharge into it. I tried to reach up to cover my mouth, but my arms were restrained. I moaned realizing at last I was in the hospital tethered to a bed.

When the whooping fit passed, I turned my head looking at my Master who appeared incredibly happy for some reason. Irritation filled me as I assumed he was excited to see me trapped in a bed at the mental hospital. What an asshole. I glared at him hatefully still unable to get enough air through my swollen vocal cords to curse him for allowing them to lock me up. He promised, damn him, I thought miserably.

He threw away the befouled tissues then walked back to me taking my restrained hand while smiling and stroking my cheek lightly. "I thought I had lost you forever baby. You almost died. They said you may not survive the sepsis. Dennis just left. Carla and Linda were here too. Everyone has been praying and hoping. We all thought but not my baby. My Niemand is a fighter. You made it back to us.

Please honey don't ever leave me. I don't know what I would do without you. I love you so much. I have been so scared." He teared up then leaned down kissing my forehead gently.

A nurse came into the room and my Master looked at her smiling. "She is awake. See I told you she would beat it. My girl is the toughest around."

The nurse looked at him appearing stunned initially then looked at me as a smile spread across her face. "Well Mister Simmons. Seems you know your lady. Hi there, Missus Voss. I am Judy your nurse. You have been one sick person, but it looks like you have decided it wasn't your time yet. How you feeling sweetie? Rough still I bet." She put a blood pressure cuff on my arm while motioning my Master to sit down so she could get my vital signs.

I tried again to speak only managing a groan. Judy looked at me appearing startled. "Oh honey, don't try to speak. They have had you on a ventilator for days. You're not going to be able to speak for a bit. Let your throat heal sweetheart. I will give Mister Simmons some paper and a pen so you can write rather than talk. You need to rest. Honey, you have just had one hell of a battle. Rest and stay quiet and in a few days you'll be on the way to recovery. Your blood pressure is back to normal and looks like your heart rate has slowed down too. The sepsis has passed. You are one lucky girl. Another few hours and we could not have saved you." She looked at me appearing relieved.

**NOTE:** *(PLEASE PAY ATTENTION HERE.) A quick word about sepsis. For those of you who don't really* know what it is, let me enlighten you. Sepsis is the overreaction of your own immune system to an infection in the unit. There are three stages to this natural response of your system when infection is deemed life threatening by your internal defenders. Mild sepsis will onset with symptoms of low blood pressure and rapid heat rate (over 120 at rest) usually without a fever over one hundred degrees. If you catch this life-threatening illness here withing twelve hours of onset then you will likely survive with only fifteen percent of persons progressing to the next stage (if treated).

If you are one of the unlucky fifteen percent or sepsis is not caught within twelve hours, the next stage is severe sepsis. When this deadly phase onsets (I had been admitted in the early part of this stage in case you are wondering) then your chances of survival are about forty percent even with treatment. Symptoms are mental changes, decreased urination, dangerously low unit temps, chills, irregular heart rate, unconsciousness, and at the end of this phase your organs, starting with the kidneys, begin to fail. Most patients with any underlying conditions, elderly or with other compromised health issues, do not survive this stage.

The final stage or septic shock is almost universally fatal. During this stage, your kidney fail, causing a domino effect of complete organ failure, coma and death withing 24 to 72 hours. At this level there is extraordinarily little hope of survival and no real treatment. Often the hospital will call all your loved ones to come and say goodbye, while your unit shuts down and death comes to claim you.

*I have had to sit with over five people who died this way. They arrived in the second stage, then progressed rapidly to septic shock. All we, or the medical professionals, could do is hold their hand and watch them drift off to the Summerlands.*

*This is a serious, life threatening reaction that can happen to anyone over even the slightest infection. One of the people I watched pass became septic over an injury from a butter knife no bigger than a paper cut. This disorder used to be called 'Blood Poisoning' but understand that is not what it is. It is your immune system literally eating itself alive in a desperate attempt to beat an infection, any infection, even a mild one can set this off.*

*So be aware. IF you notice any of the symptoms above and have been sick with respiratory ailments, the flu or had an open wound recently, then check with your doctor just in case. Better safe than sorry and you only have twelve hours to get help. After that it could mean a slow death while your loved one's cry helpless at your bedside. That is my public service announcement for the day.*

I was handed the paper and pen. In a series of questions and answers with Master Boyd I was finally able to piece together the happenings of the two weeks after our wild car chase and capture.

Master Boyd had received six days inpatient treatment on the third floor while I was admitted as a regular patient on the first. I had somehow managed to escape my restraints and tried to break him out and run away with him after only three days being a guest of Wheatly Regional. Thanks to my Bonnie and Clyde move, I had been arrested. I had been arrested and held for two hours, then set free to visit him to calm his agitation.

After being caught trying to engage in a sexual session with my Master, a nurse had threatened to call the State hospital if we pulled that stunt again. In a psychotic state I had hallucinated the nurse was my own doctor and had fled the scene telling no one where I was going.

I called Sheryl from the DCFS office and told her I was ready to go back to work. I had indeed visited with Jane and with Julia. My memories of those interactions were correct. However, the investigations that came after that were hit or miss.

Apparently, I did attend to my list of cases, but had appeared confused, babbled and was sent away on more than one occasion by the other attending officers at the scenes. For over five days I wandered from place to place suffering from the effects of profound psychotic episode, pneumonia, and a vicious UTI infection.

Master Boyd was released on Tuesday in a tizzy thanks to everyone's inability to locate or reach me by phone. Dennis, Linda, and he had searched high and low trying to find me. Wherever I went to this day no one knows.

Finally, after resting for the night Master Boyd received my phone call as he prepared to head out looking for me again. He determined my location but reported to me I was out of my head, confused. My Master had no doubt I was in a great deal of trouble. Without even attempting to reach me, he called Dennis and Randell to report my likely whereabouts. I was pulled over by the old Bulls but immediately collapsed into total septic confusion upon the traffic stop.

The ambulance had to immediately force a tube and oxygen due to my inability to breath and my failing systems. I was rushed to ICU and put on a respirator with heavy hitting antibiotics and antipsychotics pumped into my unit while everyone nervously waited to see if I would survive. My chances were less than forty percent.

For three long days I hung in the balance, unable to recover but not backsliding into a semi-coma. By day four the danger began to pass and it started to appear I would recover after all. They took me off the machines happily finding I was able to breath without aid.

I finally awoke on the sixth day after my near-death experience with severe sepsis and pneumonia. I was still labeled 'serious but out of 'critical' care for the first time in over a week.

Master Boyd could not believe that I had been so poorly treated, completely ignored and left to fend for myself by the medical personal and those around me. He found this disgusting and told me it was unforgivable.

He had immediately called a lawyer to start proceedings against the hospital for refusing to take an emergency hold when contacted by the Wheatly Sheriff's office. The Hospital administration had been informed that the police were holding the hospital's escaped, psychotic and obviously very physically ill patient.

The hospital had told the police I was fine and healthy enough to be cut loose. They saw no reason to take a hold on the individual who they had deemed healed and completely competent. Their own records indicated I was suffering extreme exposure, malnutrition, profound psychosis, and a moderate case of pneumonia the day I busted out in my hospital gown.

Ultimately the hospital would settle this case of mishandling my illness quietly out of court, but they learned a powerful lesson. Never again would they rush me from one of their beds just because I had shitty insurance.

Master Boyd used the money we won to cover the expenses of my almost two weeks of intensive care while I slowly recovered from one of the deadliest battles with my illness I had ever encountered. The price to save my pathetic life was outrageous. In the end, I was not sure I was worth the bill. Yikes!

Sheryl didn't fire me as I had expected her to do. Instead she filed for a medical leave on my behalf. Dennis had filed for a six-month catastrophic leave for Master Boyd. He didn't want my Master to be hauled in for a surprise 'fitness for duty' evaluation until it was damned sure my Master could pass reality testing and had finished his acute cycle.

My medical leave on the other hand was only for one month. As my Master followed the nurse and my wheelchair out of the hospital the final week of January, we were in a heated argument regarding my intentions to return to work immediately.

Our somewhat aggressive discussion was halted suddenly when I broke out in laughter as he opened his new car door to help me inside. It was the same model, color and make as the black car he had destroyed in our wild dash to escape from they.

Master Boyd looked at me confused. "What is so funny?"

I shook my head. "Obsessed much? Really? This is the same fucking car."

He chuckled when he realized what I was laughing at. "Oh year, well, I know what I like. What can I say? I always say, when you find the perfect match there is no need to look any further. I don't like any kind of change. New things make me nervous. Stick with what works, you know," he said while helping me hook in my seat belt.

I nodded suddenly feeling despair wash over me. "Yeah, I do know. That is what scares me."

We took off to see Maiden Mary, Seine, and my kids. I had forgotten I was even a mother and fur baby owner. I spent the ride trying to figure out how to keep this kind of horror from ever happening again. Master Boyd and I had almost lost our battle in our war against schizophrenia this time.

It was at that moment my Master smiled at me and said, "So, I figured out the Thorazine was causing my anger outbursts and my problems with sex. I quit taking that shit. Dennis has been closely watching me, but I outfoxed him. I have been cheeking that poison. It is almost out of my system now and I must tell you I have never felt better. You were right, Niemand. I don't have schizophrenia. I really wish I had found that out sooner, you know."

Uh oh, here we go again. Oh boy. Looks like trouble on the horizon of the electrical grids. Are you ready for the second round of schizophrenic stupidity? Ah, you see until May this is going to be one fucked up ride. You are about to see what happens when two idiots pair up and try to make a go of it while acute.

Were you able to understand that in this chapter I was not lucid and many of the reported happenings were not real. You see that is the real issue with schizophrenia. It is not the memory slips, the voices or even the movement disorder that will get me into real trouble. It is the misunderstanding of what is really happening and what is in my imagination. I need a normal to point out the errors in my perceptions and keep me from harming myself by falling for lies my own brain tells me. If this still seems a confusing concept to you, no worries, the next many chapters are going to take you right into a profound break with reality.

I will help all of you to understand by writing the story the way I saw it and then tell you what the normals told me really happened. It will be up to you to decide what is real and what is not. It seems easy but be careful. My perceptions are often perfect and there will be very little evidence to help you determine if my actions happened or were hallucinations. Before you get too upset understand there is nothing before the next chapter I didn't report from a realistic standpoint. Master Boyd and the others are real. It will be from this point forward that things will happen that in the end you will find out didn't.

Sound like fun? Great. Get ready to take a trip right to Mars with me.

## Chapter 76: Breaking the Shattered
## The Fall of Psycho & the Rise of Neimand
## Master Boy and Sheryl the Absent Interim

Guess who's back? Well, it sure as shit wasn't us. Oh hell no. Our psychotic break was more tenacious than even our impressive spirit in the Spring of 1999. The year 1998 had proven to be a year of surprises, tragedy and incredible miracles. One of the most impressive repercussions of that wild year had been our discovery of our deep love for Master Boyd, the rapist Keyholder.

The fact that this most misunderstood of all our Dominants shared the misery of our own inner beast only seemed to enhance our tightly bonded D/s relationship. Until it all went straight to schizophrenic hell just as the year turned and the new millennium loomed.

The D/s couple had weathered its very first emergency. Despite the many setbacks, they were ready to face life as a mating pair once more. Master and collar now carried the marks of the beast that raged within them for everyone to see. The scars on their units would stand as a testament to their failures like a roadmap of despair. Even with an atlas to their location, they were lost. Sadly, neither was willing to stop their blind dash through the hair pinned curves of madness. If only they had asked for directions, they could have avoided that crash.

The shards are spinning out of control. Simon can no longer apply his expert brake ability to this crazy train.

Ahead at the bridge between the Real and the Delusional the tracks are broken and in disrepair. Try as he might the engineer wouldn't hear his warnings. The iron horse races toward utter destruction. One by one the cargo cars will fall into the awaiting abyss, lost forever in the dank waters below. Thank goodness Simon knows how to swim.

Sheryl is sick and tired of waiting for her promised place of power. She knows the name of one who can move her up the ladder to the rung she desires. With her trusty submissive anything is possible. She will send the investigator into dangerous territory to cut the throats of her adversaries. When her precious Psycho returns, Sheryl will stab her in, errr, pat her on the back for her successful efforts.

Time to go everyone. Don't drag your feet. Fighting will do you no good. Never did help us much now did it? It is almost time to blow our last gaskets. It was going to happen at some point so don't look so surprised. Living a life of loss and exploitation has its drawbacks far deeper reaching that what you see on the surface. No one can hold it together forever, not even a Psycho.

*"Hey, stupid. Over here. Hey Niemand, over here. Psssst. Come here. Follow me. I have something that will make you feel a lot better. Hurry before that fucking nurse gets back and hauls you to the hole. You know she went to get the orderlies to restrain your schizophrenic ass. You must be insane punching her in the face like that. Strait jacket city for you kid. Just what the fuck were you thinking? Oh, never mind, before you go I have a present for you. Hurry up you damned Thorazine*

I watched my Master running and playing with the children while I sat on the old porch swing with Maiden Mary. The day was uncommonly warm for January even in this southern state. Seine laid at my feet snoozing happily. He was willing to even tolerate Master Boyd now that he had at last been reunited with me. My Maiden looked at me appearing deep in thought.

"Mother, look, I know it has been a real rough time for you lately, and for Boyd. Dennis told me about the uhm, situation and made me promise to never say anything to anyone. We need not tip toe around it. I know all about the, uhm, car trip the two of you have been on and why it happened. Everything about Boyd makes sense now. I can see the why the attraction too. That said Mother, this has been a bad time for the kids just as much you two. They are suffering with you and Boyd. It is time to think about divorcing Timmy and making that man official." She pointed at my Master as my son tackled him knocking him to the ground both laughing wildly while my daughter scolded them for acting childish.

I shook my head. "Mary, once again you are sticking your nose where it does not belong. Boyd has the mother of madness too. We can never marry. That is impossible for reasons I do not care to discuss."

Maiden Mary's eyes went wide. "Oh Mother, does Boyd agree with this? He thinks you two are going to marry. You should have seen him when we all thought you were going to die. Mother, the man almost died right there with you. I have never seen anyone love anyone so much. Why would you not marry him?"

I growled while glaring at her. "Mary I mean it, drop this now. This is my business. I refuse to discuss it."

She shook her head in disbelief. "Mother, if you don't marry Boyd you are truly as insane as everyone thinks you are. You know Timmy has been slinking around here? Oh yeah, since your little trip to wherever you two went the asshole has stopped by twice demanding to see you. He says you owe him money Mother. He is going to make trouble."

"I don't owe that fucker a thing," I snarled out.

Mary snorted. "He said you had a deal, something about selling a farm. I am just the messenger, Mother."

My eyes went wide. I suddenly recalled making a deal with my husband to sell the farm if he would outrun Master Boyd's attempts to have him served with divorce papers the Spring before. Shit, I had completely forgotten that fucking agreement and that fucking farm too. Hey wait, I need a house.

"Hey Mary, can you have Ronnie go take a look at a house for me if I gave him the address," I said suddenly.

Mary narrowed her eyes. "Of course he could Mother. You found a house for you and the kids maybe?"

I smiled while looking back at Master Boyd and the children. "You bet I may have. I will leave the address and have Ronnie call me next week. I may be able to get my kids back under one roof with me yet."

Maiden Mary looked at Master Boyd as well. "And what about Boyd? He expects you and the kids to move in with him. Mother, you are going to break his heart. Are you sure you want to throw away maybe your only chance at happiness? I mean no one could understand you like he can. He won't even care about your problems because he has them too. You both have the same disease. It is a perfect match when you really think about it. If you toy with him, he could maybe change his mind and move on, then what? Not like you have had any other takers all these years. You are going to be twenty-seven soon and all you have to show for it is what? A stupid collar, and no one to share your bed or heart."

I rolled my eyes. "See Mary that is what I am talking about. You have no fucking idea what is going on, yet you speak shit about it. Boyd is never going to leave me Mary. I could put out both his eyes with a red-hot poker then cut off his feet and he would still chase me until I say I do. He is trapped by his delusion. He can't get out of his hell, just like I am a prisoner to this fucking collar. I am supposed to just ignore the fact that his designs for me will make my life more of a nightmare than it already is. You would have me suffer just to keep from breaking his heart? What about my heart? Why the fuck is everyone trying to tell me what will make me happy? None of you even know me. Furthermore, just because Boyd and I are supposed to be schizophrenics everyone would expect us to be a natural match. Really? That is a hell of a stupid thing to pair two people up over. I will say this for the last fucking time, butt out. Don't make me say shit to you that we will both regret. And if you say a fucking word to Boyd about any of this Mary, so help me, a word of it and I will never speak to you again. I am not fucking kidding here. Stop going behind my back and talking to him about our discussions." I spit out at her angrily.

Mary looked at the ground sheepishly. "Okay, okay. I hear you Mother. I didn't mean to piss you off or anything. You are right. I don't know shit about the situation you and Boyd are involved in. I just want what is best for you, is all."

I laughed. "If that is true then let me decide for my fucking self, Mary. I know my own mind, God damn it. I must start making arrangement for grad school. Like it or not I can't stay at DCFS much longer. The job is killing me. I won't quit till I can get enough cash to start school. Boyd doesn't want me to work or have a real life. He expects me to stay home and cook and clean for the rest of my life. I wonder why the fuck I worked so hard to get a degree only to become a fucking housemaid. I mean I was already doing that motherfucking job with my collar. I am trying to get free of that shit, not be trapped in it forever. Damn."

Maiden Mary took a deep breath. "Ah, I see, Mother. I never thought of it that way. It all makes sense now. Well, you are too smart to ever be happy making cakes and darning socks that is for sure. Maybe if you spoke to Boyd and pointed this all out to him he would…"

I raised my hand to silence her. "You think I haven't? Christ Mary, he is schizophrenic. He will never listen to me. Just do what I told you and stay out of this fray, okay? This is one mess I am going to have to just endure until I can get out of it, and I will get out of it you'll see." I smiled at that.

She nodded. "No doubt you will Mother. You are like a cat that always lands on its feet no matter how high the drop. Grad school, wow, you will be like a Doctor?"

I nodded still smiling. "That is right. I am headed right for the top Mary. Just call me Doctor Nutball. I will not stop till I have fulfilled a promise I made to someone special a long time ago. Just wait and you will see. I am going to change the way people like you and me are treated around here damn it. Not even Boyd is going to keep me from it." I winked at her while she giggled.

Seine looked up suddenly while stretching. I scratched him between the ears. "I am headed back to work Monday. I will come by and pick my boy up. I could use the company. I am looking forward to hearing if Ronnie thinks this house is ready to move into or if it needs work."

Maiden Mary narrowed her eyes. "You mean you have never seen the house?"

I chuckled. "Not since I was just a teenager. It is right next door to Mary, my grandmother." I smiled evilly as Mary's face fell.

"Holy shit, you have got to be kidding. You can't be serious Mother. She will try to kill you again," Mary cautioned.

I nodded. "Probably. I am not a stupid teenager this time Daughter. Mary wasn't able to nail me into a coffin when I was less experienced at demons. Now that I am the Queen of Hell, let her bring it. Just have Ronnie check out that old farmhouse and let me know." I stood up leaning out suddenly hearing something odd in the distance.

"Do you hear that Mary," I asked still cocking my head while watching Seine to see if he was also alerted to the strange noise.

Seine looked at me and yawned. Maiden Mary listened but was also shaking her head that she heard nothing odd.

Master Boyd stopped what he was doing and looked at me appearing to notice my straining to hear into the grid. "Niemand, stop that. Don't listen to that shit. Just sit down and ignore it. They may be watching. Do you want to get into trouble again," my Master warned while glaring sternly.

I nodded. "Yeah, you are right." I sat back down trying to ignore the sound of thunder off in the distance.

Maiden Mary looked at Master Boyd then back to me appearing upset. "What the fuck? Mother, did Boyd just say the two of you are being watched? That is nuts. No one is anywhere around here."

I shot her a look of caution. "You don't know shit about anything Mary, be still. The thunder is still rolling. Boyd

93

knows what he is talking about. They are always waiting, just when you thought you were safe they come for you." I got up motioning my Master to let him know it was time to go.

I could hear 'they' threaten my Master and me just from behind the belly of the Giant. Master Boyd shot me a look of nervousness as we said our goodbyes. Seine wanted to come with me badly. He was even willing to share my attention with my Master, begging to be allowed into the black car. It was with much hesitation I had Maiden Mary cart him back into the house.

I wanted to take him and Master Boyd was not opposed to the idea. However, something told me my furry friend was safer with the kids and Mary. Being in a house with two psychotics who had just nearly starved to death forgetting they needed to eat, well not smart. We weren't competent enough to care for a guppy at that point.

Once we were on the road to the house Master Boyd looked at me appearing irritated. "You were listening to voices right in front of Mary. Jesus Niemand, the normals just locked us the fuck up for that shit. I am not in a hurry to go back. You have to stop doing that. I am making that a directive," he growled.

I snorted. "You make everything a directive Master. As for behaviors that will send us back to the hospital, not taking your medication will sure as shit assure it right fucking fast. If Dennis catches you cheeking, you are going to be in big trouble."

Master Boyd sneered. "Yeah, but he won't. I am not taking it anymore, that is final. I feel better off that poison anyway. How am I supposed to hear the transmissions with that crap fouling up my air waves? Besides, I won't give up sex with you for anything or anyone. I waited all that time. Now those stupid doctors think they are going to take that away. Fuck that."

I shrugged. "Master, it doesn't matter if we don't have schizophrenia, everyone thinks we do. If we don't do what they say, they will lock us away forever in a cell somewhere and forget we exist. I must take blood tests to prove I am minding them. Do you want to end up like that? I suggest you take the medication like Dennis tells you to. Eventually the side effects will wear off and I don't care if you are a grouchy bitch. So what? Seeing you tied to that bed bothered me. Having to endure your rough touch I can get over."

Master Boyd shook his head. "No Nicmand, it is not fair. We had to give up all our dreams already over being misdiagnosed. I can handle being a cop. I can deal with being treated like a damned kid when I am over thirty. I can even handle the damned joke I am going to be at the station now that everyone knows about me. I won't put up with being an asshole and not being able to get it up so I can fuck my beautiful wife. I have lost so much time already. I am not going to waste more waiting for the shitty medication to wear down. Look, 'they' are not going to take all I have left to make this fucking nightmare life worth bothering, with God damn it."

I looked at the floorboard feeling empathetic towards his words. "You are right Master. I must tell you I cannot stop the medication even if you can do so. They do check me every month. If I am deficit, they will come take me away. I have no choice, Master. You realize I am rendered, uhm, incapable of orgasm until the side effects calm down."

He looked at me with pity. "Yeah I know baby. I am sorry to hear that. I wondered, but if it fucks me up I kind of figured it would mess you up too. There is no way to get around the testing?"

I shook my head. "No. When I kicked in that church door, I fucked my world up. The courts own me, Master. There is nothing I can do. It is okay. I am happy to provide your special services. I can still perform, just never reach climax is all. I can still make being intimate with me worth the effort." I smiled bitterly.

Master Boyd reached down taking my left hand into his own. "The courts don't own you baby. Not anymore. You belong to me. I want you to try to remember that. I was going to tell you when we got home but since we are on the subject. Before this whole mess started, I filed for a request to have your name legally changed. I also had Katheryn file a form to stop them from forcing any future name changes without your permission. Soon you will be Niemand May legally, not just because I call you that." He kissed his ring.

I looked at him in shock. "What? Why did you do that Master?"

He chuckled. "I wanted to give you a gift. I wanted everyone to stop making a joke of you by calling you that terrible word. I figured out the only way that could ever happen is by standing up to the ones who allowed it. If your name is stable, no one can use your chronic name changes to justify calling you by a nasty nickname. I wanted you to have your identity back. Equal service for equal service, Niemand. Thanks to you everyone has stopped calling me by a false name too."

I winced. "That is true. Master. Now instead of a rapist, they will call you a fucking schizophrenic. I did you no service my love. I didn't truly earn such an honor, but I do thank you always for the mercy." I looked at him feeling a great surge of affection for his incredible kindness.

**NOTE:** *The courts had been tormenting me for years by enforcing legal identity changes without consulting me. I would just get a packet in the mailbox telling me I was no longer 'so and so,' and now I was 'what's her name.' It was so confusing and difficult to keep up with eventually everyone just called me the Psycho rather than try to remember what I was being called any given year or day.*

*My dearly departed friend Stephanie had called me the nasty moniker in high school. It had stuck to me like crazy glue due to my many years of insane antics around those small towns. I had always hated being known as Psycho but over the years I had given up arguing with everyone about it.*

*Since the judges were still scrambling my identification almost every other year, there was really no point anyway. Hell, I didn't even know what the actual legal name I was going by was half the time myself. How could I be pissed off at the simple town folk for not knowing any better either?*

*For this cruel name change practice to end, I needed a guardian to advocate in my stead. Master Boyd had cleverly hired my old Mistress Katheryn. She may have been a horrid Master but she was and is one awesome lawyer.*

*Mistress Katheryn had contacted my psychiatrist with my Master's assistance and had Doctor Baker inform the powers that be of the psychological damage and identity confusion, in someone already very confused about who they are, they were causing. The entire process was started as a feeble attempt to keep me hidden from Debbie and her goons' radars. Not like it had ever helped anyway. With Debbie's own mother Mary right there in town with me, Debbie knew my new identities before I ever did.*

*It would pass that by May of that year I would be temporarily granted court approval to be known as Niemand May. It would be a battle until 2003 to keep the courts from overturning that original ruling. Finally, that August four years later the courts granted me the name forever and stopped the automatic identity change from that day forward.*

*Niemand is the female version of the Macedonian name Alexander. It means "the defender of men." It was chosen for me by Master Boyd's psychotic inner voice he called God. My middle name May was also selected for me by Master Boyd.*

*He selected this name because it was in that month in 1997 he had consummated our unholy union in the white cell. That's right, you didn't misread that last sentence. Just like his brand, when I hear my name I have no choice but to think of the man who gave me my identity in more ways than you can imagine..*

*So, now you know. My name is a complete delusion that was concocted in the mind of a madman. The origins of my name are truly as insane as the woman who bears it. I may have shed the word Psycho, but as you all just found out, Niemand May was created for one by one.*

He narrowed his eyes at me. "It is not your fault they found out about my misdiagnosis, Niemand. Dennis told them. I know who is responsible for that. We both must stop blaming ourselves for what 'they' do. Remember we discussed this. 'They' want to see us fail. The first step is to get us addicted to their drugs. I figured it all out while you were sick in the hospital. The medication is how they control our minds. Then we aren't able to see the tapestry or hear the transmissions. 'They' know if we can't see what they are up to we can't escape them."

I nodded my head feeling a bit of fear realizing he was right. "Okay, if you say so Master. I must take that medication and there is no way out of it. I will just have to depend on you to tell me what 'they' are up to since I will be addicted to the shit pretty soon. Then I will be a hostage to 'they' again."

Master Boyd snorted. "Well for now 'they' have you but I found a way out. There is a new hospital that just opened their doors to those with so-called mental illness. It is called Harbor View. I got you signed up to go there as soon as they have an opening. Probably in May or June. This hospital will be able to clear you of your false diagnosis. The woman told me they run assessments and have the best doctors working there."

My eyes went wide. "What? You signed me up to go into a mental hospital. Why?" I almost died right there.

My Master looked at me with surprise. "Don't you want to have that diagnosis removed? This place can fix it. After they find out you don't really have schizophrenia then I can go to court and fight to have the guardianship order removed, Niemand. It was all just a misunderstanding. We both know that. Then you will be free and they will not be able to hurt you anymore." He smiled with confident pride in his plan to correct the errored judgement 'they' had forced on me.

I looked at the floorboard. "How long will I have to stay at that hospital to get them to remove the misdiagnosis?"

Master Boyd chuckled. "That is the beauty of it. You could even do it outpatient. The hospital told me they would not need to put you inpatient just to remove a misdiagnosis.

But if you did have to go inpatient it would only be for a few days." He patted my thigh smiling happily at me.

I smiled back. "Oh my God. Could this be real? I could finally get them to stop saying I am a loon? Then I could go to grad school, get a good job and live a normal life. All my dreams could come true," I shouted out excitedly.

My Master frowned. "What? Grad school? No, oh no. You don't need grad school, Niemand. I have waited all my life to have my wife with me. I am not waiting till I am old and grey to have her at home with a smile and dinner on the table after a long hard day at work. No, we will get your diagnosis fixed then get married. You will quit that shitty job with Sheryl and stay home with me. After we are legal the kids move home with us. My guardianship will belong to you. Then Dennis and Carla can't tell me what to do, and no one can call either of us loons anymore. It will be perfect. Just like I always dreamed it would be." He looked at me with a creepy glare in his eyes.

I looked at him confused. "But Master, I want to go to grad school. I want to have a job and do what normal people do. What good is being free of the misdiagnosis if all I do with it is sit around waiting on you hand and foot? Shit, I could just leave everything as it is and do that."

He reached out and grabbed my upper arm squeezing hard barely able to keep the car in the road. "Stop it. You are staying home with me, Niemand. The normals and 'they' will be looking to hurt you and you know it. Just getting rid of the lies on your records will not save you from that evil.

You go back into the world of the Real and 'they' will get you again. Only I can protect you from it. You know that. You don't belong I the world of the real any more than I do. Deal with it." He harshly pushed me backward while glaring at me angrily.

"You don't know shit, Master. I didn't escape Darlin to only end up a fucking prisoner in your House. Fuck that. I am not crazy. I never was. It was a misunderstanding. This is not fair. I want a fucking normal life. Not one living like a hermit waiting for the attentions of a fucking schizophrenic. You really are fucking schizo and you God damn know it," I yelled out staring at him with hatred.

Master Boyd pulled over to the side of the dirt road now angry beyond reason. "That is it. Get out. Get out and stay away from me. I can stand being called crazy by everyone but you. That is not forgivable. Stay away from me. I mean it." He pointed at my door.

I glared at him full of rage. "Fine by me, asshole. I never wanted to be with you in the first fucking place. If you recall, you are the one who started this whole nightmare to begin with. I would have never granted you Simon's Key and you fucking know it. As it is if you ever bother me again I will tell Dennis and you will be sent away forever, nutball." I got out of his car while he spun his tires and raced off leaving me there on the side of the dirt road while my brother raced to his Western bed.

"Psychotic asshole," I yelled after his shrinking car.

I looked around at the miles of forest and fields all around me groaning. I would have to walk a full five miles to reach Darlin. It was already dusk. It was going to be a night stroll for my idiotic ass. I cursed myself for not waiting till I was at least back at Master Boyd's house where I could have left his idiot ass in my Taurus. I turned around and started my long trek toward my long-forgotten home at the cemetery.

Many thoughts swirled in my shattered mind while I wandered down the road. After my initial cursing of my schizophrenic Master's existence, I finally began to focus on planning for my future as a normal. I decided to call my Vocational Rehab counselor Jim and set up an interview with the graduate school that had been interested in enrolling me into their Ph.D. program for Diagnostic Psychologist.

I reached the iron gates in a little over an hour. My father darkness had arrived in force happy to take me into his loving embrace as I sighed while pushing the gate open. I walked to my outhouse and went inside slowly. It was possible any kind of creature may have decided like me this shelter would make for a good place to sleep.

I found my old home empty of unexpected roomies. I chuckled as I sat down on the dirt floor deciding I would have my Maiden go and collect my car from the psycho's house. No need for me to ever see that weirdo again. It could only lead to more trouble.

My collar made a clinking noise as I attempted to get comfortable. I winced at the sound. It was time to throw that stupid thing out too. I had outgrown it. There was no longer a need to follow an imaginary Key just because some drunk railroad man said I had to. That was crazy. I was not insane, so what the hell had I been doing all that time? Well, I was no doubt stupid but schizophrenic, no. That was a misdiagnosis. Had to be.

"Psycho, what the fuck are you doing? Why are you back in Darlin again." I heard Simon say just outside the door of the outhouse.

I snorted. "I am not staying Simon. I am just hanging out till my brother wakes up. I am too tired to walk all the way to Mary's place. Shit can't a girl rest her barking dogs without criticism. I did just about die a couple weeks ago. I am not a fucking robot, wait." I suddenly recalled that I am a robot.

Simon walked into the little space looking worried. "Psycho, you need to work out your differences with Master Boyd right away. Go to this Harbor View place and listen to what he has to say. You may not want to be sick, but you fucking are. If you fall for this bullshit lie you are telling us, we are going to be finished this time. We are not a kid anymore. These little brushes with death we keep having are starting to take a toll on the unit and our mind. Please listen to me. We are in a lot of trouble. The medication isn't working. I have never seen the madness this strong before. Something is wrong here. Please, I am begging you. Get help. Tell someone the medication isn't working," he said as he sat down on the privy bench to roll a smoke.

I shook my head. "Stop it Simon. The medication isn't working because we never needed it to begin with. We are not going to put up with Master Boyd's delusions. So, bug off, will you? I have heard from the Higher Power. It is time to go to Grad School and do what Matthew wanted us to do. In fact, tomorrow we are cutting off our collar and fuck your stupid Key. We are not owned by anyone. We don't need anyone. We are normal. Go away and bug some other idiot. I am done with this conversation fool." I turned my back towards him.

Simon gasped. "Holy shit, Psycho. You must follow the Key. You can't just ignore me. I am you and you are me, idiot. Oh shit, just oh shit. What is happening to us? This bad. Wait we have been slowly breaking apart. That is what is happening. Why didn't I realize this sooner? Oh, my God, we are becoming hebephrenic. Goddess help us, we can't return if we break completely. Psycho, get help. Please get help. We will go mad dog forever." He wailed out in a scream that made my blood run cold.

I turned back around in shock. "Simon, shut the fuck up. What is wrong with you? You know what? The only one going mad dog is you. You chose Master Boyd, a fucking schizophrenic to be Master. You knew he was sick Rachel and you picked him anyway." I stood up now yelling at the top of my lungs at the very upset railroad man.

"Don't call me that name, Psycho. You know I hate that fucking name, Simon growled.

"It is who you really are, asshole. You don't fool us. Pussy! Whore! Couldn't even stand up to your mother. You're a God damned loser." I coughed while laughing.

Simon stood up more furious than I had ever known he could be. "You motherfucking demonseed. We should have fucking died at birth. I hope they lock us up and burn down the fucking cell. Hell is too God damned good for us.

I stood up squaring up against my Simon. "Oh yeah? Well, you certainly have experience watching fires burn, now haven't you. While 'they' light up our cell, you can stand there crying like the helpless pussy you really are. You remember, Rachel, like you did when you let Scruffy burn alive," I said accusingly at my inner self.

His eyes burned with deep inner rage. "That is it. I have had enough of your crazy bullshit, Psycho." He came running at me plowing into me so hard I fell out of the outhouse onto my back just beyond the door.

I grabbed his arms and began to roll with him, kicking, scratching and biting as we struggled to get control. He rolled off me and stood up landing a good hard kick to my upper right thigh. I let out a yelp. Then I tried to get up before he gained the upper hand by kicking me in my other leg.

Simon quickly jumped on my back subduing me by my upper arms holding me to his chest forcing my limbs behind my back. I screamed out in agony and anger that he was using my weakness against me. He knew my shoulders were damaged from the cat o'nine tails many years before. I had no strength in my upper unit.

"You fucking bastard. Let me go motherfucker," I yelled as I stomped on the toes of his boots.

Simon let out a yell of pain but held me tighter despite my wild struggling. "Fuck you. I am never letting go. You will mind me, God damn it. I am the Master, not your," he growled into my ear.

With lightning quickness and incredible strength, he pushed me hard sending me face first to the ground. Before I could figure out what happened much less recover to get up, he was on my back grabbing my wrists and pulling them behind me while putting his knee into my back. I felt the metal bracelets just as I heard the clicking of the handcuffs locking shut.

I winced at the pain. "What the holy fuck, Simon. What are you doing you crazy asshole." My mind whirled unable to grasp the reason my old friend would treat me with such brutality.

Simon chuckled as he lifted me back to my feet now cuffed and confused as hell. "Now that is better. You seem to listen when you have no choice but to hold still." He started to pull me after him while he headed for the iron gate.

"Hey, what are you doing? Simon, look I am sorry I called you Rachel. That was uncalled for. Stop this insanity. We can talk. What are you fucking doing man," I pled while my railroad man continued to drag me after his storming unit roughly.

Simon stopped and turned around looking at me appearing confused. "Niemand, stop calling me Simon. I am taking you home, that is what I am doing. That is where you belong. You are clearly out of your fucking mind. You need to be protected from yourself," he snarled at me.

My eyes went wide. "Christ, Simon. You are delusional. We are home. You are heading in the wrong direction." I felt fear roll through my unit as I realized my Simon had gone insane.

Simon reared back his arm and backhanded my face hard. "Niemand, I am your Master. I am Boyd, not Simon. Wake the fuck up. Stop fighting me, that is a directive."

My head was forced to the left from the blow as his words echoed in my Looper. I let out a yell while the sting raced across my right cheekbone. I closed my eyes trying to shut down the spinning confusion inside my head.

"Master Boyd? No, you are Simon. You look like Simon. You can't be Master Boyd. He left us on the road and went away." I breathed out, refusing to look at my railroad man feeling very strange and lost.

Master Boyd let out his breath. "Yeah I did leave you on the road. I went home to get my handcuffs. You are talking out of your head. I knew you would come here while I ran home. Honestly, I was afraid you were going to attack me in the car. I didn't want to get into a physical fight with you. I thought you would walk off your aggression. I see it only got worse. You just attacked me when I asked you to come home. I can see trying to give you space is a total waste of my time. You have gone completely bonkers. How could you mistake me for Simon? Niemand, you need to quit that medication. It is making you nuts. Now, come on. We are going home." He started to pull me for the gate again.

I opened my eyes and saw it was indeed Master Boyd who had subdued, then cuffed, me. I felt my eyes fill with tears. He had come back for me and was taking me hostage again. I was never getting free of this psychotic cop. If I tried to escape, he would just chase me down, handcuff me and drag me back to his house.

"I hate you," I screamed at Master Boyd.

He ignored my statement and kept dragging me to his Chevelle, finally pushing me into the passenger's side, slamming the door behind me. I sat there crying and fuming at his total disregard for my desires for a life without him in it.

We were almost to his house when he finally spoke. "Niemand, you are suffering the effects of that dope they have you on, so I forgive you. However, if you ever try to run from me again, well I will have to take more serious measures than just handcuffing you. You belong to me, and that is final. You will finish this stupid job with Sheryl, then after that you will come home for good. Since I am off work till the summer. I will come with you and help. With the two of us working, Sheryl will get to be Area Manager faster. No more arguments. No more talk of Grad school or foolishness about Diagnostic Psychology. They are twisting your mind.

Don't listen to they, you listen to me. That is a directive," he growled as he pulled into his driveway.

"Fuck you. You are a psychotic asshole," I yelled out at the top of my lungs.

Master Boyd just shook his head. "Yeah, you are gone. Okay, you asked for it Niemand. I wanted to have a nice loving reunion, but you insist on making this ugly. Have it your way. I have no choice but to give you what you request just like you give me what I want. Equal service for equal service, right?"

He got out of the car then retrieved me throwing my cursing struggling unit over his shoulder like he had done in our early days together. He kicked open his door angrily and walked us into his bathroom. He tossed me roughly onto the floor while he turned on the cold-water full blast. I tried to get up, but he snatched me by the waist and flung me into the frigid shower.

I howled out in shock as the liquid sent electric pain throughout my unit. The torment collected inside my whirling brain suddenly making everything around me brighter and clearer. Master Boyd was holding me under the facet appearing upset and concerned.

"Niemand, baby, can you hear me? Are you back with me yet? Please baby, talk to me" he said sounding desperate.

I shook my head. "Please mercy. Master no more." I cried out shivering in both terror and the cold.

He nodded then killed the flow. "Okay, now tell me who am I and who you are. Say it, that is a directive."

I stood there quivering confused by this odd request. "Uhm, you are my Master and I am Niemand, your fiancé?" My lips trembled as I wondered if I was correct in my assumption. Something was wrong here. Why was he doing this?

Master Boyd smiled then rubbed his eyes appearing relieved. "Oh thank God. I thought for sure I had lost you for good. Welcome home baby. Here let's get you dried off and out of those wet clothes. I am sorry I had to do that, but you were out of your mind sweetheart."

He grabbed a towel and handed it to me. I reached out to take it wondering how he managed to get his cuffs off without me noticing it. Master Boyd took my hand and guided me out of the bathtub while pulling off my now soaked clothing still smiling in what appeared to be gratitude.

"What is going on Master? Why did you put me in the cold water? Why did you handcuff me at Darlin? I only did what you told me to do. You said to get out of the car so I did. I don't understand any of this." I frowned feeling very confused and unsure of my surroundings suddenly.

Master Boyd sighed. "Honey, I never told you to get out of the car. You should know better than that. I would never leave you alone to be kidnapped or raped on some lonely dirt road. You were never at Darlin and I never handcuffed you. I would not do that baby. We stopped all that shit a long time ago, remember? You and I were talking on the way home when suddenly you stopped making sense. I tried to get us home, but the episode came on too fast. I couldn't get you to respond to me, and you didn't seem to know who you or I am. I dragged you in here when you started to babble and called me Simon. I didn't know what else to do other than shock you back from Mars with cold water. Was it one of your partial seizures," he said while helping me dry off the freezing droplets from my skin suit.

I stood there with my mouth wide open. "You are lying. I walked to Darlin, Master. I saw Simon. We got into a fight about me going to grad school."

Master Boyd closed the commode lid then sat down running his hands through his hair appearing agitated. "Look Niemand, it is true that I am not keen about your going to grad school, but I am not going to stop you. I only asked you to leave that damned job with DCFS if you plan to do that. The stress of both, no honey. It doesn't matter if you are normal or schizo, no one could take that kind of stress, nor should they. You neither got out of the car nor walked to Darlin. Do you see handcuffs? If I handcuffed you, where are they? Huh? Besides, you know I swallowed the key. I would have had to bust you out of them. A bit extreme don't you think?"

I nodded. "Yeah it would be. I am sorry Master. Forgive me for my outburst. My medication doesn't seem to be working."

He smiled bitterly. "Yeah mine either."

I looked at him surprised "I thought you said you have been cheeking it. That you stopped taking it on your own?"

Master Boyd looked at me appearing very confused. "I said that? Huh? That can't be Niemand. Dennis would catch me. He makes sure I take it. The only way I could keep that shit out of my system is if I were to puke it back up," he snared angrily.

I shook my head feeling very scared. "Oh Master, nothing is making any sense. I think Simon is right. I am going Hebephrenic or something. Or you are lying or I am? Oh fuck me. I don't know. I just don't know. Is this real?"

Master Boyd looked at me appearing very sad. "It is okay baby. Come here. You just got out of the hospital. You will be okay. The confusion will pass. Yes, this is real. You and I are together, that is all that matters." He reached out and took my arms into his pulling me to him as he hugged me with his face in my belly while sitting on the commode. I stood looking around completely frightened.

"Something is wrong, Master. Where are we?" I noticed the walls of the bathroom looked different somehow.

He snorted. "You are doing it again Niemand. It is going to be okay. We are home, I already told you."

My Master stood up and began to pull me into a deep kiss, first forcing his tongue into my mouth. I tried to back up feeling terror rising within. I couldn't figure it out, but something was incorrect about this situation.

Master Boyd grabbed me tight by my upper arms then not breaking his lip lock. He pushed me hard into the wall knocking my air from my still healing lungs. I gasped into his mouth starting to panic. I could feel the sounds of the grid vibrating inside my ears screaming. My heart began to race wildly as my Master pushed me to the floor pinning my unit while he began to paw and fondle me like a wanton animal.

I started screaming in terror as the walls melted away and my father the darkness rushed into the space left behind. I could see the headstones all around me of Darlin. Master Boyd was on top of me holding me down while he engaged in harsh carnal congress with my unit. He was panting in his rhythmic thrust telling me to stop my screaming and do my duty as his wife.

I looked around wildly beyond terrified that somehow, I was back at Darlin and not in Master Boyd's bathroom. I began to beg him to stop his sexual attack due to my confusion.

He stopped his thrust looking at me appearing surprised. "Niemand, wake up. Stop fighting me. Give me what is mine. That is a fucking directive." He then thrust hard making me cry out in pain.

"Where the fuck am I, Master. Help me. Please help me," I wailed out in despair as he continued taking his special services rights unaffected by my lack of understanding of the situation.

He let go of one of my arms to put his hand over my mouth. "Shut up, shut up. Too much noise, God damn it. You will wake the kids. Do your fucking job and stop acting crazy," he growled while continuing to take his pleasure.

Thunder rolled along the ground under us while lightning ripped through the darkness above my head while my Master reached his climax moaning out in ecstasy, then suddenly covering his ears wailing out that the noise had to stop or his head would explode.

The storm broke loose again sending freezing cold rain down on our engaged units. We both gasped from the shock of it. Master Boyd disengaged then rolled off my sky clad unit as I sat up trying to cover my head yelling in fright. He grabbed my arm screaming for me to get up and follow him before we both died of another case of pneumonia.

I got up and followed him through his back door into the kitchen. He stood there also sky clad, panting appearing afraid while I looked around unsure how we managed to get from Darlin to the bathroom again, then his backyard all in only a matter of moments. I looked at him nearly ready to have a nervous breakdown.

"What is going on, Master? What is wrong with us," I screamed as I fell to my ass in the kitchen floor pulling my legs to my chest rocking in pure terror.

He shook his head. "I don't know, Niemand. I don't know what is going on. They all need to shut the fuck up. I can't even think with all this fucking noise." He walked over to his table, grabbed a chair and smashed it into his cabinets in pure psychotic frustration.

Master Boyd banged it into the wall next growling and yelling for everyone to leave us alone. He didn't stop until he had broken his weapon into tiny pieces. Then he too dropped down not far from me rocking and cursing while holding his ears begging for the voices to leave him alone. I just cried in pure misery at my lack of being able to figure out what was really happening, and what was in my imagination. I had lost my location and could not find my way back home.

I fell asleep still rocking and blubbering like a child in a fetal position next to the back door. My last sight of my Master was of him pacing and wringing his hands wandering around the house appearing very lost without a stitch of clothing covering his unit that sported new bruises and fresh cuts everywhere. We had again entered the twilight zone after only a few days of lucidity.

I awoke to my Master staring into my face appearing nervous. "Niemand. We must get dressed. Dennis will be coming soon. If he finds us like this, oh shit it could be bad."

He was pulling me trying to get my groggy unit to stand up. "Okay, okay Master. We can get dressed and I will make breakfast. Did you throw out the turkey," I mumbled while following him to our bedroom.

Master Boyd groaned. "Shit I forgot. I am sorry baby. I will do it after we are dressed. Hurry, Dennis doesn't fuck around. He is always on time."

I nodded while I aided him to dress, then dressed myself with his assistance as quickly as possible. I was helping him put on his boots when the knocking began at the front door.

My Master looked at me with worry. "It is Dennis. Told you he never fucks around. Shit, we really fucked up the kitchen last night. What happened? Did we get into a fight again?" He looked at me appearing to be trying to read my mind.

"Stop trying to read my mind, Master. That is not fair as I don't read yours," I yelled at him.

He looked at the ground quickly. "Sorry baby. I forgot. Okay, never mind. Too late now. Dennis is already here." He got up as I stood from my knelt position in front of him.

"Let me do the talking. You are still messed up from the hospital. They have you on that fucking dope. Okay? Be still, that is a directive." He walked to the door with me following, my eyes down caste as he ordered.

Dennis stepped into the house looking angry. "Boyd, the Chevelle is parked sideways again. Give me those keys. You are not to drive until this cycle passes. Now go get your medication. Niemand, have you taken yours? I don't smell breakfast cooking. Are you two eating, God damn it," he barked out.

My Master shot me a look. "Uhm, we just woke up Dennis. You know, we had a long night reuniting and all." He blushed at the memory of our lovemaking.

Dennis rolled his eyes. "Damned doctor told me the medication he gave you should slow that rutting behavior of yours down a bit. God damn boy, let that girl have a rest, will you? She just got out of the hospital. Have a little respect. That kind of business can wait. Now get me those keys and then your medication. I am beat. Along night myself." He trailed off suddenly noticing the disheveled kitchen in the distance.

"What the Sam Hill?" He walked toward the destruction shocked into silence at the sheer violence of it.

He turned around to look at my Master and me as we shot each other nervous looks.

"Boyd, Niemand, I think it is time we talk about inpatient treatment for you both for a few months. The medication isn't working. Someone is going to get killed this time. As it is both of you barely survived just a few weeks ago. I am not ready to bury either of you." He hitched his pants while shaking his head.

Master Boyd gasped while looking at me in terror. I returned his look. "Dennis, look it was just a fight. We got a bit out of hand. It was better the kitchen chair than each other. See the medication is helping already," my Master feebly tried to defend his bad behavior.

Dennis looked at him sternly. "Boyd, I don't want to hear it. Knocking the shit out of a wall to avoid hitting your sweetheart is not normal. Next time maybe you'll be busting your noggin into a fence post or driving that fucking car into traffic head on. No, this is going to stop. You both get into the car right now. We are going back to the hospital and this time you are fucking staying, both of you until your heads are back on straight." Beyond angry he pointed at his squad car.

I looked at the old bull. "Hey old man, you may be able to make Boyd do your bidding, but you can't tell me what to do. I am going back to work tomorrow. I didn't beat anything up. I also am not sick Dennis. So, kiss my ass. I am not going anywhere. Boyd is staying with me too. He was just suffering some left-over shit. It has passed as you noticed. He is lucid. Leave us the fuck alone," I yelled back angrily.

Dennis snorted. "Well you are right about me not being able to send you back to the hospital, but I can and am sending Boyd, sister. Boyd, get into the car, now. Niemand, sweetheart, you need to come with us. If you refuse, fine I can't stop you. I will just pray I end up picking you up attacking cars or kicking in church doors rather than identifying your decomposing parts out in some field."

Master Boyd was sweating in full on terror. "Dennis, I am not going to the Snake Pit again. I am willing to do what it takes to not go, even hurt you." He looked at the floor appearing embarrassed to admit what I already knew. My Master was not kidding, he would kill Dennis if need be.

Dennis scoffed. "You could try boy. You won't need to go that far though. I am only taking you back to Wheatly Regional unless you want to give me shit on this. If so then I am happy to go a bit further. Want to test me Boyd? Go ahead or get your ass in the car."

I looked at my Master. "Just go with him Boyd. Shit, they won't even keep you anyway. You are lucid. They only want easy cases, silly. No reason to get upset. I will see you in a couple of hours." I walked over and kissed him while chuckling at my true statement.

My Master kissed me back. "Okay you are right. No reason to get upset. I am fine. They will send me home. Have dinner waiting on me?" He smiled bitterly at that.

I nodded. "Sure will. We are having turkey." I winked making him giggle at our inside joke.

Master Boyd and Dennis took off for Wheatly Regional while I sat down on the couch for a nap. The phone began to ring wildly. I finally got angry enough to answer the stupid thing.

"Psycho, baby girl, how are you feeling," said Sheryl on the other side.

I groaned. "Great till I heard your voice. What do you want? I will be at work in the morning. You couldn't miss me this bad, no one ever does." I yawned then coughed a bit.

"Well, I found out that the Area Manager just retired.," she said sounding pensive.

I nodded. "Well congrats darling. What are you expecting me to arrange, a fucking celebration party or something? This has nothing to do with me. So again I ask what do you want?" I growled out irritated.

There was a pause. "Uhm, I have a problem. A fellow named Harold is standing in my way. I have to have a unanimous vote to get the position. Harold hates me. He will keep me from getting the position," she said.

I rolled my eyes. "Well, I am surprised Harold wasn't blinded by your stellar personality and graceful charm. So, Harold is an issue. What the fuck am I supposed to do about it. Suck his dick and beg him to relent?" I started to laugh.

"If that is what he wants," she said flatly.

I stopped laughing feeling quite offended. "Excuse me? Fuck you Sheryl. If this is a joke, I must warn you I don't care for your kind of humor. I am not your whore."

Sheryl snorted. "You want to keep your job you fucking do what you are told Psycho. I don't care what you have to do for or to that asshole Harold. You get his vote. I mean it or you can hit the unemployment line. It is simple, the vote happens next weekend. You fix it. That is a directive."

I took the phone and slammed it into the wall several times cursing and stomping. "Fuck you and your God damned directives, Sheryl. You are the shittiest Master I have ever had and knowing who has held my collar that is quite an accomplishment bitch."

At that moment, the front door opened, and my Master came storming in appearing angry himself. He came into the kitchen looking at me with irritated curiosity. I mouthed "Sheryl." He nodded then sat down in one of the last two chairs still unbroken by our ongoing psychotic shit fits. He started to wring his hands but kept his eyes on me appearing to be interested in what was going on with my ball breaking boss.

"Psycho, look I don't care how you do it. Charm him, fuck him or kill him for all I care. Just get me that position," yelled Sheryl.

I took a breath. "Uhm, so what the fuck makes you think he will listen to me? If he hates you why would anything I do make that change," I growled.

Sheryl chuckled. "He has seen you sweetheart. The guy has a massive hard on for your sexy little ass. You get him compromised then tell you what, I will give you a nice desk job out of the field. A real nine to five. No more traveling, court or dead kids. I will even raise your pay grade. Think on it. You put up with Harold for one moment and you are set for life."

I narrowed my eyes. "All I have to do is get this asshole to vote you in and I am assured a nine to five desk job. I want that in writing Sheryl."

Master Boyd looked at me stunned while he mouthed, "Really?"

I nodded at him.

He smiled happily and sat back in his chair crossing his arms appearing pleased.

Sheryl sighed. "Fine. I will put it in writing. Okay, you will have to catch the asshole this Friday in Wells. I will arrange for a nice dinner out just the two of you. After that you work your magic on your own. Come next Monday I expect to hear my name announced Area Manager. I mean it, Psycho."

I nodded. "Gotcha boss. Are we done here? I have other shit to attend you know." Sheryl hung up on me.

I snickered as I hung up the badly busted up receiver. Master Boyd jumped from his chair hugging me tightly.

"A desk job? Eight-hour days, no more nights and weekends. That is wonderful baby." He squeezed me tightly.

I snorted angrily. "Master you have no idea what that beast wants me to do to get that promised job. She wants me to sleep with a man named Harold." I didn't even get that sentence finished.

"Fuck that. Hell no. Fuck her. You are not fucking another man. Forget it. You are my wife. You belong to me, all of you," Master Boyd bellowed out furiously.

I nodded. "Yeah, I do Master. I never betray my collar so let that shit go. I am saying I cannot get that job she is promising and she knows it. I will not sleep with Harold so that is that. Unless I can figure out another way to get him to vote her in as Area Manager."

He let me go then sat back down. "You could, I know you. Well, we can talk it over. There must be some way. I want you out of the field. It is not good for you."

I sat down in the other remaining chair. "Never mind all that. Where is Dennis? How did it go at the hospital? I see they didn't keep you. I told you they would not." I started to giggle.

Master Boyd looked at me appearing confused. "Huh? The hospital? Niemand, I just went to the station to fill out paperwork for my leave. What the hell are you talking about they didn't keep me?"

I looked at him startled. "You left with Dennis, Master. He was pissed about you breaking the chairs and beating up the walls."

My Master raised an eyebrow. "Niemand, Dennis has not been to visit yet. He comes before his shift not after it. Broken chairs? Beating the walls? Honey, are you feeling alright?"

I was just about to start calling him a liar when I looked around at the kitchen suddenly realizing not a thing was out of place/

Well, seems one of us is not with reality. The question is how much of it is my fantasy and how much is Master Boyd's?

## Chapter 77: The Reality Impaired Pair are Psycho
The Reality Impaired Pair are Psycho
### Master Boyd & Submissive Niemand
### Sheryl the Absent Interim

Are you good and confused yet? Well if not, no problem. We will just have to get more psychotic. Now that shouldn't even cause us to break out in a sweat. Schizophrenia is how we got our name, and skirting reality is our game. Go ahead and follow us right down the rabbit hole. We have such wonderful sights to show you, to quote a famous fiend of ours, if you dare. Forget everything you thought you knew. Wisdom and reason will do you no favors where we are headed. Welcome to the world behind the shattered looking glass. We are so happy you decided to join as we have tea for two.

The demented D/s couple were battling a war they could not win. Tooth and nail they were fighting for their sanity, but both were sinking fast. Without a stable lighthouse to guide them in their psychotic shit storm, the Master and submissive follow each other's lead. The tapestry tempest was fueling the waves of madness. Ever faster, the two were tossed violently towards the jagged barriers of their shattered minds. Sadly, their lifeboat only had room for one. The Dominant would be forced to watch helplessly as his beloved sank into the briny depths of insanity.

Sheryl is about to have her dreams come true. At long last she will be the most powerful in the realm. She investigates her shattered mirror, mirror on her wall. Who is the greediest of them all? Ah, our dear Master Sheryl is the worst of them great and small. She is breaking her collar which will cause her fall.

The hunter is watching her prey closely. The Psycho is starting to stagger wildly from her mortal wounds. The stalker is silently waiting for the beta wolf to fall. When the beast lays helpless no longer able to struggle, she will make off with this rare prize. The greedy has already purchased an empty mount from which to hang his first kill. The monster is eager to enjoy the spoils of his expensive fantasy. Time is running out…

We are off to the Spring that sprung in 1999. Forget about Y2K, much bigger disasters loom for the psychotic duo as their world cracks apart and minds scatter in the coming storms. Grab you gum wrappers. Stuff them in your ears. Snatch up that hospital gown and stash it under the seat. We don't want anyone to see that. Swallow the handcuff keys just in case we need them later and let's let Master Boyd drive. The man is a maniac behind the wheel. That is exactly what this trip needs; someone who knows how to go around the bend.

*"We were best friends, come on think hard, don't you remember me Niemand? We hung out every morning for coffee for the last year or so. Damn, do you remember anything about your past at all? That would scare the shit out of me if I suddenly woke up with my mind erased."* ---- **Julia visiting Niemand inpatient at Harbor View, October 1999.**

I walked over to the kitchen wall to examine it closer. There did appear to be some mild damage but nothing like I was sure I had seen when Master Boyd wrecked his chair. Wait, where are the other two chairs? I turned around to count the chairs again. My Master was sitting there looking at me strangely.

"What are you doing Niemand," he said while looking back at the front door nervously.

I narrowed my eyes. "Master, something is wrong here. Where are the other two chairs? I broke one before our vacation but there were three, now there are only two. I know I saw you bust one up last night."

He shrugged then shot another look at the door. "I don't know where it went. We must have moved it to another room and just forgot."

I nodded then gasped out loud as I noticed what I had missed due to Sheryl's rude distraction and my total confusion at the lack of damage on the wall.

"Master, why are you in a hospital gown," I yelled out in astonishment that I had not noticed his very obvious attire until that moment.

He looked down at his unit. "Uhm, I think I may be in trouble baby. I didn't want to stay, so I broke out of the restraints. They were going to put that dope back into me. I couldn't let them do that." He looked at the floor in shame.

I shook my head in disbelief. "Holy shit, you broke out of the hospital. Master, on my God, what are we going to do?

They will be coming to find you. Oh shit, oh shit." I began to wring my hands.

Master Boyd looked up startled. "You think they will come here? Shit, we must get out of her Niemand. I am not going back. I am not taking that poison, damn it."

"Yeah, they will come here. Dennis will be looking for you, Master. This will be the first place they will come looking. We have to get you dressed and get the fuck out of here right now." I rushed to his bedroom to grab clothing to put on his unit while he came running after me.

I stopped dead at the bedroom door gasping in horror. On the bed was the broken chair and the handcuffs from my memories. On the floor was wet towels and my wet clothing from the night before. How could this be? I turned to look at Master Boyd who was also staring in shock at the strange sight in the room.

"Master, did Dennis come here this morning? Did you put me in the shower? Handcuff me? Did we end up at Darlin? Tell me the truth, God damn it. What happened last night? I am not helping another moment until I know what the fuck is going on." I rubbed my eyes to make sure I wasn't dreaming this.

**What Happened the Night I Got Out of Wheatly Hospital**
**(What really happened from the last chapter)**

My Master groaned then ran his hands through his hair appearing agitated. *"Okay, I am not sure about any of this.*

*Everything is a bit fuzzy, like a dream you know? I sort of remember we got into a fight about your job in the car on the way back from Mary's home. You demanded to be let out. I told you no and you jumped from the car. You hit the ground hard and for a minute didn't move. I pulled over thinking you were dead because you were just lying there not moving. You hit your head hard, I think? I picked you up and tried to get us in the car to take you back to the hospital, but you suddenly woke up. I was hugging you grateful you were okay, but you started screaming and kicking me. I thought it was maybe because you were injured from the fall and not thinking straight. I told you we needed to get you back to the ER and you flipped out. You wouldn't get back inside the car, instead you jumped up and ran off down the road. I didn't know what to do so I came home and got the handcuffs. I thought I might have to restrain you so you wouldn't hurt yourself. I went looking and found you at Darlin. You attacked me when I asked you to come home. I tried to wake you up from your episode, but you kept hitting me. I tried to slap you back from Mars. Then things get weird in my head. I am not absolutely certain, but I think: I ended up having to put the handcuffs on because you wouldn't stop attacking me. Then I believe we started to head home. You had a seizure in the car. I raced to the house. I think I put you in the shower because you wouldn't wake up from the trance. When you woke up you wanted to dance. We went outside. Maybe you and I started to make love after our dancing. Then I seem to remember right in the middle of it you started screaming at me to leave you alone. I think you forgot who you are or who I am or something. It seems that is when it started to storm and we came back inside. I busted up the*

129

*chair because you wouldn't stop screaming at me. Then you got quiet, but I was not sure why. I remember cleaning up the mess I made. I checked on you and you were asleep. I thought I put the broken chair in the shed, but I guess I put it in here. Dennis did come by this morning, I guess? I think he hauled me off to the hospital at Wells. I took a cab home. Niemand, I am not sure if any of that actually happened. I am not even sure if we are here right now or if I am restrained in a bed on medication at Wells hospital. I am so damned confused. My brain is mixed up. God and Bastard won't let me think. I am lost. Nothing is making any sense. What are we going to do?"*

I looked at him narrowing my eyes. "I remember all that shit too, so I know it happened the way you think it did. I am not sure, but I think it did. What I don't understand is why did you lie about Dennis coming here this morning or being at the station when I just asked you about it?"

He shook his head appearing very confuse., "I didn't lie baby or at least I didn't mean to if I did. I did go the station to sign some papers. I had forgotten about Dennis and the hospital until you pointed out this stupid outfit they put me in. They took my fucking clothes, those assholes." He growled while ripping off the hospital gown.

I winced. "Master, I think we are in a lot of trouble. Neither of us have a fucking working brain between us. Let's get you dressed and then we need to decide what to do about all this."

Master Boyd nodded. "Yeah, that sounds like the right thing to do if you say it is. I confess I have no idea what is going on. I am so glad you seem to. We will just do what you think is right until my mind clears up. I guess I still have some of that fucking medication in my system. I keep forgetting shit. I am really confused, like last night. Why the fuck can't I remember it clearly? I am never taking that crap again. Fuck the medicine." He followed me into the bedroom where we quickly got him dressed in a t-shirt, jeans, boots and his heavy black jacket.

**QUICK NOTE:** *He very quickly became so confused at that moment he couldn't even figure out how to put on his clothes without my aiding him. Master Boyd was in a full psychotic episode mumbling incoherently at times and drooling a bit. He was not sure if he was coming or going. I had to get him back from Mars, so I woke him up the brutal but rapid way (backhands and cold water). It took several slaps to his face and a cold rag face bath to wake him out of his madness.*

"There, all better now Master. Can you hear me in there? I am sorry I had to hit you but you were babbling again. Look, just relax a minute and I will toss this bullshit. Those mental hospitals have no style you know?" I chuckled while I picked up the discarded hospital gown from the floor.

He chuckled. "You did what you had to do no, need to apologize. I have had to do it to you enough times. It happens. As for that stupid hospital gown, I am surprised they don't put duckies and kitties on the damned things. Look at it. What is it made of, crepe paper?" He was rubbing his now pink jaw from my backhands and blinking his eyes trying to clear his vision.

I howled at that. "I think you are right. I bet the taxicab driver got one hell of a show with my big Master in this little piece of nothing. Well, now I know you really are as good as you say you are at getting out of restraints. I heard Wells Hospital don't fuck around with the loony toon clients."

Master Boyd scoffed feigning snootiness. "Well, the driver was a beautiful woman baby. She let me ride for free. All I had to do was give her a big tip."

I picked up a pillow and hit him in the face interrupting his repeating of the fantasy tryst with the imaginary sexpot taxicab driver. "Now you are lying, Master. The girl would have paid you to get the fuck out of her car. No one would fucking have you but me. And vice versa too." I laughed.

His eyes lit up with mischief. "What? Bullshit. We are beautiful, Niemand. Anyone would love to share their lives with either of us, or the backseat of a cab."

I rolled my eyes. "Oh my God, you are fucking delusional. You do need medication if you think looks matter. Those normals know a monster when they see one. They may fuck you but the second you drool on them they run for the hills. Trust me."

He frowned at that. "Yeah, you are right. No one wants a stupid schizophrenic around. Good thing we figured out the mistake." He reached out and pulled me to him hugging me tightly. "I love you Niemand. Please don't ever run for the hills."

I nodded while hugging him back. "You can run for my hills anytime, Master." I giggled at my sexual inuendo.

Master Boyd smiled at that and then laid his head on my breasts. "I intend to my love for all my life. You are my One and Only, perfect in every way. I am the luckiest man on Earth." He pulled me into a kiss while he began to grope and pant with lust.

I felt myself giving into his interests. We both had already forgotten the serious situation his escape from treatment had put us in. I was brought back to Earth when I heard a strange crying noise in the distance. I pulled from our heavy petting now alert to the weird sound. I strained my ears while standing between his legs. He was calmly sitting on the bed fondling his 'hills' cocking his head appearing as confused as me.

"What the fuck is that noise? Do you hear it too?" I nodded to him while he got off the bed and walked to his window looking outside.

"Sirens Master, that is the sound of they," I yelled out suddenly recalling that same odd crying noise the night 'they' captured us.

He turned to look at me in terror. "They are coming. Shit, what do we do? Fuck!" He looked about the room in a panic.

I looked at him with terror. "They may check the house for you Master. Dennis is with them, I know he is. Okay, get into the closet and crawl up into the crawlspace in the roof. They will not look there. They don't know it is there. I will cover the opening with folded quits. Hurry, they are almost here. Don't make any noise," I yelled as I ran to his closet to aid him to crawl up into the small door that lead to a tiny air duct hideout.

I got on all fours so he could reach the opening. I braced and moaned holding his weight while he pulled himself into the ceiling. He got inside just as the I heard the squad cars speeding into the driveway. He looked down worried. I smiled nervously while I motioned him to close himself off. He did as I directed. I quickly pushed the piles of his mother's old quilts to the center of the top shelf of his closet to hide the small opening.

The heavy banging on the door began while Dennis yelled out, "Open this God damned door Boyd. I am not kidding. I will kick this fucker in boy."

I opened it appearing surprised. "That won't be necessary Dennis. What the fuck is the hub bub? Shit, I was just napping. Is Boyd okay? What did the hospital say? Did they keep him?" I stammered out trying to appear concerned and unaware, not that this was hard for me. Most of the time I didn't know.

Dennis looked at me suspiciously. "Niemand, you know God damned well Boyd escaped the hospital this morning. The cab company said he gave them this address and the cabbie said he dropped him off. I know he is here because you are here. Boyd would never be far from his sweetheart. I know that boy as well as I know anyone. So, cut the crap. Where is he?"

My eyes went wide. "Do what? Here? Boyd escaped? Oh my God. Dennis, I have not seen him. I was off with Mary most of the day. I just got home about an hour ago. I didn't see Boyd. Oh shit. Do you think he went looking for me when he got here and I was gone?" I looked out the door into the yard trying to appear to be seeking his whereabouts outside.

Dennis shook his head while hitching his pants. "You have always been a clever little thing. Me and Linda are coming inside to look for Boyd. Now if I find him, and you were hiding him I will haul your ass in too. If nothing else, it will give me an excuse to put your psychotic ass strapped in a bed right next to him were you both belong. You are not helping him by lying to me Niemand. Boyd needs help and here you are once again getting in the way."

I glared at Dennis now angry. "Look all you like Dennis. Boyd isn't here, I told you already. Threaten all you like. I have broken no laws. I must be at work first thing in the morning. Maybe I will head out early and keep my distance since I am such a problem for your Boyd."

He snorted. "We will find him here. You just sit your ass right there and stay quiet. Linda, come keep an eye on our future inmate here. Randell and I will search the house."

He said to my Goddess who had been standing there behind him quietly.

Dennis motioned to Randell who was exiting the other squad car, there were two in total, to come out and join him in the house investigation. I sat down on the couch as ordered while Linda stood guard to make sure I didn't attempt to flee the scene.

The old bulls began to look around the house. I just sat there with my eyes closed pretending to be tired. My ears picked up every footstep of the officers while they checked the nooks and crannies of my Master's home. When Dennis checked our bedroom, I heard him call for Randell. My heart sped up, but I didn't move pretending not to notice the excitement as the old bulls discovered the discarded hospital gown, broken chair and wet clothing everywhere.

They tore up the room looking in every corner and under the bed, even in the closet but no Master Boyd was discovered. When I heard their footsteps come out back into the living room, I finally opened my eyes sat up and pretended to stretch while yawning.

"I am really sorry I wasn't here when he came by Dennis. I thought someone would call or you would bring him home this afternoon. This medication they have me on is whooping my ass. Damn am I ever tired." I yawned again appearing very fatigued.

Dennis shot a look at Randell then glared at me angrily. "Well, it must be pretty damned good medication for you not to give two shits about where Boyd is right now missy. I know better than that. He is here somewhere or you would be very upset right now. You are not fooling me. Where is he? Tell me or so help me God I am hauling your ass down to rot in jail," he yelled out angrily.

I opened my eyes feigning fear. "Jesus, Dennis, no need to threaten me. I am just as worried about Boyd as you are. If you would stop being an asshole, I would tell you were he likely went when he came home and found me not here. That is why I am not worried. I know my Boyd. He is at the edge of Wheatly camping out. He would expect me. He told me if ever we were separated that is where he would be waiting. I am not trying to get in your way. I know you are only trying to help him get better." I tried to look sincere.

Dennis snorted obviously not buying my bullshit. "Oh is that so? Well, then load your ass up in the squad car Niemand. I would like to know how he got there seeing as how his car is sitting out there in the driveway. Did he walk do you think? I don't. Tell me where he really is or we can go downtown right now."

I shook my head. "Look Dennis you are getting angry at the wrong person here. The hospital is the asshole, not me. I am trying to help you out, but you are starting to get on my last nerve. Boyd is at our campsite no doubt. I don't even know how he got to the campsite, but I know he is not here. Look again if you want. I didn't do a fucking thing to deserve to be hauled in other than come home for a nap before heading back to my motherfucking job. The way I see it, you are the one that should not be trusted. You told Mary about Boyd. We had an agreement. So, you don't trust me? Well I am not the one who tells tales out of school Dennis," I growled out angrily.

Dennis's eyes went wide. "Huh? Niemand, I didn't have a choice but to tell Mary about that bullshit you and Boyd pulled, God damn it. You were dying and she is your Guardian. Not like I could hide what happened when she obviously knew of your condition. She needed to know all of it so you could be treated properly."

My heart skipped a beat at the discovery that Dennis was not aware that Master Boyd held my guardianship because Mary had signed it over to him. Oh shit. I just shook my head appearing still angry while hiding my true terror at this latest misunderstanding.

"Well nevertheless, I have not done a fucking thing to give you cause to doubt my word. You searched the house. Do you see a Boyd? No. I will draw you a map and you can go pick him up, but I am going to nap and take it easy. I must go back to work Dennis or I am fired. You will find Boyd no doubt. Without a car, he won't get far. I do love Boyd, but I know him. I know where he is headed and I also know you. You will catch him. That is all I have to say about this bullshit." I crossed my arms waiting to see if my bluff would be called or if I had successfully misled the old wise bull.

He rubbed his moustache then shot Randell and Linda a look. "Okay Niemand, you draw that map. I am leaving Linda here to watch you and the house. You will stay here so that if I get to this so-called hideout and Boyd is not there, well it won't go well for you."

I nodded. "He will be there no doubt. If he is not here, that is the only other place he could possibly be." I took out a paper and pen and drew a map of a place almost fifteen miles away.

I was not dumb enough to give them the real location of our secret spot. I chose another place just out of Wheatly that I had often pulled off to collect my thoughts in the past. I handed the false map to Dennis. He and Randell called Linda to follow them out into the yard to speak privately after I got another warning that they would be back to pick me up if my fiancé was not located where I said he would be. I just rolled my eyes as the three officers went out to talk by the parked squad cars.

I rushed into the bedroom and pushed the quilt aside, then called for my Master. He opened the small doorway.

"Master, they are going to be back. I will get arrested if I don't run now. Come down and sneak out the back door into the woods. Go west and meet me by the road. I don't have much time. I am going to call Sheryl and make my escape," I said feeling my heart may explode from panic.

Master Boyd told me to move while he crawled out then dropped to the ground. "Okay Niemand, I have to go now. Linda will likely want to come back inside. You had better hurry. Dennis is not stupid. He'll come back if he said he will." He kissed me quickly then sprinted out the back door before Randell and Dennis had even finished giving Linda her orders in the driveway.

I took a deep breath then headed for the phone calling Sheryl hoping that just this once the old bitch would be of some use to me.

"What the fuck do you want Psycho," Growled out my interim Master.

"Uhm, I need you to tell the cops I have an emergency case to attend right fucking now. Like now," I said praying Linda and the old bulls would give me just a few more moments to work out this clever plan of escape.

"Huh? Tell the cops. Why? What is going on Psycho," said Sheryl now sounding concerned.

"Look, I don't really have the time to explain but if you don't tell the officer I have to come in to work right now they are going to hold me for God knows how long. Then I won't be in tomorrow or maybe ever. Just help me out please. Call me back in ten minutes and say I have an emergency and if I don't come right way I am fired. Could you do that please," I whined a bit.

There was a pause then. "Okay, fine. Ten minutes. When you get to the office you call me back and tell me what the fuck is going on. I mean it," she snarled.

"You bet boss. Got to go. Ten minutes." I hung up the phone and headed back to the couch just as Linda let herself back inside.

My Goddess closed the door looking at me with pity. "Mother, you and Boyd are in a lot of trouble you know. Dennis is really pissed off. If you do know where he is, I

140

would fess up if I were you. He isn't playing. Not after the stunt the two of you pulled last time. You both almost died. This is serious."

I rolled my eyes and sighed. "Damn, you too Goddess? Where is the faith around here? Look, I already told everything I know. I am trying to help but damn it, I didn't help Boyd get out now did I? I was not involved this time, yet everyone is trying to take me down river with the psychotic asshole. This whole thing is ridiculous. Dennis should be kicking the hospital's ass not mine."

Linda nodded. "That may be so, but we all know wherever you are Boyd is. You are here so where is Boyd?"

I shook my head. "That is a good question, but I can only answer what I know."

The phone began to ring. I excused myself and picked it up knowing full well it was Sheryl.

"Hello? Oh, hey Sheryl what's up boss," I said loudly pretending to be surprised to hear from her.

"Okay Psycho I am calling back, now what," she said sounding a bit irritated.

"Oh no. Seriously? Now? Boss, look I have a situation, oh? That bad, yeah, I understand. Hey, I need you to tell this nice officer that you need me there or well they won't let me go. Yeah, I know it is my job but. Okay, let me get her on the phone." I yammered on as Sheryl sat there quietly listening to my false conversation with her.

"Linda, can you come here a second. I have an issue," I yelled out to my Goddess.

She came into the kitchen and I handed her the phone.

"This is deputy sheriff Linda Hendricks. How can I help you,' Linda said while looking at me appearing confused.

Linda got a sudden look of concern on her face while listening to Sheryl then said, "Well Mrs. Voss is being held for questioning in the whereabouts of Boyd Simmons, Ma'am. I am sorry but she needs too, oh well but we can't allow, no, no we don't think she hurt him or anything it is just we thinks she knows where he is and she is not talking. What? Oh well, no she is not under arrest formally. What? Ah no, that won't be necessary. Couldn't this emergency wait? Oh, I see. Yeah, I suppose that would be a problem. Okay, look can I get your word that when this case is completed you will send her back our way? Alright, yeah, I hear you. Got it." Linda handed the phone back to me looking very angry.

I took the receiver. "You get your ass to the office now and call me, God damn it. If you know where that asshole is, then tell them and then get the fuck out of there. This is bullshit. That fucker is going to get you fired. You hear me? You get out of that county and stay out of it. I will get another worker to handle Wheatly until this shit settles, you hear me," Sheryl growled out angrily.

I nodded. "On my way boss. Call you when I have assessed the situation. Bye." I hung up the phone and headed to grab my purse and keys for the Taurus while Linda followed hot on my heels.

"You better hurry up or Dennis will have your ass. You do what you have to do and get back here right away," Linda yelled after me as I scrambled to grab my stuff.

I opened the door to leave, looked back at her smiling. "Dennis won't even think about me Linda. He will find Boyd where I told him he likely is and forget I ever existed, just like he and everyone always does. See you later Goddess. Oh help yourself to whatever you can find in the fridge. I think there may be a turkey in there if Boyd remembered to put it back before it ruined." I took off in a sprint and was gone from the driveway rushing to pick up my Master before Linda could respond or Dennis could return to stop me.

I took a right headed turn west down the old dirt road and was just barely out of sight of Master Boyd's house when I spotted him walking down the road in full view. I pulled up next to him and he turned to look appearing to not recognize me at first. I rolled down the passenger side window while he stared at me with a vacant look on his face.

"What the fuck are you doing Master? What if Dennis or Linda had come by instead of me? Fuck, get in the car. We have to hurry before they figure out what I just pulled." I pushed open the door and he stood there looking a bit lost.

"Why am I walking down the road? Where are we? What is going on," he said while wringing his hands staring at the ground avoiding eye contact.

I blew out my breath in frustration. "Get in God damn it. I will explain it while we haul ass. Master, they will figure out what I did. Once they do, they will be looking for us. We have to go."

He looked up at me startled with a sudden return from wherever the hell he had been in his head, "They are coming? Oh shit. Go, go, go." He jumped in barely getting his door shut as I took off throwing gravel headed for the county line.

I made sure to follow all the posted speed limits and road rules headed for Cumberland by bypassing Wheatly. This added a full thirty minutes to our scramble for escape, but I couldn't risk running into the old bulls headed back to Master Boyd's once they realized my misdirection. Master Boyd and I let out our breath in relief as we crossed over into Cumberland county. We were not out of the woods, but we were at least half-way there.

Neither of us had said a word during our frightening flight out of our home territory. As we traveled toward the DCFS office my Master smiled and looked at me lovingly.

"Thank you baby. You really do love me to do this, I could hear what Dennis said. They were going to arrest you. I owe you one." He reached out and stroked my cheek.

I snorted. "Ah, do you think being arrested scares me, Master? Hell, I hang out in the white cell every other weekend. Dennis will have to step up his game to get me to shake in my platforms." I laughed at that.

My Master looked at the floorboard wincing. "Yeah, we have arrested you a lot over the years. Dennis and the others hurt you all the time. I hated it so much. It must stop Niemand. You should never have been beaten or treated without any respect like that. They treated you like a criminal. Then hauled you away to the Snake Pit like one too. No one ever stood up for you…. That is all going to change now. I am here for you always." He leaned over and kissed my cheek.

I giggled. "Lot of fat good you have done me Master. No offense but seems to me you are no better off than me these days. When push came to shove, they took you down like a monster too. You need to face the facts, you may not want to admit it but they all think we have schizophrenia. That makes us public garbage. You know what they do to garbage?" I looked at him to see if he understood my language.

Master Boyd looked out the window appearing to be in pain. "Yeah I do know. They take it out and dump it for the buzzards as far as possible from decent folks."

I nodded. "Exactly. Now that they all know about you, well welcome to hell Master. You thought being called a rapist was bad? Shit, that was nothing. Everyone will think you dress in your dead mom's clothing and kill people talking in her voice, or worse." I sighed.

Master Boyd looked at me appearing surprised. "Do they really think that about a schizo? No way."

I nodded. "Yes way. Where do you think old Stephanie got that name Psycho? She used to say 'this is my friend Psycho. She is all like Norman Bates and stuff.' She liked that word stuff, damn girl. You know, Stephanie killed herself a few years ago over a breakup. Now that was truly a Psycho thing to do. To think she called me that, when really, she was the nutjob all along. I would never kill myself over losing a man. Geez, there are more of them. What a crazy thing to do." I chuckled bitterly at that true but sad statement.

My Master looked at me appearing in a trance. "That was not a crazy reason to kill herself. Maybe the guy was her One and Only, Niemand. If you left me, I would not be able to go on. I would maybe choose to do what your friend did. When you lose the reason for living what is the point in going on?"

I looked at him narrowing my eyes. "Really? you would kill yourself just because I fucking moved on? There are billions of women on Earth, Master. You could do better, trust me. Killing yourself over a woman or man is stupid. There is always another one out there somewhere."

He reached out suddenly grabbing my upper arm squeezing so hard I almost drove into the ditch. "No there is not. You are my one and only. There can never be another woman for me nor man for you. We are a pair for life. If you tried to leave me, I would hunt you down. You would never get another chance to run from me again. Do you understand me? You will never try to run away again, that is a directive. Do you hear me?" He continued to squeeze until I yelled out in agony.

"Yes, Master, I hear you. Mercy please. I am not going anywhere. I swear it," I yelled out almost in tears from the pain in my right arm from his grip.

He released me when I yelled that out. "That's better. Where are we going? Dennis will be looking for us soon. I hope you have a plan," he said appearing to have already forgotten his sudden outburst of violent anger.

I sniffed back my tears trying to ignore his volatile aggressive move toward my discussion of a person's right to end a relationship that is not working for them. "Uhm, I have to stop by the office and call Sheryl right quick. Then we can find a place for us to stay till this blows over. Eventually, Dennis will realize you don't need to be in the hospital, surely he will?"

Master Boyd nodded. "Yeah he will. Okay, sounds like a plan. Maybe a motel or something? Just for a while somewhere quiet. I go back to work in June." He began to wring his hands again.

I arrived at the office. It was with great relief I found no other employee had decided to come in on a Sunday to catch up on files or reports. I parked and Master Boyd and I went inside to Jane's office and my desk.

I flipped on PC while I called Sheryl to fill her in on the situation. Master Boyd pulled Jane's office chair over to sit next to me wringing his hands and appearing to be in a mild trance.

"Hey Sheryl, I am in Cumberland. I plan to rent a place here or in Wells or one of the other counties until they find Boyd. I am in no mood to deal with the Wheatly cops. You know how the boys in blue can be about one of their sons. I have missed enough work over this shit. I am done with it, so no need to start up any crap with me." I rushed on before she could start her verbal assault.

She sighed. "Well, about time you started talking some sense. That's my girl. You stay out of Wheatly. Get yourself a nice quiet place to rest when you are not working. Mary can watch the kids and Seine till this all settles down."

I gasped. "Oh shit. I forgot the kids and Seine. Mary, oh hell's bells. This is not good for them." I put my head into my hand rubbing my eyes hard.

Sheryl snorted. "Kids are tough they will get over it." This is your fault anyway. This is what you get for hanging out with a man. They are nothing but trouble. I have warned you so many times, but you must learn the hard way. Let this be a lesson to you fool. Stay away from Boyd and everything will be fine. Now I have faxed over your next cases. Get on them first thing in the morning. Go get some rest sweetheart because your fun and games just ended. You have a lot to do, and it was all due yesterday. Bye." She hung up.

I hung up the phone while looking at PC who was staring at Master Boyd with a look of shock. "Psycho Tron, who the fuck is this," he said narrowing his electronic eyes.

I giggled. "PC, this is Master Boyd. You have heard me talking to him on the phone a thousand times. Well this is him."

Master Boyd stopped wringing his hands and looked at me with surprise. "Who the fuck are you talking to Niemand? Did Bastard or God say something to you?" He looked around the room straining his eyes.

I pointed at PC. "No Master. This is PC. He is my co-worker. He asked me to introduce the two of you."

PC smiled brightly. "Ah. Well I am jealous but hey, the better man won right? Hey, wait, why did he call you Niemand, Psycho Tron?" He suddenly looked confused.

Master Boyd was staring at PC appearing afraid. "Did you hear something? Shit baby I think maybe I am hearing voices again. Do you have anything to put into my ears? I don't want to hear them anymore." He wrung his hands and rocked slightly.

I nodded. "Okay, both of you, I am in no mood for all this craziness so before it even starts, just don't. Master, let me go to the break room and grab some earplugs. Jane keeps a stash in there because she likes to sleep at her desk. PC my name is Niemand, that is why he calls me that." I got up headed for the breakroom to get the ear plugs.

When I returned, I found Master Boyd pacing and mumbling in an agitated state. I handed him the ear plugs. He took them putting then into his ears watching out the window while speaking under his breath to God. I shook my head watching him briefly. I then went to turn on Fax chuckling at my Master.

"Schizophrenic idiot," I said under my breath while smiling as Fax whirled on spitting out his lies into the tray.

I picked up my case load and groaned. "God damn, I will never get this all done." I walked back into the office and sat down in front of PC.

"Psycho Tron, uhm, your Master is uhm, well his motherboard has landed if you catch my drift." PC winked at me then rolled his eyes.

I giggled. "Yeah I know PC. Oh well, sucks to be me, right? Hey, do you know of a motel where he and I can hang out for a bit? The cops are looking for him."

PC wrinkled his nose. "Uhm yeah out on highway 37 there is a cottage motel. Nice and quiet there. I believe they rent by the week and the cottages are widely spaced. Private you know. That should work?"

I smiled. "Oh yeah. I had forgotten about that place. Sleepytime Cottage Village would be perfect. Okay let me call them." I picked up the telephone book while Master Boyd continued to pace and wring his hands talking a bit louder than before to no one.

PC giggled. "You know seeing Mr. Nutball there reminded me of a great joke. You did say he is a cop right?"

I nodded without looking up. "Yep, just like me."

PC nodded. "Okay so this friend of mine is a police detective and he was recently diagnosed with schizophrenia because he kept questioning himself. Get it?" PC burst out laughing which shook the walls.

I looked up startled. "Stop laughing PC. You will wake up Dude, idiot."

Master Boyd stopped pacing looking at me in terror. "Wake up Dude? Huh? He is here too? Shit! We have to get out of here."

I growled. "He is not here. I told PC to stop laughing so he doesn't show up Master. Everyone just shut up and calm down please. I can't think."

Master Boyd grabbed the sides of his head. "Fuck, neither can I. Shut them up. Shut up, shut up," he started yelling completely off his rocker.

"That is it. I have had enough of this insanity." I got up and clobbered Master Boyd across the face with the phone book knocking him almost to the floor I hit him so hard.

"Wake up nutball. Calm the fuck down." I started to hit him again, but he backed up.

"Stop hitting me. I heard you the first time." He backed toward the wall watching me nervously as I went back to the phone to call the motel.

PC watched me appearing rather startled. Master Boyd sat back down rubbing his face glaring at me appearing irritated but he was back from Mars, at least for that moment.

The motel told me they had a cottage available in the forested part of the grounds and quoted me a price. I told them I would be by in the hour to pay for the next two weeks. I hung up the phone and entered my password to start my CHRIS program. PC whirled while I checked in as the DCFS investigator effectively ending my medical leave.

"Will two weeks be enough time," said Master Boyd still rubbing his jaw and glaring suspiciously at me.

I nodded. "If not we can get two more. They said it is off season. So, we have plenty of time."

PC grinned. "Ah, that sounds like heaven. A cottage in the woods. Hey, have I ever told you this one? So a blue man gives you a pineapple, a horse gives you a blender, and an ant gives you a lemon. With all that what, do you have?"

I shook my head sighing. "Okay, I don't know PC. You have a way to make pineapple and lemon juice? Yuck, by the way."

PC grinned big. "Uhm, no. You have Schizophrenia Niemand. Just so you know, Master Boyd isn't the only loon around here. You are in more trouble than you admit. We are so fucked." He winked while smiling wickedly.

"Asshole, I am not. You are a liar." I switched off PC now feeling very irritated at my damned co-worker calling me false names.

Master Boyd jumped at my sudden outburst. "What the fuck? Who are you talking to Niemand."

I glared at my Master. "Fucking PC. I am sick of everyone trying to tell me I am fucked up. I am not fucked up. I am fine, God damn it. Do you hear me PC? How about you, Fax? Simon, you too. All of you bastards need to shut up. I am not schizophrenic."

Master Boyd looked away as if finding what I said a bit unrealistic. "Uhm, okay, sure baby. You are not schizophrenic. Wow. Yeah, so you're talking to the computer and fax machine. Totally normal." He started chuckling at that.

I snorted "Oh? You want to talk about not normal? Uhm, who just broke out of the psycho ward? Wasn't me. Hey, what is God saying to you right now? Hmmm, cause I know everyone can hear the voice of God. I am totally not schizophrenic. Just saying, cuckoo bird."

He stood up fuming. "I am not schizophrenic. Take that back."

I stood up glaring back at him with hate in my eyes. "Neither am I. So you take it back first."

Master Boyd's look softened. "Okay, yeah, I take it back. Sorry baby. I don't know what got into me. You didn't deserve that."

I nodded "I take it back too. We are just stressed out is all. They are getting to us. We must stop fighting each other. That is what they want us to do."

He nodded. "Yeah you are right. They are trying to control our minds and to set us on each other and pick us off one by one. Pretty smart. That is what I would do if I were them."

I smiled. "Okay then let's agree no matter what we trust each other and never let they come between us."

Master Boyd walked over hugging me tightly. "You got it baby. We are in this together. Us against they. They won't get us this time." We kissed then headed out to the car for the motel.

I had Master Boyd hide in the floorboard while I checked myself into the cottage under one of my old identities from years before. I still had the old driver's license that had not expired. I drove us to the cottage and slipped him into the small outbuilding. My brother the sun had set almost an hour before. It was easy to hide our entry in the darkness without any of the scattered other cottage residents noticing the strange couple's arrival.

The cottage only had one large living area with a kitchen/dining room attached. The only other room was a bedroom with a tiny bathroom and stand up shower. It was not much more than a fancy shed with a bathroom and stove, but it would serve as a much better hideout then our last vacation spot had.

We covered the television with a blanket so 'they' couldn't use it to find us. Yeah we thought TVs were and are tracking devices of they. We unplugged the tiny microwave to keep it from impeding the transmissions. Yes, we believed that too. Still do, not kidding, I hate microwaves.

Once we had secured the small cottage Master Boyd called in his special services rights. I pretended to be frightened and unwilling much to his thrill. He appeared to enjoy it greatly as he chased me playfully till he cornered me in the small bedroom. I was still very weak from my near-death illness. He didn't have much difficulty subduing me for his lustful interests due to my inability to resist his strength.

Unlike his failed attempt while in the hospital, this time he took his privileges with great vigor several times throughout the night. He was no longer hampered by the side effects of Thorazine. This sudden recouping of his manhood helped to reinforce his belief that the medication was designed to harm us, not to help us. Master Boyd decided we would never take Thorazine ever again and he never did and soon enough neither would I. You'll find out how we managed that, just hang in there. Everything will be discussed in time.

**QUICK NOTE:** *We apparently had already engaged in successful carnal congress the night before but neither of us could recall it clearly. The first night in the cottage we both were aware enough, we were not in a heavy episode, of the situation to remember it properly in case you were wondering.*

The next morning after providing special services to my Master yet again, the horny bastard, I dressed and got ready for my first day back to work in weeks. He wanted to come with me, but I finally convinced him that Dennis may come looking for me. My Master finally realized, like me, he would have to hide out completely for a bit until everyone stopped suspecting me of knowing his whereabouts. I kissed him goodbye after reminding him he could not wander the grounds under any conditions. I got into the Taurus and headed to Julia's for morning coffee. She was the first item on my list, much to my irritation.

I pulled into her driveway deep in thought of how I could end these horrid morning sessions with the most annoying person I had ever met, just under the evil clique that is. Julia was sitting in a lawn chair in her yard watching me appearing slightly humored as I got out of the car.

"Well look who has risen from the dead. How you feeling Psycho," Julia called out happily.

I glared at her. "I was feeling great till I saw your name on my to do list. Why are you still insisting to Sheryl that I come here every fucking morning? This is utter bullshit you know." I slammed the car door walking toward the dumb bitch.

Julia chuckled. "Oh, now you are hurting my feelings. Where have you been Psycho? Sheryl says you were sick, no kidding. That was pretty obvious the last time we saw each other, pneumonia, right?"

I rolled my eyes while chuckling. "No, Julia you got me all wrong. I was off in Hollywood launching my career as an actress. I actually did quite well. In fact I am such a good one you will hardly even know I don't give two shits about you or your problems. I am going to act like I care, and you can act like you are a victim. Shit, I bet there is a daytime television hit in this whole fucked up situation you have me hijacked into. I will be sure to call my agent soon as we are done here. I could make you famous, darling. Now let's cut the crap, shall we? How I am doing has never mattered to you before, so let's go inside and drink your fucking coffee. I have real work to attend, and you are wasting my time and getting on my last nerve." I gave her great big fake ass smile.

Julia started to clap slowly while smiling back. "Wow, you really are good at acting. You'd never even know you are psychotic as shit. Unless you know what to look for that is."

I stopped smiling and glared hatefully. "Fuck you Julia. I am not psychotic, and you can stop trying to play mind games by saying it. I know your fucking game sweetheart. Never going to happen, got that? Sheryl does not have the authority and even if she did, I would never kneel to you. So, forget it," I sneered.

Julia's eyes went wide. "Huh? What the fuck are you talking about Psycho? Kneel to me? Sheryl doesn't have the authority to do what exactly? I am not playing mind games. You can deny it all you like. I have seen you. You are schizophrenic and I don't know why you are trying to hide it from me. I am not going to tell anyone. Shit the last thing I want to see is you fired."

I walked over and grabbed Julia by the collar of her shirt and reared back my hand. "Say that again, call me that again. Go ahead, I dare you. I will knock your teeth out sweetheart.

I've done it before, I have experience. Say it again. You won't be telling anyone anything without a fucking head."

Julia trembled in terror while cowering. She put up her hands. "Okay. Okay, I am sorry. I didn't mean it. You are not psychotic or schizophrenic. I am really sorry Psycho. lease let me go."

I pushed her backward and she fell over with her chair,. "There I let you go Julia. You know what? I really don't feel like coffee this morning. I think I will pass but fuck you so much for the offer." I walked back to my car and sped off while Julia was getting up off the ground glaring at me.

I sped to my next assignment in Jessieville. I had received a report of a three-year-old who had been molested by her biological father. I found the small single-family home and pulled into the driveway wondering how angry Sheryl was going to be that I had pushed Julia onto the ground. I was rather surprised I was not already being called or paged off the hook. It was then I noticed I didn't have my pager. I was deep in thought trying to recall where I had misplaced those items as I knocked on the door.

It opened and a tiny little girl with big brown eyes and stringing brown hair answered. She smiled at me sweetly. "Oh hi. Guess what? My daddy put his mouth on my pee pee and it feels very funny." She grabbed her private and giggled.

I raised my brow bridge thinking I had found the correct address apparently. "Oh? Well, that sounds like something to talk about. Is your mommy home honey," I said while smiling.

She shook her head still smiling sweetly. "Nah uh, my grammy is here though," she said in her baby talking voice.

I nodded. "Ah, let me talk to your grammy then? Then you and I can play a game. Won't that be fun," I said sounding excited.

She nodded. "Yes, let's play." She grabbed my hand dragging me behind her into the house where a middle age woman who appeared very worn was standing looking at me with sadness.

I shot a nervous smile at the woman. "Uhm DCFS investigations Ma'am," I spouted as the little child continued to drag me to her room.

The middle-aged lady nodded then turned to follow us. "Yeah, I have been expecting you."

I sat down as instructed by the child while her grandmother waited just outside the room. The little girl told me a story of how her father would put his mouth on her 'winky' and move his tongue making her feel 'funny' and then would insert his fingers making her cry. I wrote down the horrors this little three-year-old girl told me of her molestation feeling very sick to my stomach. Her offender was her actual biological father, not a stepdad, not even an uncle. Biological parental molestation and sexual abuse is rare, but since I personally have endured such a thing I know for a fact it happens.

The child was too young to understand the stigma, trauma, nor did she know society believes she should be ashamed. It was good to see. I knew a bit of work would fix this young girl's mind so that in time she would not ever feel that way if no one ever did anything stupid like make her feel guilty. She was just a baby so she had not picked up the understanding of shame. No girl deserves a rape nor should she ever feel guilty about it. Society is responsible for that bullshit by making a victim take the responsibility while giving the offender excuses. For the record, fuck that shit, grrr.

I finished my interview with the baby then with some difficulty escaped her friendly clutches to speak to her grandmother. The lady was very worn and appeared upset, as would be expected. She offered to sit at the kitchen table to tell me her side of the story.

"So where is her mother and the offender right now? Missus, I didn't catch your name," I asked as she poured my coffee.

The lady chuckled bitterly. "You can call me Maggie. I am Dot's grandmother. Her mother Candy is in jail, and her rat bastard father Kenny is in the hospital."

I looked up startled. "If Kenny is in the hospital then how did he molest Dot? Why is Candy in jail? Was she in jail when this all happened?"

Maggie put my coffee in front of me and sat down sighing. "Oh, well you see when Dot told me what Kenny did, I made the mistake of calling Candy at work. I told her what Dot said Kenny did. Candy came home and waited behind the front door with a two by four. When Kenny came in from his job, well my girl beat him within an inch of his life. The cops hauled her to jail and took him to the hospital. I have been here watching after Dot ever since this all happened yesterday. My girl Candy is a scrapper you know. I should have known better. Anyway, I can't afford her bail so I am doing all I can to help out. Please don't take Dot into custody. It would kill Candy. I promise I won't leave until Candy gets out no matter how long they keep her. She was only protecting her baby." She broke down crying.

I got up and patted Maggie on the back. "It is okay Maggie. Calm down, I am not taking Dot. I need you to do two things for me though. I need you to stay here with Dot and I need to know the jail in which they are holding Candy."

Maggie looked up. "Thank you so much for letting Dot stay. They, the cops, said I would have to go to court to get her out of foster care…"

I interrupted her. "You would Maggie. So, answer my questions and I will get this all fixed up. Now please, I don't have much time before I have to take Dot into custody."

Maggie raised an eyebrow confused by my statement, but she gave me the name of the jail holding my vigilante momma. I told Maggie to stay put and rushed off to the local jail house. Once there I spoke to the cops and found out Candy was able to post bail. I paid it out of my own pocket and had Candy released into my custody.

The jailor brought out a pretty woman of only twenty-three with long sun colored hair. She was only about five one like me and thin for a lady who just had a child only three years before. Candy looked at me with big brown eyes in shock when she found out I was with DCFS. Her eyes got even bigger when the jailor told her I was the one who freed her from jail.

"Why would you do that," Candy said in surprise.

I chuckled. "It is a pleasure to meet you too, Candy. Uhm, can we discuss this in the car? I must hurry. We can interview on the way to your house if you would be so kind?"

She nodded then did her best to keep up with my rapid stride as I practically ran to my car. I knew I had to get this mother back in the home before the hour was up. If I could not, the child Dot would go into foster care due to lack of legal guardian protection in the home.

Candy and Maggie were unaware that with the offender running around out of jail. The hospital didn't count as a jail and the child was under five to make matters worse, I would have to follow the law or go to jail myself. It was unfair but that is the way it is. I, the demon of the state, would be forced to remove Dot crying and scared out of her mind. I viewed this as punishing a mother who defended her child and a child who was an innocent victim.

Once I was speeding Candy back to her home, she told me that she lost it when Dot told her what Kenny did. She started crying saying she never wanted to see Kenny again or, she had to be honest, she would likely finish the murder she intended to commit in the first place.

I nodded in sympathy. "I know darling. Look, don't say that to anyone else, okay? If they ask, tell them you are sorry. But divorce Kenny immediately and if you can file and get an order ending his ability to see Dot I can close this case without it going on your record too. You only have thirty days. If you can't I have to send you to the caseworkers. Darling, once they get involved it is hell to end them. You did the right thing. You protected your child. I don't want to see you punished for it."

Candy nodded. "I got that loud and clear. Why did you bail me out? I mean that was expensive. I am grateful but all that just to keep my girl out of foster care and keep a case off us? Really?"

I smiled bitterly. "No, that is not why I did it Candy. Honestly, you are the very first mother I have ever met who beat the fuck out of the asshole who hurt her child. I admire you. You are a hero to me. It would be wrong to let you rot in jail, take your baby, and see you punished for doing what all these other monster mothers didn't do. Can you get that divorce quickly?"

Candy sat there with her mouth open in shock for a moment in a daze finally appearing to hear my words. "Uhm, I doubt it to be honest. I only have a shit job at the quick stop. Kenny made all the money Missus Voss. I will get one, but it will take a while. I am sorry I want that asshole gone now."

I pulled into her driveway with fifteen minutes on our clock to spare. "Okay, here is the number of a lawyer I know. Her name is Katheryn. She will get you set up. Tell Katheryn to send me the bill. You need to file immediately if you mean what you say. I will close this case on you in thirty days if you and Katheryn can get that order. She will know what to do and how to do it." I wrote down the number for Candy.

Candy looked at me again appearing surprised. "You can't be serious? Every mother doesn't protect their babies? This is a joke, right? You would do this for me? Missus Voss, I don't know how to thank you. I just, what can I do?" She looked at me tearing up with true gratitude.

I smiled. "You can pay me back by filing for that fucking divorce and protecting Dot from any more horror. I know I can depend on you. You are one in a million Candy. I hope you don't take offence, but I hope to never see you again, darling, except in passing on the street."

She took the number smiling. "You bet. Thank you again. I will never forget this. May God bless you Missus Voss."

Candy got out of the car while I looked at her. "Afraid not, but thanks so much for asking. Call Katheryn." I pulled out and raced to the hospital to meet with the sorry ass father that just threw away a beautiful wife and loving daughter for twisted lust.

Kenny was busted up, hee-hee-hee, with a broken leg and various other injuries. Candy was quite a tigress. I sat down next to his bed glaring at this man.

He was about five ten and had green eyes. His hair was brown and stylish. Though his nose was broken and face swollen, I could tell he was handsome. I could not for the life of me understand why this father, who was good looking and blessed with a gorgeous wife, would resort to molesting his three-year-old girl.

"Kenny? Got anything to say before we file charges officially? You can have a lawyer present, but to be honest you have no shot. Dot is very believable and we both know you did it," I said sounding short.

His eyes teared as he looked at the ceiling appearing shamed. "Yeah, I did it like Dot said I did. I don't know what got into me. She was dancing around in her little pink tutu and doing this seductive dance. Then she jumped into my lap grinding herself into me. I could tell she wanted me. I knew better but she was just so damned sexy. I didn't mean to go that far, but she kept asking me for more. You know she was loving it. I was just seduced by her."

I stood up slamming my folder loudly making Kenny jump from the noise. "Enough. Dot is fucking three-years old Kenny. No fucking three-year old is seductive. You are sick. She is your fucking daughter. Jesus, okay, you know what, doesn't matter. In prison your cellmate will find you seductive as well. I hope you think of what you did to that helpless little baby while Bubba does it to you. Cry all you want. Understand Bubba will not be able to help himself either. Good day to you Kenny. See you in court." I left the sobbing child molester to make my phone call to Sheryl and report my findings and to have Kenny officially arrested for child molestation.

## HAPPILY, EVER AFTER

*Candy did call Katheryn, and she did get a permanent restraining order put on Kenny. She was divorced within the ninety days allowed and eventually remarried. Dot went to counseling and did not appear to suffer significant effects from her trauma. Last I heard she was doing well and happy as always. I was able to close this case in less than thirty days and keep this family out of the cross hairs of DCFS thuggery. Thank the Gods.*

*As for Kenny, he did five years hard time in the state penitentiary. His parental rights were terminated while he was in prison. I am not certain, but I think the cellmate seduced by his charm was named Rufus, not Bubba.*

*Interestingly, in all my years working with DCFS and cases of child abuse, Candy was the only mother who ever did this for her daughter. In every other case of sexual abuse by a father or stepfather the mother always took the offender's side and blamed the daughter. That is why I remember Candy and why I helped her in any way possible. She really is my hero. To this day I look up to the mother who proved she is the one. Bravo Candy. Love and big hugs to you girl.*

After calling the local cops after filing for Kenny's arrest, I stood around waiting for Sheryl to call me on the hospital pay phone. I had left her a message to let her know

I couldn't find my cell phone anywhere. Where did that fucking thing go?

"Psycho, Julia called me about your bad behavior this morning. You want to keep your job I expect you to be at her house with an apology and better manners first thing tomorrow," growled out Sheryl.

I rolled my eyes. "Jesus Sheryl, I have work to do. The woman doesn't even work for DCFS anymore. What are you doing to me? I don't have time for this bullshit."

"Make time sweetheart. That is a directive. Now on to my next beef with you. Where is your pager and cell phone? Did you fucking lose them? How the fuck did you do that? If you have, then you need to have the new secretary file for replacements and I am taking the charge out of your check. That is ridiculous losing office property like that," Sheryl said sounding irritated.

I made a fake 'stroking' motion with the phone. "Yeah okay whatever. Anything else boss? Want me to go pick up your dry cleaning and groom your fucking dog too?"

Sheryl snorted. "Stop being a smart ass. Oh, get to the office. Jane says there is a cop there looking for you. She said to tell you Dennis wants to have a word, whatever that means."

I groaned. "Fuck me, alright. I will file with the secretary for a new pager and phone after I deal with that noise. Kiss, kiss grouchy momma. Bye." I hung up wishing I could just disappear off the face of the Earth forever.

I walked to the car noticing all the codes lighting up on the hospital walls. That made me a bit nervous. It seemed 'they' had something to say and wanted me to hear it badly to be bothering me at work. I walked out into the parking lot and almost screamed. The entire world was covered in the tapestry webs and the transmissions were flowing like waterfalls in every direction. Maybe Simon was right. I had never seen the world of the delusional this bad before. Not even back when they first said I have, wait a minute, could I have schizophrenia?

Nah, just kidding, that was just a misunderstanding.

## Chapter 78: Do Not Disturb
## Master Boyd & Submissive Niemand
## Sheryl the Absent Interim

Double, double toil and trouble. Fires burn and cauldrons bubble. Fair is foul and foul is fair. Do you sense it? Danger is in the air. Run, try as you might. Insane or not, who knows which path is right? Welcome to the nightmare of the waking dead. Please don't stress, it's only in our head.

The Dominant is pacing in his personal hell. The submissive is rushing towards her two-fold grave. Both are wandering without a sense of time and space. It seems though while everyone seeks, no one is really looking. The D/s pair will hold on to each other begging for mercy, but they forgot just how subjective that really can be when granted by a normal.

Sheryl is tired of being a Master to a collar who doesn't mind. She plans to teach that insolent Psycho a lesson. Sheryl has let the power seduce her. Now she will pay a heavy price, at the expense of her most prized investigator.

Dennis has loved his son since the day he was born. No matter what horrors have befallen the cursed boy, the old bull has guarded the lost soul. He only cares that the misunderstood Master be saved from himself. He has always been able to push the schizophrenic ward to do as he was told until Master Boyd found his One and Only that is.

My, my, my. What do we have here? You are all back begging for more of this psychotic abuse? Really? Wow, you

169

are tough ones indeed. Well, who are we to argue. Seriously, can you tell us who we are? We forgot. Oh never mind. That is not important for this chapter. Grab that golden seal in case they pull a drug test later. Don't forget to back up all your data for PC. Wrap that electrical tape up nice and tight. We wouldn't want us to have any screws loose, now would we? Time to fly. Does anyone remember where we put that fucking turkey?

*"Look at me, you psychotic motherfucker. Don't you see mom and I are busy? Besides, it is your fucking job to do the shit I don't have time to do. I told you this already. Damn you are one forgetful bitch. I left the damned thing next door after a few drinks last night. Gus says he has it. Just knock on the fucking door and he will give it back to you. It's going to get cold tonight and I need that God damned jacket. Quit whining and follow my fucking orders or you will find yourself back in the loony bin."*
--**Mistress Julia yelling at Niemand, Baltimore, Maryland, May 2000.**

I raced past the tapestry webs hoping none of them would stick to the Taurus and pull me into the vortex swirling above my head. This was bad, something was wrong here. For some reason I couldn't recall Simon calling for a 'healing of the shattering.'

I didn't have time for this. Dennis was waiting at the office and my case load was spilling off the page into the seat next to me. I could hear the screams of all the children calling out for aid. I rubbed my eyes trying to erase the visions of chaos all around me.

"They are coming. Run Neimand, run. Hahaha," a voice called out from the void.

"Loser. Loser. You can't even remember you name, fool. Who are you," whispered another.

I screamed out in terror gasping for air. The whirling was so loud. I felt myself being pulled inside. Numbness spread through my unit as the drool began to pour from my mouth. I couldn't swallow while my brain tilted just a little too far to the left.

"No, no, no. Not now. Please Goddess, not now," I yelled out slurring my words slightly as I grabbed the steering wheel holding on tightly against the coming catatonic stupor, I needed to pull over and fast.

I whipped the Taurus into the ditch throwing it into park. I could not get my scattered thoughts in order. I was completely ignoring the probable damage to the front of the car from my sudden nosedive into the rut. Helplessly I sat there while the Dopamine dried up in my brain. All I could do is brace for the coming psychotic seizure as my eyes rolled back into the head and my bladder released into the cloth seat. Shit, that is going to be nasty. I wish I hadn't drunk all that coffee with Maggie.

The minutes seemed to slow down while the Real was pulled into the world of delusions. I sat there staring mindlessly into the empty field while the cows walked to the fence to examine the curious sight just beyond their reach. My cogs slipped and screamed inside my head. I could not get a single coherent thought to settle in my now barren memory.

I have no idea how much time passed in the Real world. In the delusional, it was eternity when finally, someone pelted a rock at my unit. One thump, two thuds my wheels began to turn in the right direction. My machine began to re-boot, the rocks kept hitting me harder and faster. I turned my neck slowly with only a bit of consciousness returned to my control.

At the glass was a figure. Many colors whirled about as it moved to hit the encasing around me. It was making noise. I blinked slowly trying to move my limbs, but my veins were filled with thick molasses. It was painfully clear I was going nowhere fast.

More noise. "Hum, buzz, could, hum, what, help." The thing was trying to communicate with me from behind the window, that is what that is, but where am I?

"Do you need help, Ma'am?" Suddenly I understood the creature's language.

I blinked reaching up with my half dead hand to wipe my wet chin of drool, "Humm, nah, uhm, ah, shit," I slurred out unable to make my words so this thing could comprehend my needs.

"You are in the ditch, Ma'am. re you hurt," said the young man with curly ash blond hair as he banged on the window again.

I shook my head slowly now finding my legs were back in my command. "Nah, I'm finish, I am finally, I am uhm, fine." I searched till I found the correct term.

The young man narrowed his eyes. "Ma'am you are drunk. I have called the police. They will be here in a minute. Just sit still. You have been unconscious for a bit."

Police? Uh oh. I sure knew that word. I had to get the fuck out of there. They were coming.

I sat up feeling suddenly very capable as I started the car and began backing out of the ditch scaring the young man. He went running back to his truck parked in front of my wrecked Taurus. He was screaming for me to stop. I ignored him as I backed into the road put the car in drive and tore off from the scene of my own accident sweating and swearing.

"Shit, God damn it. Fuck me. What the fuck," I yelled out angrily pushing the dented Taurus to speeds slightly faster than the posted fifty-five. I was doing eighty actually.

I was still cursing myself for that little oops moment when I realized I was about to miss the turn off for the DCFS parking lot. I whipped the ailing car into the drive nearly slipping off into the drainage ditch squealing tires and sliding in sideways. Dennis was outside the office with Jane. The two of them got to see that Dukes of Hazzard moment as I found a space and parked the busted-up Taurus.

Dennis and Jane came running toward me both staring at the mangled front end in horror. "What the Sam Hill,

Niemand? What the hell happened to your car." Dennis pointed at the mess that used to be my ride.

I shrugged. "I hit a cow Dennis. You know they are always flying around this time of year. Pesky creatures. This was a big one, but they slip up on you so fast, you know. Oh well sucks to be me. Guess I will have to get a better bug screen on the next car. What are you and Boyd doing here? Have you got a case in the area?"

Jane's eyes went wide. "Did you just say cows were flying around, seriously? Oh shit, she is talking crazy again."

Dennis looked at Jane nodding. "Yeah, maybe, but I know this gal. Clever little thing. She is playing dumb. I have seen her do it before. Niemand, you know God damned well Boyd is not with me because he slipped his restraints down at the Wells Hospital yesterday. I came here to find out where you have hidden him. Stop the shit and answer me. I mean it."

I looked at Dennis in shock. "He did what? Are you kidding me? Is this a joke Dennis? I am too busy for tricks. Did Boyd put you up to this? You tell him this is not funny. I am not quitting my fucking job and that is final. Excuse me, I must go file for a new pager and cell phone with the secretary. You want to play games Dennis you can do it without me. Jane, uhm, I need to rent a car maybe? Oh, and if the police come by. tell them I didn't kill that fucking cow. I saw the fucker get up and fly away. The God damned thing was fine." I pushed past the very stunned duo headed to file my paperwork with the new staff member. I was not awaiting an answer from Jane.

I walked into the back offices and found the office of the new secretary. I opened her door and the young lady was on the phone. She smiled at me motioning to sit down while she finished her discussion with a client.

I sat down keeping my eyes downcast while stealing glances at her. She was very petite with light brown hair pulled into and elaborate hairdo. Ringlets hung everywhere at almost impossible angles. She wore a pair of brown turtle shell framed glasses and had big doe brown eyes. Her face was heart shaped with pouty full lips and an ample bust. I smiled to myself thinking she was quite the looker. I decided I wouldn't mind getting to know her a lot better. I snickered.

She hung up the phone still smiling sweetly. "Hi, I am Sheila. How can I help you, uhm?"

I didn't look up feeling quite sheepish as dark thoughts about this pretty woman crossed my busted brains. "Uhm, oh yeah, where are my manners. I'm Niemand, the DCFS investigator with the State boys. Sheryl is my contact boss?"

Shelia grinned. Damn was she hot. "Ah, we meet at last. I only started a week ago, but Nora told me all about you. It is a real pleasure Niemand. Oh, uhm, Nora said they called you Psycho? Which is the right way to address you, hon?"

I blushed. "Niemand is my name Sheila. Look, I hate to bother you, but I need to file some paperwork to get a new pager and cell phone? I seem to have misplaced mine."

She frowned at that. "Oh, okay. Yeah, I have the forms. I am sorry to hear that. They will charge your paycheck for losing State property. Are you sure you wouldn't rather look a bit longer before filing?"

I shook my head. "No Sheila. I must do this right now. My job won't allow me to be without those things for long. Can you put a rush on the order? I am alright with paying for it. Sucks to be me you know." I grinned still coyly looking at the floor.

Shelia nodded. "Alright Niemand, if you need it done, I am your girl." She reached into her filing cabinet.

"I wish," I breathed under my breath.

She turned back still smiling. "What did you say hon?"

I shook my head. "Nothing. Thanks for the forms. Catch you around the office, maybe someday if I could ever be so lucky." I took the forms from her and got my ass out of her office before I said one more inappropriate word to this Goddess on Earth. She was a fox.

I was still trying to calm down my girl boner for the sexy Sheila when I walked into Jane's office and saw Dennis sitting at my desk. That was better than a cold shower. I growled while I glared at him.

"What now? Geez Dennis, I have work to do man." I looked over at Jane who was sitting at her desk shrugging that she was helpless to make him leave.

Dennis shot a look at Jane then back to me while rubbing his moustache. "Okay Niemand, I am just going to come clean. I don't want to have to commit Boyd. If I do that, you understand his career is over. Boyd can't be a police officer if he can't carry a gun. That means I can't commit him or file anything on him other than a missing person report. That also means I can't legally haul you in for impeding my investigation since I am not claiming him as an escaped mental patient. You are too smart to fall for my threats; I should have known that. We have known each other a long time. Hard to bluff when we already know all of the other's tells." He looked at me appearing sad.

I shrugged. "Okay, so what the fuck are you still doing here then Dennis? If you can't do anything to me for not knowing where Boyd is, because I don't know, then why are you bothering me?"

He looked at the floor. "I am here to beg you to tell me where he is. Niemand, I love Boyd and he is very sick. I am terrified he will not survive this cycle. I have never seen it this bad. He is in a lot of trouble. He was already too thin. You saw what he did to his head. If I lost him, damn it girl, it would kill me. I can't, I just won't lose him. Please, find it in your heart to tell me where he is so I can help him. I need him to sign himself into the hospital voluntarily. That is the only way to keep it off his record. There I have put my cards on the table. I have shown you mine, now show me yours." He smiled bitterly at his using my own words to speak to my heart.

I looked at the old bull realizing he truly loved my Master. This whole mess was tearing this tough old cop apart. Pity for the officer rushed through me, but I could not betray my collar. Master Boyd asked for my defense and protection. This was a tough spot for both that old bull and for me.

"Dennis, I don't know where he is. However, I will do my best to look when I can. I will also do you the favor of telling him to go home if he does show up or call," I said while looking at the floor feeling a bit bad that I could offer no other comfort to this worried guardian.

Dennis sighed loudly then rubbed his head. "Well, I do know you know where he is. Boyd would never leave your side. He is hiding and you, no doubt, are helping him. Just do me one favor if you will not turn him over, have him call me please. Maybe I can talk him into coming home if I cannot talk you into helping me bring him in. Do that for me will you, sweetheart? I need to know my boy is at least alive for now." He stood up and nodded to Jane then walked out of the office appearing beaten.

Jane looked at me harshly. "You are a demon. Why won't you tell that man where his son is hiding, Psycho? How could you be so damned mean?"

I snorted. "Damn, everyone is riding my ass. Look bug off will you Jane? I have shit to do. If I wanted your opinion, I would beat it out of you." I turned and stormed from the office after Dennis feeling very angry that I couldn't seem to figure out how to solve this complex issue of my hidden Master without someone getting their feelings or worse hurt.

I found myself running after Dennis. I felt the need to tell him I would get Master Boyd to come home.

Julia's called out to me from behind me. The confusion of hearing that harpy's voice distracted me from my task. I turned to look, sure I was hallucinating again.

Julia was standing in the doorway of Nora's office. "Hey Psycho, over here. Where you headed?"

I rubbed my eyes trying to clear them of this very strange sight. "What the fuck are you doing here," I said out loud without thinking as I watched Dennis get into his squad car and pulled away.

She snorted. "Well I came by to visit old friends. I was bored. Hey, what happened to the Taurus? Did you hit someone?"

Nora came out into the hall adding to my nightmare. "More like what did she hit. She drives like a maniac."

Julia giggled. "I know I have seen it. So hey, do you need a ride somewhere? I was just headed out. Looks like you need a new car. It would be no problem. I have nothing else to do."

I let out my breath. I found myself wishing for death as I realized Julia was my best hope, other than walking, to get to a rental lot. It was obvious that my vehicle was a not going anywhere until it was fixed.

"Yeah, okay yeah, if you are offering, I suppose I have no real choice. That Taurus isn't getting far," I said with my shoulders dropping in defeat not unlike Dennis's had only moments before.

"Your welcome Psycho. God damn, don't thank me all at once. You tend to be a bit ungrateful, did you know that" said Julia as she put on her coat while I followed her to the parking lot.

"Stop fucking calling me Psycho, Julia. My name is Niemand. Thank you, I guess," I yelled out very irritated at this annoying woman.

Julia stopped turned and glared at me angrily. "Fine. I will respect you by calling you Niemand, but you will start respecting me back by cutting out the smart-ass remarks. That is going to change or so help me you can fucking walk to the rent-a-car. I'm had all I am going to take of your nasty attitude. I cut you slack because your, well, you know."

I looked at her full of hate. "No, I don't know Julia. Why don't you enlighten me," I spat back.

She rolled her eyes. "Different. That is what you are, but just because you have issues does not give you the right to treat everyone like shit."

I started to laugh like the loon I am. "Oh my, you got it all wrong, Julia. I don't treat everyone like shit. Only you." I stopped laughing appearing suddenly aggressive.

I decided I was ready to just fucking walk after all. I was in no mood for her preaching to me out of church.

Julia shook her head. "Christ, just get in the car Niemand. I have feelings too you know."

I looked at her small red Acura Integra car. "Could have fucking fooled me." I got into the passenger's seat as she unlocked the doors.

Julia sneered. "Oh that would not be too hard now would it? I think it may be best we keep our thoughts to ourselves. I think we will get along better that way."

I nodded while chuckling. "Finally we agree on something Julia. Your wish is my command."

She and I traveled to the only car rental business within miles. I was promptly denied due to my lack of a credit card even though I had the cash. What the fuck? I stood there fuming, angered beyond imagination when Julia came walking over holding her cell phone out to me. I looked at her confused by this strange behavior.

Julia rolled her eyes. "Sheryl is on the phone, Psycho. She wants to talk to you."

I glared hatefully at Julia while I snatched the phone. "Yeah, what now?"

Sheryl snorted. "That is what I was going to ask you, Psycho. What the fuck? Nora, Jane, and now Julia have all called to tell me you wrecked the Taurus. God damn it, what are you DOING."

I held the phone away from my ear looking bitterly at Julia standing there with a smug smile and her arms crossed.

"Uhm, it was a cow. It flew right in front of the car Sheryl. I uhm, well the cow is okay. The Taurus lived up to its name and tried to fuck the old girl but she busted him in the nose."

Sheryl interrupted my weird confabulation (the making up psychotic stories in case you forgot), "Psycho, stop being weird. Listen to me. Julia is going to loan you her Acura for the week. I will take the payment for the rental out of your check and give it to her. In the meantime, call a wrecker and get the fucking Taurus fixed, you fucking idiot. Jane said that fucking cop was snooping around again. Do you know where fucking Boyd is? Fess up if you do. Call the wrecker, get back to work or so help me I will fire your ass." She was yelling so hard she was breathless.

I winced as her words pieced my eardrums. "Okay. Okay, got you, boss. Cool your blood. Fuck. Color me gone." I handed the phone back to Julia who was grinning at my ass chewing. She could hear Sheryl screaming from feet away no doubt.

Julia got back on her phone and walked off so I couldn't hear the conversation. Like I cared. I sighed and ran my hand over my forehead finding I was sweating like a whore in church.

I looked up and saw the flowing electrical grid racing across the blue sky. I groaned. The damned thing was lower than it had been the day before. If it kept falling at that rate, I would have to crawl to keep it out of my head. Yikes!

"Well, looks like my car is all yours till the Taurus is fixed up," said Julia suddenly.

I flinched from her voice, startled out of my watching of the lowering power grid. "Uhm, yeah looks like it. What are you charging me for it?" I looked at her expecting to hear some ungodly amount. That bitch, it was higher than I ever expected.

"Oh, I don't want your money. I told Sheryl having your company without the tart comments every morning is payment enough. And maybe a lunch out occasionally when you have a lighter case load." Julia smiled her cat smile at me.

I sighed. "Could this day get any worse. Fuck, look, just charge me, will you? I am not okay with seeing you in the mornings. Can't you make real friends? What is wrong with Nora? Call that nosy bitch. I have too much to do. Fuck I never see my kids as it is. I have a life too you know. Why does everyone seem to think I don't," I yelled out to deaf ears.

Like it or not I was stuck in a devil's deal with the annoying ex-foster mom. She drove us back to her place. Julia handed over her keys and reminded me that I needed to call the wrecker and not to be late for nine in the morning coffee talk. I groaned but took the keys and tore off to deal with my case load.

I worked every single case on the list. Amazingly I made it back to the office just as the other staff was heading out for the night. Sheila was coming down the hall as I was headed to Jane's office to check Fax. I almost hit the floor seeing her in full view like that. The woman was a living, breathing vision of beauty. I looked at the floor as she walked up smiling at me.

"Ah, Niemand. Hey great news hon. I got your new pager and cell phone approved. It is on your desk waiting for you. I even filed a special form, so they only took fifty bucks for the pager. I told them the cell phone was broken when we got it." She winked at me smiling over her mildly criminal but kind act.

I smiled back still looking at the floor feeling my heart speed up. "Thanks a bunch Sheila, you're a real doll. I owe you one."

Sheila looked around then leaned in close. "You bet you do and I intend to call in that favor one day. I will be seeing you real soon Niemand," she whispered into my ear.

I almost fainted feeling as if I was caught in a siren's song. Without another word she walked away. I just stood there staring at her like a creeper. I felt hypnotized while I watched the gorgeous woman's hips swinging seductively as she went out the door. I blushed feeling a mix of longing and extreme interest in getting to know this woman better.

"What are you doing out here, Psycho," Jane's monotone voice broke me from Sheila's strange provocative spell over me.

"Uhm, I was just, uhm, saying hello to the new secretary. That's all I was doing, nothing else," I stammered out like a love-struck idiot noticing my words sounded as clumsy as unseasoned high divers doing painful belly flops.

184

Jane's eyes went wide. "Uhm, you stay away from that new secretary. We can't keep staff as it is. Shit you'll have the poor thing running away in seconds. I mean it. The wrecker came by. They said the Taurus will be ready next week. They said the damage is cosmetic. You got lucky."

I nodded. "Sure I did. I am stuck in Julia's car and her fucking kitchen chair over it. Anything else Jane? I have shit to do."

Jane nodded., "Oh yea they brought your new computer in today. Lucky, I didn't get a new one." She took off down the hall.

Her words looped around my head refusing to go into my ears. "New computer," I ran into her office. My eyes almost fell out of my sockets. Sitting on my desk was a brand-new PC. My friend was gone. He had been sent to the dump stamped as obsolete. I leaned on the doorway for support feeling all the air being sucked from my lungs.

I finally walked over and flipped on the switch praying to the Goddess that PC was still there. The screen whirled on. No PC. I flipped it on and off. My friend was gone. They killed him. I began to weep out of control. I didn't know what I was going to do without my PC.

"What the fuck, Psycho. Stop that. PC is gone," I heard Simon say behind me while I cried like a child into my arms in front of the empty computer screen.

"Fuck off Simon. They killed PC. He was obsolete. I am next. They got him. I wasn't here to protect him. He told me. I didn't listen and now he is dead," I wailed out in agony.

Simon snorted. "Stop it. We are losing it. PC was us. We are still here."

I shook my head. "That is a lie. You don't see him, do you? Oh Gods, what am I going to do? I wrecked the Taurus. I got myself indebted to Julia. I have Master Boyd wandering like a loon at a cottage. I have Dennis broken hearted. I haven't seen my kids in forever. I think Seine forgot I exist. I let PC get killed. Oh Christ, Simon, I am fucked. So fucked." I got up and began to pace wringing my hands.

Simon appeared upset., "Look, stop this right now. Go back to the cottage with Master Boyd. You need him now. This will pass. It is just a bad day is all."

I looked up at Simon angrily. "Bad day? Are you fucking kidding. Jesus. I looked at the empty computer with irritation growing inside.

Simon read my mind. "Oh no, Psycho don't. They will get you for that," he screamed while putting himself between me and the imposter computer.

"Get out of my way Simon. This delusion must go. If I kill this lie, then they will bring back PC." I intended to throw the new computer onto the floor.

"No, Psycho think. He is in the dumpster out back. Go get him. Leave this one along," Simon screamed red faced begging me to listen to him this time.

186

I stopped trying to get around Simon. "Wait. You are right. He is out back in the dumpster. I will take him back to the cottage. I can hide him out with Master Boyd. Good thinking Simon." I took off for the back door of the building.

I found my beloved PC almost at the bottom of that huge green dumpster. I recognized his ID numbers. His monitor was cracked but otherwise he seemed no worse for wear. I smiled as I carted his heavy ass out of that garbage bin. I joked that he weighed a fucking ton for an airhead.

I watched until no one was hanging around in the parking area. Then Simon and I hauled PC into Julia's Acura and raced to the cottage I shared with Master Boyd. I was not done with my paperwork, but this was an emergency. I needed to save my friend.

I arrived at the cottage just a little after seven. I noticed only one small light was lit inside. I picked up PC and went to the door knocking while announcing it was me and not they. Master Boyd opened the door immediately looking worried. I noticed right away his forehead was bruised up. He looked at PC and raised an eyebrow.

"Where have you been, Niemand? I have been worried to death. I thought they got you. What is that?" He tried to hug me, and I almost dropped PC.

I looked at Master Boyd feeling fear rising. "Please Master, I have to get PC inside. He is hurt. Can't you hear his heart is fading."

Master Boyd stepped back letting me inside appearing confused. I gasped as I looked at the walls of the cottage. In the dim light I could see that every inch of the living room and kitchen was covered in numbers, equations and geometric figures my Master had drawn with a pen.

I shook off my shock recalling my dear PC's plight. I plugged him into a power outlet. I flipped his switch, and nothing happened. His screen was black. I put my ear to his face and heard nothing. PC had expired. There was nothing I could do. He was now in the Summerlands with Matthew and Mother Delleh. I knelt there beginning to wail again forgetting about Master Boyd who had been watching the entire scene in confusion.

"Niemand, what has happened? Why are you crying baby? Please tell me. What is wrong?" He knelt next to me.

I looked at him feeling intense agony "Gottverdammt. Die Monster haben ihn getötet. Ich hasse sie alle," I screamed out in German beyond upset.

**QUICK NOTE:** *this is a language I had always forbidden we speak to deny my childhood trauma of D/s training at the hands of natives of that country. Translation: God damn. The monsters killed him. I hate them all.*

Master Boyd blinked in terror. "What? Huh? Niemand baby, did you just speak German?" He grabbed me trying to shake the crazy out of me.

I shook him off. "No, he is dead. No!" I stood up and began to pound my head into the equation riddled wall closest to my now deceased friend.

Master Boyd grabbed me to prevent my head banging. "Stop. Baby stop. What is going on? Who is dead? Tell me know, that is a directive," he screamed into my ear holding my struggling sobbing unit close to him.

"PC Master. I told you. The office staff killed him. See, he is dead. I can't go on without him. They take everything. I can't have any friends. Why did they have to kill him, Master? He never hurt anyone. Oh Gods, I want to die. Kill me. Mercy, kill me." I pointed at the cracked computer monitor falling limp in his arms into a full-on crying jag.

Master Boyd sat down holding me while I blubbered incoherently. He rocked with us trying his best to console the insanity within me. I watched Simon walk over to the now quiet PC and remove his hat appearing to honor our lost friend. That only made me cry harder. I understood one of us was now destroyed. Who was next? Fax? Looper? Simon? Dude? Perhaps me?

It took some time to for my wailing to finally quiet down. Master Boyd didn't let go. He sat patiently waiting for my episode to pass. When he heard my sobs subside to sniffs and gasps, he looked at me with pity.

"I take it that is your computer from work. The one you called PC. Baby, they have broken it. I can take it to a computer tech when we come off vacation. They can fix it and you can have your PC back, but you will have to wait

189

till they stop looking for me. Please don't cry. PC is not dead. He is broken like us." He smiled bitterly.

I looked up at him with some mild hope. "You think they can bring him back? That is not possible Master. The dead don't come back. Sometimes the living don't either." I noticed his right eye was blackened. He had been head banging too.

He nodded. "Yeah that is true. How did work go otherwise? I have been so worried. God said they got you. He told me you were gone forever. I didn't know what I was going to do without you, but now you are back. I don't like us being apart so long baby." He hugged me tightly again.

"I wrecked the Taurus, Master. Dennis came looking for you. He was very upset. He wants you to come home. I think you had better call him. Master, I am worried his not knowing you are safe is bad for him," I said while sniffling.

Master Boyd shook his head. "Niemand, today I remembered why I had to run away from Wells. Baby, they planned to have me ride the lightning. I heard the doctor tell Dennis. I broke out of the restraints because I can't go through that again. Dennis told them to do it. He said they should do it. I couldn't believe he would let them do that to me, but I heard him," he trailed off sounding broken hearted.

I gasped. "Ride the lightning? Are you sure Master? I mean we tend to get mixed up. Dennis wouldn't ask them to, surely he wouldn't, would he?" I thought back to Dennis's face yesterday morning when he saw the mess in the kitchen or whatever he saw that set him off.

Master Boyd nodded as he lifted my chin so I would look at him. "Yes, he did tell them to do it. They want to put that poison in me and run electricity through my brain again. I can't go back baby. You of all people understand that."

I nodded. "Yes Master, I do. I am sorry I didn't know. Master you could call Dennis from a pay phone. You could do that and make him feel better. Tell him you are not going to go back to the hospital, then stay here with me. We can stay here forever if you want. I don't care where we live. I think I may be in a lot of trouble. Simon says, he says, I am going Hebephrenic. I saw the tapestry today. It got the Taurus trying to reach me. If it gets me I will be lost." I teared up again at my darkest of confessions to my Master.

His eyes went wide. "Oh no, how long do we have? Harbor View can fix it in May. Can you hang on until then baby? The last time you got Hebe, oh baby…I can't lose you again. I remember that. Dennis almost didn't catch you in time. You ran into the traffic. Please stay with me. They take the Hebephrenic to the Snake Pit and you know what happens there." He took my hands looking very frightened.

I looked at the floor. "Yes, I am aware what happens. It has happened to me there already. I almost didn't make it back from the vortex last time. If it gets me again, oh Gods Master. They already got PC. I'm next I can feel it." I started to groan feeling the earth below us rocking gently.

Master Boyd pulled me into a passionate kiss then looked at me smiling lovingly. "Okay, it is dark. Let's go find a pay phone and I will call Dennis. That will make you feel better. Then we can go to the office and you can finish the paperwork I know you have. I will sit with you. I can't go on your calls, but I can spend the nights with you. We will be together as much as we can until this mess is all back to normal. The cycles pass, they always pass. We can do this together."

I shook my head. "As you wish Master. Just realize mine don't pass for a very long time, sometimes years. You should know that as my Guardian. Dennis doesn't know that does he? That you are my Guardian? Master, he is going to be angry when he finds out. He will make you give it up." I looked at the floor feeling unsettled by that knowledge.

Master Boyd stood up while taking my hand and helping me to my feet chuckling. "No he won't baby. You keep forgetting, I can pick my guardian too, just like you can. He makes me too angry I can always find some asshole willing to take the damned position." He winked.

I smiled as I realized he was right. Dennis could push him around, but only for so far. We went to the Acura and this time I let him drive. I didn't like Julia, so if my schizophrenic fiancé were to wrap her fucking car around a tree then so what.

We decided to drive to Wells just in case Dennis found a way to bug the phones. It was also important no one around recognized us in case there was an APB's floating around out there. Wells was a much larger town than Wheatly or even Cumberland. It was unlikely that two very thin, dirty, bruised up schizophrenics would be noticed hanging around a pay phone. Master Boyd and I decided the one-way hour trip was worth the effort for the added protection.

My Master called Cathy at the station. The crazy bitch was so excited to hear his voice he almost couldn't get his message out to her before the call ran out. He finally got her calmed enough to tell her he wanted Dennis to come to the station to take his call in thirty minutes.

He and I sat on a park bench watching the large town bustle about even at the hour almost mid-night. A few passersby stared at us looking suspicious or nervous but most people ignored us. Wells had a population of 90k so it was much bigger than the sleepy towns of Wheatly, Carter or Cumberland that didn't even have 5k between them.

My Master and I felt safer blending in with all the movement and noise. For a change we didn't stand out a bit. That was very nice. He and I laughed and talked about the various sights and sounds of the chaos around us while holding hands on the bench. We were so involved with the excitement that Master Boyd almost forgot to call the station thirty minutes later.

## WHAT MASTER BOYD TOLD ME WAS SAID DURING HIS PHONE CALL TO DENNIS FROM WELLS IN FEBRUARY 1999

My Master looked at me appearing a bit pensive, "Hello, Cathy? Is Dennis there yet?" Cathy immediately patched him through to the awaiting Dennis.

"Boyd, son, where are you? I have been to hell and back looking for you. You are not well. You need to come home right now so we can help you."

Master Boyd shook his head. "The cycle will pass Dennis. It always does. You are just going to put me back in the hospital. I was fine staying home, but I am not going back to the hospital."

"Boy, you are down under one hundred and fifty pounds. You need to be in the hospital so they can get you back to a healthy weight. Have you even eaten today?"

My Master looked at me appearing confused. "Uhm…I think so."

"See you don't even remember, do you? Your medication? Are you taking that? I know you aren't because I have it Boyd. Think son. You are killing yourself."

Master Boyd scoffed. "No I am not. The cycle will pass and I am not taking that shit anymore, Dennis. That crap is fucking with my mind and you know it. If it was so damned great, then why is everyone freaking out? I was taking it when I left on vacation you know. Fat good that did."

"Okay you have a point there Boyd. The doctors obviously screwed that up. We will get you a different medication, but you have to come home for them to do that."

My Master growled. "You mean like ECT? I heard you give them permission, Dennis. You were going to let them light me up. Fuck that. I am staying on vacation until this cycle passes and that is final. I only called so you wouldn't worry. I am fine, better than fine."

"Boyd, you don't understand. Your psychosis is not responding to the medication at all. They need to jump start your chemicals. It was only a few treatments then they would have you all set and feeling better in no time. I only agreed to it because it is what is best for you."

"Fuck that. No ECT. Jesus, Dennis, you ever had ECT? No, so stop telling me it is for my own good. You don't know shit about it," my Master yelled into the phone.

"Okay, come home and I will promise you no ECT. Boyd, I mean it come home now and I will not let any of them do it. I promise."

My Master chuckled "Yeah sure Dennis. You think my memory slips that bad? You said that when you dumped me off at Wells too. Well, this time you can't fool me. I will be back in time for work in the summer and when my cycle is over. I will handle this one on my own. I will show you and Carla I don't need a fucking Guardian."

"Boyd, God damn it. Listen to me. You can't handle this on your own and you fucking know it. We have been through this before. How many times have you banged your head into the wall today? How about those walls? Bet wherever you are there is some redecorations there, maybe a bunch of numbers?"

My Master narrowed his eyes. "Fuck you, Dennis. I have this under control. I will show you. I don't have schizophrenia. You have been lying to me. I figured it out. So this is goodbye until I am done with this stupid cycle. See you in a month or so. Stop bothering to look for me too. I don't want your help." My master hung up the phone.

Master Boyd appeared a bit agitated. He stood next to the phone wringing his hands looking at the ground.

"What is it Master? Did Dennis upset you?" I walked over to him hugging him as he flinched at my touch.

"Niemand, when did we last eat something?" He looked at me appearing afraid.

I shook my head. "Uhm, the turkey? We ate the turkey."

He nodded. "Yeah, but how long ago was that? A week?" I had in fact been over thirty days.

I laughed. "No silly. We would be skeletons by now. We must have eaten today. We just don't remember it."

Master Boyd looked down at his unit then to my own. Our clothing was hanging on us like oversized circus tents we both had become so rail thin. He was down to one hundred and fifty pounds at six foot one and I was down to around eighty-seven for five foot one. Both of us were severely underweight and starting to show signs of malnutrition.

He shook his head. "We are very thin baby. Let's find something to eat and not tissue paper this time."

My eyes went wide. "Master. We can't. It is how They get us. The food is poisoned you know that."

My Master's jaw began to grind in nervousness. "They can't be poisoning everything. Other people would die to. There must be safe food somewhere. Food they never thought to poison?"

I nodded. "There is but you won't like it Master."

He smiled. "Try me."

I chuckled. "Well if you are ready to go native, allow me to show you where the street people find supper." I grabbed his wrist taking him down alleys until we found a dumpster behind a restaurant.

I pointed at the big green garbage bin. "In there is food that they poisoned but it has been laying around long enough that it has lost its potency. We must find the kind that is both inert and not rotten yet. You still up for this task Master?" I narrowed my eyes at him in a dare.

My Master smiled wickedly. "Follow me baby. Hell, all those years I tried to get you to go to lunch or dinner with me, I was trying too hard. Shit, I should have just said want to go dumpster diving." He laughed as he hoisted himself up the side of the bin.

I chuckled. "Now see that is how you tempt a lady, Master. I totally would have jumped at that offer."

He stepped inside then reached down to aid me to join him. "Now you tell me. You are a bit too high brow for my taste." He pulled me up.

I winked. "You still manage to spoil me Master. Now, watch me. This is not my first rodeo. Don't eat anything till I get a look okay? Sometimes it can seem right but is messed up."

He nodded. "You lead this time and I will follow my Queen. Oh, hey you just stepped on my breakfast." He pointed at a smashed half eaten sandwich under my platform laughing.

I giggled. "Hey, that is mine. I stepped on it first."

In true schizophrenic street dwelling style, the two of us dug around in that dumpster. We didn't stop hunting until we had packed our pockets with eatable items to last a few days. We likely hadn't even collected three to four thousand calories between us. Master Boyd ended up eating the leftovers of a hamburger while we searched, and I enjoyed a soiled chicken patty sandwich with a bit too much catsup on the soggy bun. Welcome to the eating experience of most schizophrenics. We all have been here once, twice, some all our lives. Even the well protected Master Boyd can say he dumpster dined a few times in his day.

We went back to the car and sped back for Cumberland. He and I yapped about subjects only a schizophrenic could ever understand. The discussions were illogical, tangential, circular and at time incoherent. The food made us feel a bit giddy, but it helped to brighten our usually despaired moods a little. Master Boyd teased me about being a psychotic and I accused him of being all 'Norman Bates and stuff.'

We pulled into the DCFS parking lot still giggling like kids as we went inside. My mood immediately darkened when I recalled my beloved PC was gone. I stopped at Jane's office door staring at the strange computer feeling emptiness fill me to the point of agony.

"Niemand? Baby, what is wrong," said Master Boyd as he tracked my eyesight to the computer.

I shook my head. "Nothing Master. You said you can get PC back from the dead. I believe you. Until then I still have Fax and Simon, I guess." I walked over and sat down in front of the strange monitor.

He grabbed Jane's chair and rolled it over next to me. "Let me help do something? I do paperwork all the time. Maybe we can make it go faster then go back to the cottage and fool around." He giggled uncontrollably.

I narrowed my eyes. "Why wait? Let's fuck on Jane's desk. Then we can go befoul Nora's too. I hate those bitches."

Master Boyd's eyes went wide. "Wow, uhm I can't believe I am going to say this but we better not. You know how we get. If we break something questions will get asked." He appeared disheartened that he just turned down a chance to have sex.

We divided the paperwork between us. He sat next to me filling out my forms while I entered the proper screens on my CHRIS program. We raced through the work like a well-oiled team despite our glaring psychotic symptoms.

Master Boyd often would have to wring his hands, got up to pace mumbling to God or Bastard from time to time and would bang on his forehead with the palm of his hand. I would giggle, rock and I drooled a bit while trying to finish all my work before my brother the sun could rise from his eastern bed.

By five in the morning we had finished all my back logged cases. He smiled while looking at the floor when I thanked him for aiding me in this difficult task. I decided he would need something in payment for his service.

I got up and took off down the hall leaving my confused Master while I collected several tablets of paper from the supplies room. I returned and presented him with more appropriate background for him to write his letters, lists and numbers onto rather than the walls of the cottage.

He thanked me appearing genuinely grateful to have the gifts. I was about to put back on my garbage can smelling jacket when my Master dropped half his tablets into the floor when he stood up to stretch.

I bent down to assist him in picking up the falling items when he suddenly grabbed me from behind. Before I could realize what was happening, he forced me to my knees on the carpet in Jane's office floor.

My Master was fast and strong in his subjugation of my unit to his carnal desires. I tried to get up, but he had no difficulty pushing my weakened unit back to all fours while he disrobed me from the waist down and began taking his special services without explanation, hesitation nor warning.

I had no choice but to endure his lustful engagement while I watched the door nervously hoping he didn't take too long. Normally, I would have been fully involved in this enjoyable romp but I was aware sometimes some of the office workers would come in early in an effort to leave early. My anxiety overwhelmed my interest in the baser act of lovemaking.

My lack of full attention irritated my Master. His easy, gentle stride suddenly became violent, strong and rough. That got my attention. I groaned out in pain and pleasure which encouraged his aggression.

As usual, we ended up in a fast, brutal session that ended with his loud crying out in ecstasy and my moans of painful cramping. I was now only taking half does of my medication but an orgasm for me was still impossible no matter how vigorous my Master got. This fact was wearing on his last nerves. He didn't like our new one-sided intercourse. Yeah, he may have been crazy, but in that area he was wise.

As we re-dressed from our office indiscretion he voiced his irritation at this unfortunate situation. "Stop taking the medication. I don't like that you are not cuming, that is bullshit. Sex is one of the only joys we can have Niemand. It was wonderful when we were both off. That crap numbs everything. Not just our brains." He reached down and gave me a hand back to my feet.

I looked at the floor while I buttoned up my pants. "I know Master. But the blood tests, they will catch me. Last time I fell under level I got a trip to the Snake Pit. The side effects will wear off. They always do. In a few months I will be able to reach the top of the mountain again, Master. Please be patient with me. I still have some pleasure, just not the orgasm."

Master Boyd scoffed. "That medication makes the males eunuchs and the female cold fishes. It wasn't enough they sterilize you, now they take the fucking joy out of, well, fucking. That is not right. They are sadists, the whole lot of them. They do it because they think we are not in enough hell as it is. They block our only door of escape. Niemand baby, stop taking the meds please. They are slowly destroying your mind, and sex drive. Besides, they are not helping you anyway. You are still schizophrenic as hell."

Now I was pissed. "What? You didn't just go there. Look who is talking, fruit loop. Writing all over the walls? Who is schizophrenic much? Fuck you," I yelled out angrily as he picked up his note pads.

My Master's blue eyes clouded with a storm. "Fuck you. I am not fucking schizophrenic. I didn't just have a funeral for a God damned computer monitor, Psycho," he yelled back.

I started fake laughing. "Ah, well that may be. But at least they aren't strapping me down to hospital beds and taking me off work. Didn't they say you need four hundred volts through your noggin to bring you back from fucking Mars, Mister Paranoid."

Master Boyd rushed me grabbing my upper arm and dragging me behind him to the car beyond angry. I whimpered finally realizing I had perhaps gone too far this time. He stuffed me into the passenger's seat. The look on his face told me I had better shut my big mouth and behave for a bit while his anger cooled. He tore from the empty parking lot leaving rubber and screeching the tires loud enough to make me cover my ears.

He didn't say a word while he rushed us back to the cottage trying to beat my brother the sun. We pulled into the driveway just as the yellow orb began to peek over the Giant's belly. My Master got out, then ripped open my door grabbing my wrist and roughly dragging me inside.

He took me by my upper arm to the small bedroom. I started to cry, sure he was going to wail the piss out of me for my insolence when suddenly he stopped and flipped on the light.

I gasped in horror as the walls lit up with my own handwriting. Codes and symbols of my own design were on the walls from top to bottom.

He leaned up against the door stop, crossing his arms. "Well, who is schizophrenic?"

I dropped to my knees. "We both are, fuck me."

Master Boyd growled. "Well, you may be right Niemand. Just thought you should know if I am one then so are you. The evidence is right in front of our noses, isn't it? Do you remember doing that? Because I sure as shit don't recall adding my own artistic touch in the rest of the cottage. You may as well quit the medication. If you are doing this shit on it, what difference is it fucking making? Hmm, you take it and act like a fucking loon and can't have an orgasm. You don't take it and you act like a fruit loop but at least you can enjoy a good fuck." He stormed from the room to the kitchen to get a drink of water from the facet while I stared in terror at the hundreds of scribbles on the painted wood all around me.

Simon came into the room investigating the marks of madness., "Oh shit Psycho, this is bad. You and Master Boyd are gone. It is too late for both of you. I think you already know that. He sure does. You can take the medication if you want. It is over. Soon they will leash us to the floor. You'll ride the lightning and the vortex too. Randy says hi. Maybe this time he'll bring a friend? Ah, we made it almost twenty-seven years. Don't be too sad. No one expected us to go this far." He sat down on the bed to roll a smoke, but his hands were trembling.

I watched him feeling very frightened. "You really think there is nothing that we can do? Simon, please, we need help. They got PC."

He stopped his task. "Nothing. The shards are loose and The Chosen One is kicking too many asses. Now with PC gone, Psycho Tron will go septic. Hey, how are those wrists of ours? Feeling the urge to poke a few wires in, are we?" Simon glared angrily at me.

I nodded. "You know we are Simon. We already have the wires purchased, don't we? We have hoarded them somewhere. Psycho Tron will do it soon, won't she," I said already aware of the shards tendency to do shit behind my back.

He looked into the living room. "This is what happens when there is not a normal around to keep us from floating away. Master Boyd loves us, but he is as fucked up as we are. There is no chance now. Better get to Julia's on time. You have that dinner date with Harold too in a couple of days. Go out in style baby. Drive this train right into hell sideways. I will see you at the bottom Psycho. If not, well then it has been a pleasure to know you. What a fucking ride." He chuckled bitterly.

"Wait Simon. What do you mean see me at the bottom? Are you leaving me?" I could barely squeak out the words.

He smiled looking very sad. "Yeah, I can't see us anymore, only hear us. I am guessing where we are located but it is getting harder to find us every day. I came to tell you I am lost and so are we. Our connection has weakened. We are losing touch, sight and soon I fear sound will be gone too. I can't hear our Looper anymore, nor Dude. Only Hannah is left. Psycho, we are breaking apart this time. The shattering is too wide. I will stay as long as I can but our time is running out." I looked and shuddered as I realized for the first time that Simon was transparent.

"Oh my Gods, this is not happening. No, no, no Simon. Make this stop. It has to stop. I don't want to go mad dog. Please Simon, fix this," I screamed out in pure terror.

Simon just smiled at me appearing to not hear my pleas. Master Boyd on the other hand heard them loud and clear.

205

He came running when I fell to my face in a full psychotic fit.

## MASTER BOYD'S DESCRIPTION
## OF WHAT HAPPENED NEXT

*"I ran into the room and found you on your face moaning. I rolled you over, but your eyes were moving rapidly from side to side, you were drooling and non-responsive. I ran to the sink grabbed a bowl, filled it with water and ice then returned and started shocking you back from Mars. After nearly two bowls of ice water the best I could get is you repeating every fucking word I said. So, I stripped your clothes off and jumped into a cold shower with you. You came out of it screaming, clawing and wild as a bearcat. I had to restrain you while you kicked, sputtered and cursed incoherently. Immediately, you tranced on me again. I ran to your purse and pulled out the Lorazepam and forced two of those nasty bastards down your throat. I began the ice bathing again, and finally after almost half an hour you began to tremor. You had been sitting like a damned crucified Jesus for the entire time. How do you keep your arms up like that? Anyway, when you started to respond to your name, I took you back to the shower and we had another cold shower together. You are back. You are, right?*

I nodded feeling stiff, cold and empty. "What time is it Master," I said feeling my tongue was thick and clumsy.

He looked at his watch., "Uhm guess I should have taken it off in the shower? Not waterproof apparently." He chuckled looking embarrassed at his oops moment.

"So, your belief that lasted thirty minutes could actually be two weeks is what you are saying?" I moaned out thinking I was surely fired.

Master Boyd shrugged. "Yeah, guess I have to face that dirty little fact. I confess, I have no idea what time, day or year it is baby. Your guess is good as mine. I already lost my job as a trucker. Guess you won't be waiting tables anymore either. I think we may be dead. I haven't seen anyone else in years. Was it always like this? I can't seem to remember, well, anything."

I looked at him moaning again. "Oh hell, who the fuck are you Mister? Did I fuck or fight you? Or both? Oh, my Gods, where the fuck is my God damned shit." I tried to remember my thought to finish it, but nothing was coming through.

Master Boyd snorted. "I am your fucking husband. That is who I am, and you fuck and fight me. Wake up, Niemand. This is not real; it is not real. Say it with me. This is not real." He grabbed my face.

I nodded. "Yeah this is not real. It is a delusion. Wake up Niemand…wait…is that me or you?" I looked at the strange man who just said he was my husband.

He chuckled. "Do I look like an Niemand to you?"

I shook my head. "No, but this isn't real. Anything is possible. Did you put the turkey back into the fridge, Master? Carla is gonna be pissed if you left it out. We still need to get those Christmas presents out of the car. Hey, have you seen Julie? She was just here with Joni or was she with Circe? Huh, that is weird I didn't know Ginger knew them, but Barbara told me that Tammy was asking about them. Hey, don't forget to water Zeppelin. Wait, Master Boyd? Oh shit, are we at home? Or in the office? Shit, I am late for lunch at Mistress Katheryn's office." I tried to stand but the dizziness made the world spin.

Master Boyd grabbed my hand then kissed his ring. "Baby, the pager is going off. It is in your purse. I have been telling you that for the last several minutes, but you are babbling. I think you are confused."

I nodded at him. "You bet your pretty baby blues I am, Master. Hey, did you know I dreamed I used to live in a cemetery and they called me Psycho, weird. This fat little doctor told me I have schizophrenia. That is funny." I staggered into the living room and grabbed my vibrating pager out of my purse looking at the walls.

"Hey Master, someone wrote on the walls. Wow, what a crazy fucker that must have been." I chuckled as I noticed it was a call from Sheryl recorded at seven forty-five am only five minutes earlier.

Master Boyd babbled something incoherently from the bedroom while pacing., "Maste I am going to call Sheryl back. I have a new cell phone. I am going to leave it here for you with my pager number in case you need me today. Let me call the bitch to see what she wants."

My Master peeked into the living room. "Did you just see Bastard run through here? He is supposed to be getting me a glass of water." I pointed at the sink then dialed Sheryl's number.

"Yeah, what now," I growled rubbing my forehead with a headache from hell.

"Just making sure you remember to go to Julia's this morning. Then you get down to Jessieville. We got a bad one out there. The kid is already carted off in a pine box. The brothers killed the offender. I need you to interview those boys to find out what happened. The mom is still there. See if she is in danger or if the boys are. Got that?"

"Yes boss. Oh hey, have you seen the new secretary down here? She is uhm, really great." I giggled feeling very mean by mentioning another woman to my failed Master.

Sheryl snorted.. "I heard she thinks she is hot shit Why?"

I snorted almost breaking out into laugher. "Well, you heard right. She is hot as a firecracker. Buh bye boss." I clicked off the phone then walked back into the bedroom to give the phone to my mildly agitated Master.

I handed the cell phone to my Master reminding him not to answer it but to call the pager immediately if it rang. He nodded still mumbling but appearing mostly logical. He gave me a kiss while I gave him the last of our dumpster dining delights from my pockets. He took the food and started eating ravenously. I walked out placing the 'do not disturb' placard on our cabin door. I giggled realizing there was no need. We were already as disturbed as anyone could possibly get. I looked down giggling wildly realizing I forgot to redress from our catatonic cold shower. I was standing in broad daylight sky clad.

My brother the sun glared far too brightly into my psychotic eyes. All around me I could hear the loud noises of the electric grid, the spinning vortex and forest creatures doing their best to warn me of what I already knew. I was going Hebephrenic. Half of my Simon sat in the passenger's seat smiling at me. His legs were gone and his upper unit transparent. I knew he couldn't see me anymore. He had lost his way which meant I was doomed. When my Simon is lost, so am I.

Our Master was also lost in the maze inside his head. We were all trapped in the webs of the delusional tapestry. The end was coming for us as surely as the spring storms. I sighed realizing I had given it a good fight, but no Psycho could handle the weight of the normals who thought I should solve their problems.

I went back inside and quickly put back on my garbage drenched clothing then left the cottage to start my day in a world gone insane as Sheryl's top DCFS investigator once again.

Flying cows? Dumpster diving cops? PC is dead and Simon is disappearing? What the fuck. Okay, this is fucking insane. Uh huh. Very. This is only the beginning of just how crazy this spring got. So, strap on your drool buckets and put on your helmets. We are going psychotic professional style. It is about time, don't you think? Hell, we have been battling this shit for twelve years while not winning a shit ton of those skirmishes either. Oh well, sucks to be us. \

# Chapter 79: The Area Manger
## Master Boyd & Submissive Niemand
## Sheryl the Absent Interim

On and on we go, where we stop, only Simon knows. Our buddy PC was the first of us to find peace in the void. Simon is ailing, and Fax is gossiping less every day. Psycho Tron is lost without her friend, and The Chosen One is pissed off. Things are getting out of control fast. We had always depended on the powerful Thorazine to keep us from falling off the edge of the world.

In the last months of 1996, the company who made that sanity stabilizing drug had started to cut corners. By December 1998, the Thorazine pills in the couple's prescription bottles was sugar with a few chemically sedating agents thrown in to make it look like all was well. No one was the wiser that the medication had been packaged with a lesser potency than the dosage required. Two schizophrenics in a small dust bowl town would feel their borders to the unreal weaken in unison. The March Madness of 1999 had taken a full two years to slowly build. It was a nightmare the D/s couple would never forget.

*Ah, you wondered why did the touched pair go deeply insane at the same time? Well now you know. An unscrupulous big company's desire to save a couple of bucks took Master Boyd and Psycho to Hebephrenic hell.*

Julia is patient. The submissive is an easy mark, but the ex-foster mom must wait her turn. Sheryl is not done with the hapless Psycho yet. The failed Master knows there is still a bit of blood in that psychotic turnip to squeeze out. She watches with her cat like smile. Julia has big plans for that collar. All she had to do is sit and watch. Her time is coming. The new millennium will mark the beginning of a new era of success for her, and the end of everything for the schizophrenic once known as Psycho.

Dennis is a wise man. He knows his ward well. Niemand is the key to his plan. Everything revolves around the delusion of Master Boyd's One and Only. The storm in Master Boyd's blue skies is picking up force. Thunder shakes his ground and lightning will strike his soul.

Speaking of Keys. Simon grows weaker by the moment. His connection to the real is breaking up. The railroad man has lost his way. He holds on while the train begins to derail. His injuries from this wreck will be significant. This tragedy will only yield five survivors. Wandering through the wilderness, lost and bleeding these remaining shards will have to rebuild the iron horse with their bare neurons.

***Turns out that the metal Will while unbreakable, could be badly bent.***

Alrighty then. Off we go again, hurry. We must move fast this time. They are coming again. Shit, we thought we had lost those buggy bastards last time. Grab that note pad, will you? Master Boyd drew us the map on it. Can you read that scribbling? Us neither. What the fuck. Damn looks like we are lost. Okay, now if you are lost in the woods, how the fuck do you get out? Ah, easy, build a fire and burn them down, hahaha.

*"Psycho honey, why are you covered in blood? Can you tell me where you have been? It is okay. No one wants to hurt you but you must tell me where all the blood came from. The police are right outside. They will shoot you if you don't let me help you out of this mess. You have to tell me; whose blood is it?"*
**--Jane trying to end the standoff between police and Psycho during Hebephrenic psychotic fit at DCFS office, May 5th, 1999.**

I stood there looking at the shack. I re-checked the address on the report. The mailbox numbers matched. This had to be the place. An old half-starved pit bull stretched lazily staring at me. He was chained to the side of the small building. His doghouse was almost bigger than the family home that was nothing more than a fancy outbuilding. Flies buzzed around his ears. He snorted but made no effort to come at me while I knocked on the wooden door to this hovel. I watched him watching me wondering where I had gone so wrong. Why was I a DCFS investigator and not a psychologist?

The door opened and a short very dumpy woman with greasy brown hair stood there with her back to me yelling at her partner. "Billy. Billy, hide the pot God damn it. It is the cop's idiot. Put it under the couch cushions. Shit hurry up before I have to open the door. You know they will break it down."

I stood there in disbelief. Did the woman not realize I was standing there watching Billy hide the dope while she held the door half open? I cleared my throat hoping she would recall I was standing there during this most bizarre scene.

She turned around to stare at me her eyes cloudy with the side effects of heavy marijuana use. "Oh hey, how are you doing Ma'am. What can I do you for?"

I shook my head feeling a headache coming on while heavy pot smoke rolled out the door right into my face. "Uhm, I am Missus Voss with DCFS investigations. I had a report of child abuse for this home. Are you Patty Strong?"

The short heavy-set woman nodded. "Yeah that is me. Child abuse? Huh? Not me. Billy, hey asshole, did you hit Stephen, you fucker," she growled at the tall, skinny man now stuffing a big bag of pot under the couch cushions right in front of me.

He turned to look at her appearing in a daze. "Shit no, Patty. I ain't even seen him all morning. Why would I hit him? Fuck woman. He ain't my kid." He sat down on the beat-up blue couch that now held their drug cache.

Patty looked back at me. "Nope. No one is abusing Stephen here. Have a nice day." She started to close the door on me.

I grabbed the door. "Miss Strong, here is the deal. You can let me in and we can talk all friendly like or I can call the law down here and you will get arrested for possession.

Then I can talk to you in jail. There are your choices. Up to you."

Patty looked back at Billy who shrugged. "Yeah, okay, come in then. What was your name again," she said appearing mildly tranced.

I shook my head. "Doesn't matter. I need to see the child Stephen please. I want to speak to him alone, then you, me and Billy can chat. You good with that?"

She nodded appearing a bit pensive. "Sure. Stephen, boy come here. A lady wants to talk to you," she yelled out as I walked into the small home.

All around on the floors and tables were papers, garbage, dirty clothes and dishes with half eaten food. Flies buzzed around my head and the smell of weed and dankness filled my nostrils. I noticed I felt a bit dizzy. The concern I was getting a contact high from the enclosed, small quarters occurred to me.

I groaned under my breath, hoping I didn't show positive on my monthly medication blood test with a bit of THC too. Billy sat on the couch staring mindlessly at the TV that was broadcasting a basketball game. He was so high he barely blinked. Patty sat down next to him already appearing to forget I was standing there waiting on her son. I rolled my eyes realizing me and Master Boyd had our shit together better than these two potheads on our worst psychotic days.

A boy of eight came running into the main room. There were only three rooms in the whole house. He had tan hair cut in an ugly mullet fashion. Stephen wore a dirty baseball team t-shirt, shorts and was barefoot. His overall health appeared good, but he was dirtier than me. He was so filthy I could barely tell he was Caucasian. He had a huge cut across his forehead and bruised arms that were in the exact pattern of finger and thumb marks. I winced realizing this kid was coming with me. Someone was beating his ass. I feared what I was going find when I got a look at the rest of his unit too.

I smiled at the boy. "Hi Stephen, I am Alex. Can you come outside with me and talk a minute?" I feigned being happy to see him.

He narrowed his eyes then looked at his mom "Can I go outside with this lady momma? She wants to talk to me."

Patty nodded not even bothering to look away from the television. Stephen looked back at me staring me up and down. "Yeah sure. What do you want anyway?"

I chuckled. "Just want to talk to you about stuff. Let's go visit your dog and you can tell me about him or her?"

Stephens eyes lit up. "Yeah that is Bella. She is great. Best Pit Bull in the county. Let's go then. I suppose you have a male you want to breed her with. I get one of the pups just so you know." He chattered away as we left the house.

I stood listening while Stephan bragged to me about the great qualities of his dog Bella. Bella was happy to see him, and he petted her the entire time. I asked a lot of questions about Bella's pedigree and her ability to welp without difficulty. He loved that I understood the finer points of breeding a good Pit Bull line.

Finally, after I was sure we had a good rapport going I broached the real reason I wanted to speak with him. "Uhm, so do you want to tell me who put those marks on your arms and your head. Did Bella do that?"

He looked up startled. "Hell no. She would never. She is a great dog."

I nodded. "Well, someone did it. I hoped it was not Bella."

Stephen looked at Bella appearing afraid suddenly. "I ain't supposed to talk about it you know."

I knelt down to pet the worn-out Bella. "Oh, I know. But you see there are those who say Bella is doing it. I am here to make sure she doesn't get the blame, you know. No one is listening. You tell me who did this and I will make sure Bella is protected."

He looked at Bella, then to the door. "They will hurt Bella if I don't say, won't they? Everyone thinks a Pit Bull is mean, but they ain't you know."

I petted the calm Bella. "I know they are good dogs, but there are those who think they bite. You have marks and someone told. I must answer for who did it. I really like Bella. If she is innocent, I must give the cops another name you know. Then I can make sure Bella is safe."

Stephen nodded. "I know you will take care of her. I can tell you love dogs too. Okay, it is Billy and mom. They get high sometimes. They don't mean to do it. My momma is sick you know. She gets depressed and nervous. The dope, it helps to calm her, but I get loud and sometimes I have to be hit you know?"

I nodded looking at the child with pity. "Neither you nor Bella should have to pay for your mom's sickness. I will need to take you to see some people who will help you be safe from Billy's anger and they will help your momma get better too."

He looked at the ground. "And Bella? What will happen to her?"

I smiled. "I bet we can make sure she is safe too. I know a place she can go until you are able to come home. You can go see her all you like, and she will get loved and healthy again. She needs more food and some treatment too. You want to come with me, and take a chance for a better life for you, Bella and your momma?"

He looked at me tearing up. "I just want my momma to be well, and Bella safe like it used to be before Billy came here. Can you make that happen?"

I took the little boy's hand into mine. "I am going to try Stephen. Now you stay here with Bella, okay? I must call some people who will get rid of Billy and take your mom for help. I also need to call to get the doggy hotel for Bella, then you and I are going to see the doctor and get you fixed up. After that we will go meet a nice family that will give you a place to heal up. I know this is scary, but you are tough. I can see it in you, like Bella. You are a pit bull too."

Stephen smiled while tears ran down his cheeks. "Yeah, I am a pit bull too."

I called the police and had Patty and Billy arrested for child abuse, endangerment and possession. I took Bella and Stephen to Doctor Coussins and set her up in a long-term kennel while Stephen let the old Vet know his desires for a pup. Yes, again out of my own pocket. DCFS doesn't make provisions for the poor pets left behind when a family breaks up. assholes.

I then took Stephen to the ER. I held his hand while he was stitched up. His little unit was covered in cuts and damage from being beaten with a piece of barbed wire (yeah, you read that right). He was brave, a little pit bull to the end. I never left his side.

After he was patched up, I took him to meet his new foster family the Upchurch couple. Right away it was clear the match was good. I hugged my little pup Stephen goodbye and rushed off to my very next emergency. There was never a dearth of children in need of help out of their family's hell.

## NOT HAPPILY EVER AFTER

*My poor pit bull would not live to see his manhood. The child called Stephen lived with the Upchurch family off and on for five years. His mother was in and out of Rehab, and thanks to her need to date bad boys, Stephen was returned to Patty's custody repeatedly only to be picked back up to be sewn up due to chronic physical abuse at the hands of his mom and her shit men.*

*Thanks to years of abuse and instability he picked up a lot of self-hatred. Then sadly he developed a methamphetamine habit at the age of twelve. Yeah, that young. In 2005 I received word that Stephen had passed away from an accidental overdose of various hard-core drugs. He was only fourteen years old.*

*He is sadly one of the many children I lost thanks to the system refusing to end the failed family and offer him a chance at adoption into a stable home. Repeated foster care, beatings, and probably worse got to him. It would get to anyone. He was just a little child. How the fuck was he supposed to deal with it?*

*No matter what anyone says I know he fought a good fight. In the end, my beloved pit bull just couldn't win the dog fight against the demons his mother created within him. I pray he found the peace in the next world he could never win in this one. Oh and one more thing I would like to say about this. Fuck the lazy heartless DCFS caseworkers and fuck the judges who let this shit happen.*

**PS:** *Stephen and Bella were reunited, and she lived with him till her death two years later. As for Patty, who gives a fuck what happened to her. I sure as shit hope whatever it was it fucking hurt a lot.*

It was Thursday. I had been rushing about all week attending the dozens of hard-core violent cases in my county catchment while battling my own oncoming psychotic blow

221

out. Master Boyd had managed to keep his numbers, symbols and lists on the paper pads I had given him.

While I worked during the day, he was doing his best to clean the walls of our psychotic bullshit when he could remember to work on it. My Master had managed to get at least some of it erased. He and I both decided we would have to repaint the rooms if I could recall I needed to buy the fucking paint.

At night, my Master and I would drive Julia's car to the DCFS office and complete my mountains of paperwork generated by my daily cases. He and I were doing an amazing job keeping up my caseload. It was taking us both to hide my deepening psychotic state from the powers that be. Those caseworkers and other co-workers that worked by my side, however, no longer believed me of sound mind or unit.

I was not bathing, eating, sleeping nor was I taking my medication properly. I often forgot the useless pills not even recalling I had a disease called schizophrenia in the first place. I smelled to high heaven of garbage, sweat from my random psychotic fits, and my wig was never brushed. Jane had called Sheryl to complain of my disheveled, thin appearance, and constant tangential conversations with herself and other staff members.

Sheryl had of course told Jane that I was bizarre but not dangerous. If I kept doing my job there was no need to be concerned. Jane, who was now the DCFS office manager in Cumberland, was more than upset by this obvious neglect of what she viewed as a serious situation developing. She had complained to the higher ups but again, her report was lost in the piles of paperwork at the main state office.

She was to receive no aid despite her chronic demands something be done about me. Jane's only recourse was to order me to stay out of the office during regular work hours, so I would not be able to upset the clients and staff members. Jane meant well. She just didn't have the power to do much about what was coming.

Julia was enjoying the show. Every morning I had to sit at her kitchen table unraveling at the seams. She would assault me with questions about my personal life and other private business. She seemed to get a hard on over my irritation and discombobulated responses to her nosy inquires. I wondered if I was being paranoid or if the vibes I was getting off her were correct. It was like she was thrilled to watch me losing my struggle with reality. Why anyone would hope to see another go mad was beyond me. But then again, everything was starting to become a source of confusion. Not much was making sense in my world anymore.

Dennis was calling me almost every day on the cell that Master Boyd kept at the cottage with him. He would page me, and when I called him back half the time it was because my Master was upset at the chronic ringing of Dennis's harassment by phone. I would call Dennis back and demand he leave me alone. The old bull was no fool. He noticed I never called back using the number he had used to reach me. He was now sure Master Boyd and I were working together.

He and I were getting so disorganized psychotic it was taking the use of both our heads to keep my Master's whereabouts a secret.

Luckily, Dennis had to work his shifts at night and rest during the days. He only had two days off a week to stake me out full time. I was careful on Tuesdays and Wednesdays (his nights off) to keep my weary sights on the tailing bull officer. Dennis watched me like a hawk unaware that I was aware of him. Thankfully, there had not even been any close calls due to my vigilance and a few lucky breaks of losing Dennis in heavy traffic.

Despite his best efforts, he was unsuccessful in catching me slipping back to the cottage in the first weeks of Master Boyd's second vacation. I realized Dennis was going to continue to be a serious problem if I didn't watch my back. That man was not only clever, but he was also tenacious, and I was septic psychotic. That fact did not bode well for my continued success at shaking the hell-bent Guardian.

That Thursday Sheryl had called me to give me a lecture about 'getting her the vote' from this Harold fellow no matter what I had to do. We had argued about her misuse of her rights as my interim Master. She could not order me to sleep with anyone and did not have leash rights. My true Master had ordered monogamy to the Key. Sheryl was super pissed off but unable to sway Simon's ruling on this subject. I told her I would attend this dinner date with the idiot Harold but more than that was out of the question.

She had hung up on me informing that my failure to get her the position of Area Manager would result in my immediate termination for my various and numerous infractions. The writing on this wall was clearer than that of mine and Master Boyd's at the cottage. I was boned. Sheryl had made it very clear that Harold would only agree to give her the vote if he got into her investigator. I decided to have a talk with Master Boyd about Sheryl's demands.

I will not bother to repeat what he had to say. Not that you have not heard such language, maybe even worse, since I started writing my story honestly raw, but because you already can imagine. My Master was not going to share his One and Only with anyone in any capacity.

He also didn't want to see me keep my job with DCFS, so there wasn't even the argument that I could be terminated to use as leverage with him on this subject. I do not betray my collar. This was obviously the end of my career or so it would have seemed that way at least.

That late afternoon I finished my last case in Wells and rushed back to the office trying to get through the door before closing time even though Jane told me not to come around until afterwards.

I needed to get some forms, yeah that is it, from the new secretary Sheila. It wasn't because I wanted to stand there drooling over her good looks or listen to her sexy voice. Nope, it was totally innocent. Uhm, hi Niemand, this is Reality. Reality would love to meet you. Why do you keep running from him?

I rushed through the DCFS building's front door out of breath. The intake secretaries looked up while narrowing their eyes. I saw them start to whisper to each other and giggle while shooting me looks. I knew they were making fun of me. I didn't care. I was well aware of the universal dislike of my person by every fucking staff member in that office except for the only one that mattered to me, the beautiful Sheila.

I just glared at the gossiping bitches and went into the back hallway to the sounds of their laughter as the door shut behind me. Jane was leaving her desk and headed home. She looked at me wide eyed as we walked by each other. She stopped dead in her tracks demanding that I let her speak to me for a moment.

"Psycho, get a fucking bath. Brush your hair and change those nasty clothes. It has been a fucking week. I am sick to death of it. For Christ's sake eat something. You look like a damned scarecrow. You know Sheryl and the State office may think this is okay, but I am not putting up with it. You come here tomorrow looking like that and I am hauling your ass to the ER for a psych evaluation my fucking self and let Sheryl fire me. God damn it is horrid. Someone needs to do something before you kill yourself or someone else," Jane growled.

I looked at the floor giggling uncontrollably at her anger outburst. "Liar, Liar, pants on fire, hang you with a telephone wire." I chanted under my breath nonsensically.

Jane rolled her eyes "Jesus, you're fucking nuts. It is like talking to a wall. Get a bath, eat, and stay the fuck out of the building during regular office hours. I mean it." She stormed off to the parking lot leaving me still giggling and chanting.

I shrugged then continued to Sheila's door hoping the Goddess had not called it quitting time yet. I knocked and smiled as she called out 'it's open.' I step inside finding the beauty sitting at her desk looking over files.

She looked up and smiled. "Niemand. Ah, what a pleasant surprise. Have a seat. What can I do for you?"

I looked at the floor blushing slightly. "Uhm, I wondered if you could get me a few more of the D-42 court report forms. The copy machine has been on the frizz. I took a couple of little ones into care today. I need to file with the courthouses by morning you know. The judges depend on my reports so they can figure out what's up or down, you know." I caught myself trying to sound more important than I really was. Huh? That is not like me, but this girl was fucking hot.

Sheila smiled at my mild attempt to brag. "I bet. I have heard a lot about your hard work out there in the fight against those nasty child abusers. You are like a real superhero. I don't know how you do it. Aren't you scared? I would be." She batted her eyes at me.

I shrugged while smiling appearing flattered. "Nah, just doing my job Sheila. I bet you would be great at it. Nothing to it. It is easy to hate those who deserve it you know."

227

She frowned. "No, I don't know. All I ever hear is the gossip in this horrible place. Everyone here seems to hate you but you seem so sweet. I don't get it." Shelia looked up at me with her big brown eyes.

"I am not people friendly, Sheila. That is okay. I don't care if they hate me. I am only here to work, not win popularity contests. If they all did their fucking jobs properly, they also wouldn't have time for idle chit chat. Not my problem that they misunderstood this job is not about them, it is about serving the public." I smiled again stealing a look at the beauty.

Sheila laughed out loud in a voice that sounded like wind chimes. "You are so great Niemand. I think I am falling in love here. Hey, if you are ever free I would love to go and get a cup of coffee. You know get to know each other a bit better."

I almost hit the floor in surprise. "A cup of coffee? With me, uhm, are you sure? I mean wouldn't your boyfriend, errr, girlfriend be angry," I stammered out like a buffoon.

She giggled at that. "I don't have either yet. Of course, I am sure. I have never been surer of anything. You know, you should take me up on my offer. Ich würde dich gerne fesseln. Dann bestrafe dich, bis du bettelst zu sterben." She grinned at me wickedly.

*German translation: I would love to tie you up. Then punish yourself (you) until you beg to die."*

228

I looked up in full horror. "What did you just say?" I could barely speak as I began to tremble.

Sheila laughed wildly. "Oh, I think you heard me the first time. Ich habe dir Haferflocken gemacht hast du Hunger? Du siehst sehr dünn aus. See you soon, Rachel." She picked up her purse then pushed past me headed out for her car still laughing at me.

*German translation: I made you oatmeal are you hungry? You look very thin.*

I stood there too terrified to move feeling as if I may piss myself in fear. How the fuck did she know what Debbie used to say all the time? I began to suspect the evil secretary had access to my psychiatric records. She was taunting me. I began to feel angry as I realized this was a mind game the damned woman was playing. Well fuck her. No one is good looking enough for me to tolerate such cruelty. I decided that I would end this bitch somehow.

I rapidly left her office mumbling threats of what I planned to do to that horrid woman when I just nearly ran smack into Dennis.

"Where you headed there Niemand? Off to see Boyd? I am sure he is missing you by now." Dennis smiled knowingly at me.

I growled with more irritation than I would like to admit. "Dennis what the fuck are you doing here? I am working woman. Still looking for Boyd huh? Well, not my problem. I have cases to get to."

Dennis put up his hand to end my attempt to lie. "Knock it off Niemand. I know you are full of shit. No way you would still be unmoved about the fact that Boyd has been missing almost a week unless you knew right where to find him. I only came by because I was dropping off a prisoner at the Cumberland jail. Seems the old boy found his way into our county but belongs here. I wanted to give you something for Boyd." He reached into his pocket and took out a prescription bottle then attempted to hand it to me.

I looked at his hand as if he were trying to hand me a wet dildo. "What the fuck are you doing? If you give me his medication what the fuck will you do when you find him?" I backed away from his hand.

Dennis chuckled. "You are one hell of an actress, I will give you that one. Be that as it may, take the pills please. Make sure he takes them. Maybe it will help wake him up to the danger he has put himself into. Since I can't get the two of you to listen to reason at least I can get his medication to him." He tried again to give me the bottle.

I shook my head. "I am not going to take that Dennis. I don't fucking know where he is. I don't need his medication."

He scoffed. "Okay, then if you won't take it, I will just leave it here on your desk. You tell Boyd that Carla is worrying herself into an ulcer and I sure do miss having our little chats. Take care Niemand. See you both real soon." He walked into Jane's office dropped the bottle on my workstation then headed out of the building leaving in his squad car.

I walked to my desk and sat down. I knew I had to wait a bit to be sure Dennis was far enough out of town before I hazarded a trip to the cottage. I laid my head down onto my arms feeling sick and scared. Sheila was against me. Dennis was trailing me. Jane wanted to send me to a hospital. Sheryl wanted to sell me out to a guy named Harold. My Master was going insane. My Simon was almost nonexistent anymore. PC was dead. I was feeling more alone than ever. Suddenly a voice called my name.

"Psycho? Is that you?" I looked up to see a short man of about five six standing there staring at me from the door.

He was balding, with an oversized nose. He had a potbelly but was well groomed in an expensive suit and tie. He wore a pair of glasses and held a suitcase. I assumed this fellow was one of the State workers from the capital.

I glared at him. "I don't like to be called that please mister. I am Niemand. Who are you?"

The man looked at the floor smiling sheepishly. "I am Harold. Sheryl said I could find you here. I know we have a date tomorrow night, but I was in town early. I thought I would come by see if you were interested in going out tonight instead?"

I leaned back in my chair looking him over with suspiciousness. "So you are Harold. Sheryl says you are holding up the vote to making her Area Manager."

Harold pushed up his glasses appearing irritated. "Yes, I don't think Sheryl is the right one for the job. She has a history of poor employee relations."

I chuckled at that. "Ah, that I can believe. However, you my friend are looking for great relations with a certain Psycho to overlook Sheryl's little problem. Or did I misunderstand Sheryl?"

Harold looked around the room appearing worried someone may hear my discussion. "Well that is a rather direct way to put it, but yes. Sheryl said you will be happy to trade services for my vote. I uhm, seem to recall you were not quite as thin or rough looking but never mind. I am still interested. I mean no offence by saying that, but I see you are an upfront kind of gal. I like that. Honesty is always the best policy." He smiled nervously.

I stared at him harshly. "I would agree with that. Okay, sure we can go to dinner right now. Then I assume you have made arrangements for a hotel room or something?"

A smile spread across his piggy face. "Yeah, I have a room. We could just skip dinner and get down to the, uhm, business."

I shook my head. "Oh my, how romantic you are lover boy. But you see I expect dinner before I fuck you, errr, get fucked. Why should Sheryl get all the bennies, eh?" I smiled bitterly at the whore dog.

Harold frowned. "Oh okay, sure. I was told I get the whole night. I have brought some stuff. Sheryl said you are okay with kinky? Is that right?"

I rolled my eyes smiling wickedly. "Oh you have no idea, Harold. I am going to rock your world darling. When I am done with you, you'll be a ruined man for a long time to come."

Harold looked at the floor giggling. "Damn, that sounds hot. Okay, ready to go?"

I nodded. "Yeah. Let me close this shit hole down. I will meet you at your car. Be there in a second?"

He nodded eagerly. "Alright, I am in the yellow Camaro." He took off headed for his car.

I sneered. "Of course you are freak." I said out loud to no one as I opened Master Boyd's pill bottle and took out four antipsychotic pills smiling as I slipped them into my pocket. Buh bye Harold.

Harold drove me to a local diner. I made sure to ask to sit in the outside area. When I was sure our food was close to being ready, I excused myself and went inside. I found our server and asked her if I might talk her into allowing me to take our plates out myself as a joke on my man friend.

The old waitress thought it very funny and was happy to allow this unusual request. I stopped at the door and slipped the four antipsychotic pills I had broken into tiny pieces at the office into Harold's mashed potatoes. I then took the meals to our table much to Harold's humor. He enjoyed being treated like a prince quite a bit.

I sat there not bothering with my food while this dweeb talked nonstop about himself. He was a real creep too. As time wore on the discussion turned from his bragging about his greatness to what he planned to do to me when we got to his hotel. He informed me that he wanted to dominate my unit by torturing my various lady parts and forcing me to deep throat his prick. I just smiled and told him I couldn't wait for his manly touch while secretly planning to murder Sheryl.

I patiently watched him eat the laced meal without even breaking a sweat. Harold was so self-absorbed about his vile desires he never noticed the foul-tasting pills. It only took about forty minutes for his eyelids to start to drop. I noticed a bit of drool in the corners of his mouth as he suddenly appeared very sleepy. His words slurred and he started to slump. I began to giggle when the waitress came out and asked if maybe he had too much of the cheap wine.

I told Harold to give me his keys while I paid for the meal. The waitress and I helped him into his chick magnet joking with each other about what a lightweight he was unable to hold his liquor. I got behind the wheel and drove Harold and I to his hotel room.

He leaned on me slurring, drooling and mumbling incoherently as I walked him to his room. I searched his pants and found the room key. I let us in, closed the door and aided him to his bed. I found his black bag full of various foul instruments used for sexual torture.

I wrinkled my nose but pulled them all out and scattered them about the room. Then I went to the near unconscious Harold and moaned loudly into his ears while I stripped the troll's unit of all his clothing. I threw his outfit all around the room laughing while he moaned back mocking my own fake sex sounds.

I have to say upon seeing his tiny prick I realized why he seemed to think he needed to torture a female to feel like a man. Oh well, he was just out of luck this time. I was not going to put up with this shit, but I was not stupid. Harold would think he got a good fucking, and he would be rendered unable to get it up for at least a week. He would be numb all over for longer.

When a normal takes Thorazine it creates a dreamlike state. All I had to do was make him think he was having sex by noise; evidence and his memory would be too fuzzy to know I had played a trick on him. Harold was fooling around with a professional whore. Hey, I know what I was so no need to sugar coat it. I had been playing this bullshit game with fucktards since I was only a seven-year-old girl. I knew exactly how to make someone think they were getting what they didn't. Even my deep psychotic state could hamper my hard-core street savvy. This asshole never stood a chance.

I called a cab and left the dumbass naked, moaning, and nearly unconscious from the antipsychotics in his bed. His room looked like someone had a BDSM party but forgot to put up their toys.

I chuckled the whole way back to the cottage barely able to control my amusement at the whole crazy experience. Sheryl would now have her fucking vote. I didn't betray my collar and Harold got what he had coming. For a change all had gone in my favor.

I picked up my Master and told him the tale while he drove us back to the office. He laughed at my clever deception but warned me to never be alone with a man like that again. Master Boyd lectured me about how Harold could have driven me right to his hotel, tied me up and raped me rather than take me to dinner.

I had not considered that. A chill ran down my spine as I realized being near Hebe meant soon, I was going to be helpless against guys like Harold, and worse.

Master Boyd and I finished my paperwork early that night. He reminded me that I had forgotten the paint for the walls yet again. We decided to drive to Wells and hit the Wal-Mart super center and purchase the needed materials. We took off without any hesitation fearful we would forget our plans if we didn't move quickly. We were aware it was rare lately that both of us were mildly lucid at the same time (as sane as either of us ever could get that is).

He and I didn't think to maybe buy food or other supplies while at the store. Instead we stuck to the purchase of brushes, paint and drop clothes. We were both eager to repair our mess, and to cease having to see the evidence of our illness glaring at us in every room.

The moment we got back we began to feverishly work on the project. It took us the rest of the dark hours, but by sunrise the remodeling job was mostly completed. The color was not a perfect match to the original paint, but it was damned close. Master Boyd chuckled as he told me the cottage owners would probably ask each other for years if it was just in their imagination that the room used to be a darker maroon.

My Master of course took his special services the second we had finished our work. He didn't seem to realize I had not slept the entire night. I did my best to appear interested in his adoration of my unit, but I was quite irritated at having to service him, then get dressed and rush to Julia's fucking coffee appointment.

Unfortunately for me, my acting job with my psychotic Master was not as Emmy award winning as it had been with Harold. Master Boyd recognized my lack of enthusiasm.

"Okay Niemand. That is it. Stop the medication now. That is a directive." He growled staring into my eyes while still coupled with my unit.

I winced at his directive. "Master you know I can't. They will catch me."

My Master rolled his eyes. "You know when you have your appointment. Just beef up the few days before silly. Stop taking it the rest of the time. I am sick of not having my wife enjoying being with me. I can tell. This is bullshit." He disengaged from me now fuming at my refusal to listen to his demands.

I sat up looking down at the mattress under me. "Master, I think you may have a point. The medication isn't working anyway. Okay, I will start to cut back on it for you. I will be free of it in about two weeks. Is that okay?"

Master Boyd looked at me smiling happily. "Yes, that is my baby. Okay, don't take it today, but take it tomorrow. Miss every other day for two weeks. Then it can be like it was on our trip to California. You remember that rest stop outside Vegas, right? That was amazing." He kissed me deeply hugging me tight.

I nodded. "Yeah, that was pretty fucking awesome. Okay, look we need to dumpster dive again. Jane jumped my ass about my weight or did Sheila? Shit, someone did. Oh hell. I think I was supposed to shower too." I whined realizing it was too late for that now.

Master Boyd looked over my sky clad unit. "Why shower? You look fine to me. Maybe just brush your hair and change your clothes? Do you have any other clothes?"

I shook my head. "No, neither do you Master. Someone told me I smell bad."

My Master chuckled. "You smell like sex with your Master." He jumped on me smiling diabolically while playfully knocking on my back while kissing and fondling.

I tried to push him off me. "Seriously Master, the person said they are going to put me in jail or something. Shit, I can't remember but it was a real threat."

Master Boyd groaned. "Why the hell can't everyone just leave us alone? Jesus. Seems to me everyone just wants to threaten every time we don't do what they say. You know what? We should just shoot everyone who utters another damned order at us. That would get us some respect I bet."

I laughed loudly. "Oh you bet it would Master. Plus we would get three hots and a cot for life too. Hey and the next time we ride the lightning it would be for keeps. Instead of frying our brains they would fry our ass."

My Master laughed too. "Three hots and a cot. Hey, did you say we went dumpster diving? Did we have anything left? I am starving."

I slapped his chest lightly. "God damn, you have the memory of a sieve Master. I said we need to go to Wells tonight and dive. Ugh, I really must go. Queen Julia is waiting. Fucking flying cows. You know I hate them." I pushed my Master off as I got up to start to dress.

He reached out and slapped my bare bottom. "Hurry up and bring that ass of mine home. I miss you terribly when you are gone. Bastard and God are not very good company. I prefer the fairer sex."

I growled. "Again, I don't have time for more sex, Master," I yelled misunderstanding his statement.

Master Boyd fell back on the bed as if wounded. "We never have sex anymore damn it. If you keep on running off, I will have to rape you," he said appearing to forget we had just had intercourse only moments before.

I snorted. "Well you sure have experience at that now, don't you Master? I will give you special services when I get home tonight. Then we go to Wells. Write that down so we don't forget?"

He looked at the ceiling appearing to trance. "Yeah, okay. I will write it down or Bastard can. Did you hear that? Thunder, watch your step it could be icy. Will you bring me back something to eat later? We could go to lunch or maybe that place with the pancakes? If the road is clear of ice. Do you think it is," he said tangentially.

I shook my head. "Get some rest Master. I think you are tired. I am headed out now. Write down whatever I was talking about or something. Oh well, I love you. Call if you need me." I kissed him while he stared at the ceiling unblinking.

"Yeah, okay, …be safe. Tell Bastard to write it down." He closed his eyes appearing to be ready for rest.

I yawned and stretched as I left the cottage to get into Julia's car. I winced as my brother the sun glared into my very weary eyes. I groaned against the heavy fatigue as I pulled out headed to my first appointment of the day. This time, I was glad to be going. I needed the coffee.

I pulled into Julia's driveway to find the woman out in her yard in a lawn chair waiting on me. I looked at the pager clock worried I had lost time somehow. It indicated I was right on time. A bit of fear that perhaps it was the right time. It crossed my shattered mind that I may have missed a few days doing Gods know what.

I got out of the Acura looking at the ground and wringing my hands feeling stressed. "Julia? Why are you out here?"

She laughed. "It is a nice day. I wanted to get some sun. You got a problem with that?"

I shook my head as I approached her still wringing and keeping my eyes to the ground. "Hey, I could really use that coffee if you would be so kind."

Julia paused. "What? No smartass complaints or digs this morning? You feeling okay Psycho?" She chuckled at calling me that name.

I started to get angry but the terror rising within blocked it. "Uhm, yeah, just tired. I need a bit of coffee is all. Can I please have a cup of coffee?" I hoped this time she would just let it go and get me the fucking java.

Julia wrinkled her nose. "Yeah, but you know what? You also need a shower pretty bad and a change of clothes. Jane called Sheryl bitching about it. I see you didn't listen to Jane's warning. Unless you were planning to go back home and change after our coffee. Psycho you are rank."

I shook my head feeling very nervous suddenly. "I don't have any other clothes, damn it. Can I please have a cup of coffee?" I started to pace and wring unable to calm my inner fear demon.

Julia smiled while she watched me a moment. "Yeah, let's go get that coffee Psycho." I followed her inside grateful that she didn't make me wait longer for my desired drink.

Julia told me to sit down while she handed me a cup of the dark liquid energy. "Uhm, you drink this coffee then go to my bathroom, strip off those clothes, take a shower and put on the robe hanging up on the back of the door. I want you to bring me those nasty clothes. I will wash them while you visit. Got it? You are not leaving this house looking like a street person, no arguments. You know if you don't do something, Jane is threatening to haul your ass off to the State Mental hospital right?"

I looked up from my coffee startled. "Can she do that," I yelled out feeling my heart start to pound in my chest.

Julia smiled while nodding. "Damn right she can. She is a state DCFS worker. She has a duty to warn and if she says you are a loose cannon she can ask that an emergency hold be taken. So, ready to take that shower and wash those clothes or do you want to be a smart ass about it?"

I got up wringing my hands but practically ran to her bathroom to follow her wise instructions. I couldn't imagine what would happen to me if I were sent back to the pit with my Master stuck alone in the cottage with no one around to help him.

I jumped into her shower after handing Julia my soiled clothing. I even washed my nasty wig then used her blow dryer to restyle the real hair piece. I applied my makeup taking as much time as possible in her bathroom to avoid having to visit with the pushy ex-foster mother. I really did hate Julia to the core. Something about the woman just seemed, well off.

I watched in the mirror as the haggard looking schizophrenic began to morph into someone I could sort of recognize. I was very thin, and my face was bruised from several head banging sessions. My white powders helped to hide the blue and yellow marks of madness from my visible skin suit. In less than one hour I smelled personally presentable and my clothes were in the dryer recovering from their own much needed bath.

Try as I might, I fell asleep at the kitchen table waiting for my outfit to finish the wash cycle. Julia was droning on about how great her home state of Maryland is. I was not only bored to tears by this subject, but I also had not slept more than two or three hours a night in over four days (and none the night before). Even my impressive psychotic energy could not protect me at that level of sleep deprivation.

Julia would shake my unit till I would wake up. Every time I would appear startled out of my mind. She would have to calmly remind me who she was, where I was located, what day it was and what time of day it was. Julia would laugh each time truly enjoying her let's scare the shit out of the Psycho game.

I had already been very aware that my memory was starting to slip severely. There is no way to know how much was due to lack of rest or how much was due to my strengthening illness symptoms.

No matter the cause, I knew I couldn't keep ignoring the problem. Sooner or later I would end up missing for days, then turning up having no memory for where I had been or what I had been doing for that matter. Worse, I feared I would wander off and never return, not alive anyway.

I was thoroughly irritated with Julia when my clothing was finally ready to wear again. I dressed quickly and hauled ass citing an imaginary emergency. I knew I should be grateful to the woman for her help in keeping my ass out of the mental asylum but damn she was such an annoying asshole.

My thoughts turned to Sheila while I tore off down Julia's dirt road. I felt that gal also deserved a bit of a lesson. Her nasty trick of going through my psychiatric records was simply deplorable. I decided that no matter what Jane said I was going to the DCFS office to demand that Sheila stay out of my private, confidential business.

I pulled into the parking lot sideways as was habit those days. I had the attention span of a gnat and the memory of Swiss cheese. I would nearly miss the damned turn off only recalling my destination moments before it was too late.

That often happened when the sight of the old brownstone walls of the DCFS complex would kick my holy shit that is where I was going retention back into gear.

This time when I came into the waiting rooms out front, the attending secretaries only stared appearing very surprised. I suppose they had never seen a clean schizophrenic before.

I scowled at the gossipy bitches then tore off to the back offices ready to kick Sheila's ass. Jane came out of the break room just in time to see me pushing my way through the new secretary's door without knocking.

Sheila looked up at me seeming a bit surprised but smiling sweetly "Oh my Niemand. Uhm, can I help you," she said in a patronizing voice.

I sneered at her hatefully. "Fucking right you can help me asshole. I am going to tell you this one time, Stay out of my business. The next time you nose into my records I will tear you apart. You hear me bitch? I am not kidding. I don't know if you did it on your own or someone put you up to it, but when I am done fucking your pretty face up, I will hunt the other fuckers down. Try me, Sheila," I yelled while knocking a bunch of her files onto the floor.

"Psycho, stop that now." Jane's voice yelling out behind me caused me flinch and turn toward her.

"Jane, you stay out of this. Sheila is getting into my private records. That is a breach of confidentiality you know.

She doesn't have the right." I growled out while pointing at the now frightened looking beauty.

Jane looked at Sheila then back to me. "Psycho, I told you to stay out of this office during working hours. This bullshit is why I wanted your ass out of here. Now you pick up those files, get into your car and leave now."

I glared at Shelia who was now smiling victoriously. "Seriously Jane? Did you just hear me? She is going through my fucking records. That is not legal. You are going to throw me out and not punish her for it? Tell her Sheila, don't you fucking lie either. The bitch knew my birth name. I never say that name Jane. I have proof right there." I glared at Jane crossing my arms waiting for my vindication for this obvious crime against my person.

Jane took a deep breath then blew it out. "Psycho, no one is going through your private records. They are not even located at this office. Even if they were, no one would have access but me."

My eyes went wide. "You mean you are in on this bullshit too? You fucking told Sheila my name. Well, fuck, to whom else are you spreading my business?" I couldn't believe the betrayal.

Jane rubbed her forehead. "Oh my God does my head hurt. Why do I get all the fucking screwballs? Psycho, who the fuck is Sheila," yelled Jane.

I shook my head. "Oh so now you are going to try to play the I don't even know Sheila when she is sitting right the fuck there. Do you really think you can fuck with my head now that I know your God damned game? Wow. You are all a bunch of assholes aren't you. Do you guys go to special classes to learn that bullshit or does it come naturally?" I snorted angrily while pointing at the stunned Sheila.

She looked at Sheila then back to me. "This is a file office, Psycho. There isn't even a chair for a Sheila person to sit in. You are pointing at the wall. Honey, I think you need to go see Doctor Holcomb. This is getting not good when you are seeing imaginary people so bad they make you this angry. I mean it was bad when you talked to your computer. That I could handle. But tearing up the filing room is where I draw the line."

"Jane forget it. I know that you are messing with me. Sheila is right there. Look damn you. She is the new secretary. Jesus, Jane, you need medication. I think you may be schizophrenic or something." I stood there dumbfounded that Jane was going to persist in this lie.

Jane groaned. "Oh for Christ sakes. I am not going to stand here in an empty room being diagnosed with schizophrenic delusions by a delusional schizophrenic. First, it is too fucking early. Second, it is too fucking weird. Last, this is Sheryl's baby. Let her raise it. Get out of this building Psycho or so help me I'm calling the cops right now." She pointed down the hall appearing angrier than I had ever seen her.

I looked back at the silent Sheila to send out another threat and almost had a heart attack from sheer terror. Jane was right. There was no chair, no beautiful Goddess. Just a bunch of stodgy old files and piles of paperwork laying on an old work desk. Dust and cobwebs covered everything. No one had been using this storage room for quite some time.

I stood there with my mouth wide open and my eyes fixated on what was not there.

"Psycho, get out. I mean it. I am calling Charlie," said Jane as she started for her office.

I shook off my shook and rushed for the Accord without hesitating another second. It felt like mice with tiny frozen feet were running through my scalp and upper unit while I scrambled for the car.

This couldn't be happening. I had been hallucinating a sexy secretary. What the fuck was happening. This had to be a mistake. Even Sheryl said there was a new secretary. I was just in the wrong office, misdirected that is all. Yeah, that had to be it. Sheila was real. Likely she used a false name to fuck with me is all.

As I started across the parking lot Sheryl yelled out for me to stop. She had just pulled into the driveway. She had a short stubby, middle aged woman with tightly curled black hair and a witchy chin.

I stopped upon hearing my failed Master's voice. I waited till she limped up bringing the severe looking lady with her.

I stood there wringing my hands looking at the pavement feeling very agitated at the nasty joke Jane and Shelia were attempting to play on me.

"Ah, Marcy, this is Psycho. You two have already met, right?" Sheryl said to the strange lady with her.

Marcy looked at me appearing surprised. "Uhm, no Miss Fressman. I have not had the pleasure yet I confess. Psycho is always out in the field. I have heard interesting things about her though," said Marcy as she stuck out her hand to shake.

I just stared at her hand rudely refusing to take it. "I have never met this woman in my life, Sheryl. Why should I even care," I growled now irritated at this weird encounter.

My failed Master chuckled "Oh? Well, that is odd Psycho. You see Marcy is the new secretary here in the building everyone is abuzz about. I thought you said you met her. She has been here over a week."

I looked up at Marcy now very stunned. "Uhm, a week? This is the new secretary, Marcy. Ah, okay, you sure?" I reached out and shook her hand but barely realized it while my mind whirled in horror at this latest discovery.

I had created my own secretary. One of my own shards had played the role of helpful, friendly and sexually charged secretary. Worse still I didn't recognize it. I was becoming as delusional as Master Boyd ever thought to be. This is bad.

Marcy giggled. "Gosh I hope I am, sure. Otherwise I have been coming to the wrong office for the last week. Well it is great to finally meet you Psycho. I will see you around in the halls I am sure. Miss Fressman, thanks so much for the coffee. Oh, and congratulations again on the appointment. Wow, Area Manager, that is so neat."

Sheryl smiled at me wickedly. "Yeah it is about time. I certainly had to wait long enough. It was my pleasure Marcy. Good luck with the job. Oh and watch out for Nora. She is a gossip."

Marcy nodded then waved as she walked toward the office leaving me alone with the new Area Manager, my failed Master Sheryl.

I shook my head now feeling sick to my stomach over the discovery of the Sheila delusion and hearing that Sheryl was now the most powerful woman this side of the State capital thanks to my Harold trick.

I wrung my hands harder as Sheryl got close enough to speak where no one would hear us.

"Well, I guess you know I am here because I got the call early this morning. I am Area Manager. Oddly, the vote was slated for Monday, but Harold called them this morning and relented his veto. Wonder what happened there?" She smiled at me bitterly.

I shrugged. "Humm, beats me."

She leaned in closely. "I intend to, Psycho. I happen to know you fucked that stupid prick. You betrayed your collar. How dare you. I told you no dicks."

I stopped wringing my hands and looked at her as if she had sprouted a third eye. "Huh? You said to do whatever it took, Sheryl. Besides, did you think Boyd had a vagina? What do you mean no dicks?"

She snorted. "I am not even getting into it with Boyd. You were with that dumbass before me, and I know he is using his badge to keep you hostage, so he doesn't count. This is about Harold. I said do what it took, but I assumed you would recall your promises to my collar, bitch. I didn't mean you could just go fuck him to near death. He called me this morning, Psycho. He told me you were so good in the sack he couldn't even get out of bed. He took the day off due to, what did he call it? Oh yeah, fuck fatigue. You fucking whore. How could you," yelled Sheryl.

I started to chuckle in disbelief. "Ah, silly me. You are acting pissed because you don't want to honor our agreement. That is dirty Sheryl. You promised me a fucking desk job with a forty-hour week if I got you that fucking vote. Well congrats Area Manager. You got the God damned vote. Pony up and fuck your complaints about how I did it. All that matter is you got the fucking position."

Sheryl growled, "Yeah, from you taking it in the doggy position. Sick bitch." She suddenly took a deep breath and appeared to calm down.

"You know what? Never mind. You are right. I got what I wanted. You can have that desk job. It will take me a couple of days to assign it. I still must be sworn in. Now, despite the misunderstanding over Harold, seeing you is wonderful.

251

Well except that ugly collar. I am still pissed you cut my pretty one off for this ugly piece of shit." She reached out and stroked my shoulder appearing loving suddenly.

I shook my head. "I am really sorry about that. Boyd and I were, uhm, having issues when that happened. We didn't have the right. I am grateful you are not too angry about that."

I was feeling generous towards Sheryl thanks to the fine news that soon I would never have to see another broken child or raped little girl. I needed to be out of the field. Now, finally, I was going to be saved from sure destruction of chronic severe stress. Not to mention the endless hours that stretched on never ending in its ungodly scheduling.

Sheryl smiled. "Well, I am glad you said that. I have a new collar at my hotel room. Come with me to my car and let's go get it. It is nice and thin, barely noticeable. It is my gift to my best girl ever. I am so proud of you."

I looked back at the Accord. "Well, okay. I suppose I could spare some time." I was unsure if I should accept this gift but the idea of having a less cumbersome collar was too tempting to pass up.

I followed Sheryl to her rented Jeep Grand Cherokee. She didn't even take off out of the parking lot before producing a key to remove the bulky metal ring. She unlocked it and removed it throwing it into the back seat while I rubbed my now freed neck enjoying the sensation of being uncollared if only for a few moments. Sheryl started the jeep when both our pagers went off in unison.

I looked as did she realizing this was a serious call. It was from the Jessieville police station. Sheryl called the number and was told they had a child involved in a domestic violence situation. The mother was being hauled to jail, and the little girl appeared to have been beaten by both parents while they drunkenly fought each other. Sheryl told me to take off for Jessieville and she would see me later that afternoon for dinner and my new collar.

I jumped into my Accord to head for Jessieville to save my kid. I looked in the rearview mirror admiring my lack of silver necklace. It felt really nice to be free of that heavy burden. I smiled wondering what would happen if I just kept driving and never came back for the new collar or for Master Boyd either. The horizon beckoned me seductively. I was just so tired of everyone and everything. It would have been so easy if only I could just let it all go and just go.

Uh oh, something smells and it sure isn't me, not anymore. I got the shower and my clothing is clean for a minute. Well, no worries, this peaceful moment will not even last for a full day. Want to see what happens next? Well me too. Just kidding.

Two questions to consider before we move on. Were you surprised that I drugged Harold? You do realize I could have killed that man I am sure. In my defense I was acutely psychotic, and this possibility didn't even occur to me. Do you see just how dangerous psychosis can be realizing that fact? Yes, yes he could have died at that dose especially if left alone, not that the bastard didn't deserve it. I stand by that statement.

Why do you think I created the sexy secretary Sheila? Want to take a guess?

Now let me give you a hint. In the past I had been feeling very left out and lonely. I became delusional that Stephanie, who was a real person, came and helped me escape the Sloan's and clean up Darlin cemetery. I had imagined she was there for three days due to extreme loneliness, and fear. I needed a friend, so I made one up and believed it. Know that most of my delusional shard 'people' fill a need that is being neglected in my life. What did Sheila's appearance provide and can you guess why she turned on me?

## Chapter 80: Master Blaster
## The Fall of Sheryl the Absent Interim
## Master Boyd & Submissive Neimand

Now there is something in the title that looks great for a change. Goodbye Sheryl. Oh wait, just because she fell as a Master does not mean the old heifer is gone from our life now does it? Well, the remaining story of Sheryl's time with us is an odd one for sure. The Master who didn't reign, didn't serve, but stayed in our world till the day she died. A boss and a menace to her bitter end. Sheryl's harm to us was so wide ranged and long lasting that to this very day, her marks are still on both our unit and our mind. Of all who ever held our key she was the most destructive. We served her well, but she never gave us anything in return but the nightmares that still haunt us in the darkness.

Ready to find out what can blast a Master? Oh, come on. You know this must be fun. Aren't you already having the time of your lives? Just think, two vacations, excitement around every corner, and don't forget the sex. It's it almost good enough to die for. Just ask Harold. Old Sheryl sure did. She is not happy that when she gave directives they get followed, sort of.

Grab that clutch and throw the car into high gear. We are going to need to make a quick escape. Make sure to bring your lightning rods. We wouldn't want to be accidently struck in case our plan fails. Now, we all need to get our stories straight. Put on your poker faces and let's tell some righteous lies. If you stick with us, we will get you right out of this mess. We are professionals, trust us.

*"I am not sure if I am remembering this right, but were you my Master before the nothing? You are called Boyd, right? Oh, please dear God let my memory be right this time. If you were my Master, I am in a lot of trouble. I think Julia may have kidnapped me from the hospital. She sold me to Master Gus. Master Gus is planning to do horrible things; I can't even say them. Those monsters are out looking for me because I escaped last night. If they catch me, oh God, I am begging you for help. I am hurt; I can't stop the bleeding. Please Mister, I will do anything you want if you will help me. Please, I am so scared."*

--**Niemand's desperate phone call to Master Boyd from a West Virginia bus station, May 2000**

I finished my emergency in Jessieville. It took a full three hours to return to Cumberland. I was not looking forward to being recollared, but without my circle of silver, I stood no chance at survival outside of an institution. My memory was not so poor I had forgotten what happened the last time I went without my collar for more than a few weeks. I was aware my mental health was far too fragile to dare try to go without my delusional security blanket too long. I put the petal to the metal to get the dirty deed of being locked in done and over.

I pulled into the hotel and went inside to get Sheryl's room number. The woman behind the counter informed me that she had checked out over two hours earlier. I stood there dumbfounded and asked her to check again. The lady stubbornly told me Sheryl had left and she was not going to check on something of which she was certain. I left the lazy bitch while grumbling under my breath about people not wanting to work for their money.

I drove back to the DCFS office to call my failed Master. Sheryl would let me know what room she was in. Likely, the shitty staff at the hotel had pissed her off and she went to another one in town. The office had just closed for the night. I was grateful to miss Jane and Sheila just in case she wasn't really a delusion.

I still wasn't completely sure. I didn't trust Jane, Marcy or Sheryl to be honest. I decided it could be a big nasty trick the four of them were playing on me. Getting me to question my sanity was an old game many had played before. From Master Julie to Mistress Circe, I couldn't put anything past a normal in just how low they would be willing to go to fuck with my mind.

I walked into Jane's empty office and dialed Sheryl's cell phone. I let it ring but she didn't answer. That was odd. I called again with the same result. I sat there in confusion. Sheryl always answered when I called. I couldn't ever recall her not picking up the phone. I called her pager and left my number. I sat there staring at the phone waiting. She would get to me. Maybe she was in the shower.

The phone rang. I gasped then picked it up realizing that her lack of immediate response had frightened me for some reason. The sound of the alert that she was answering my hail sent relief through my unit.

"Hello, Sheryl? Where are you," I said trying not to sound irritated or desperate.

"Uhm, no. Is this Psycho? This is Cheryl from the Well's DCFS office. We spoke about Missy Links a while back. Do you remember me," said the woman's voice.

I narrowed my eyes. "Yeah how could I forget. I suppose you have called to bitch me out for reporting you and Paula for fucking up that case," I snorted angrily while fearing that her holding me on the phone could be blocking Sheryl's call back.

Cheryl cleared her throat. "Uhm, no. I was kind of was pissed about it at first, but you were right. That child could have died. Paula wasn't doing her job. Look that is not important and not why I called. Can you head out her to Wells right now? It is an emergency."

I sat there dumbfounded. "Huh? I don't know who you think you are Cheryl, but I don't just rush ninety miles to visit case workers who claim emergencies. Especially after hours. Good day to you, Ma'am." I slammed down the phone shaking my head at the gall of that idiot.

The phone rang again. "Hello Sheryl? Hey, what the fuck is going on. Where are you," I sputtered into the phone.

"Uhm, no Psycho it is Cheryl again. Look don't hang up. I need you to come to Well's right now. Sheryl is here. It is important. She told me to call you and tell you to get

258

your ass here right now. I am not sure what the hell is going on, but she is demanding you come and says if you don't you are fired. She said to tell you there is a private problem here. She doesn't want everyone to know about it. Does any of that sound familiar to you? I sure hope so because she is super pissed about whatever is going on," Cheryl spoke rapidly trying to get me to listen.

I sat there in surprise. "Sheryl is there in Wells? Is she okay?"

Cheryl cleared her throat again. "Uhm, Psycho, she is like freaking out or something. Look can you please just come right now? I don't know what to do with her. I think the chemo has done something to her mind. I don't know. Anyway, just hurry," She hung up the phone.

I got up and rushed to the Accord. Without hesitation I took off to Well's wondering if Sheryl had slipped a loop. I had read somewhere once that chemotherapy can make some people foggy brained or even go psychotic. I admit, I was a bit scared to find out just how sick Sheryl had become. I once heard that crazy folks can be dangerous.

I arrived at the DCFS office in Wells in record time. I barely parked the car before I was rushing for the building door knocking with all my might. I had worked myself into a terrified frenzy that Sheryl was in big trouble. Cheryl came to the door with a worried look on her face. She unlocked the entry and told me to follow her to her private conference room.

I walked behind Cheryl Taggert. She was five seven and had long brown naturally curly hair. Her face was wide, and her eyes small and hazel in color. She was thin without curves or any significant signs of femininity. The thirty something lady looked more like a teenaged boy than the mother of two she was.

We walked into a large room that had a half-moon shaped desk with several chairs parked all around it. I looked around not spying Sheryl anywhere.

"Okay so where is Sheryl. Cheryl, look what the hell is going on," I said while she walked over and sat down in one of the chairs.

"Have a seat Psycho. I am not really sure but we are going to find that out right now I think." She motioned me to sit down.

I shook my head. "I prefer to stand. Out with it, Cheryl. I don't like this bullshit. Where is Sheryl, damn it."

Cheryl reached under the desk then produced my bulky collar. She laid it on the tabletop. My mouth almost dropped to the ground.

She looked at the chunky circle of silver than at me. "Sheryl gave this to me. She told me to hold it. Said that you belong to it? She said she was going to teach you a lesson by loaning you out to me for a while till you realize the mistake you made by not minding her. Look Psycho, I don't know what any of this is about. I am freaking out right now. What the fuck is going on?"

I groaned out in horror. "Cheryl, Sheryl, has tossed my collar to you. Please tell me this is a joke."

Cheryl looked at me with fear. "What does that even mean? Shit, Sheryl came her in a huff. Threw this thing at me and said for me to put it on you and you must do what I say. She said you had to do something called submission? Then told me in a couple of weeks she would come back and collect you. What kind of crazy shit is this?"

I closed my eyes listening to my heart pounding hard on my chest plate. "Cheryl, Sheryl is finished. She can never come back for me. That is the rule. Only one chance. The dumb bitch has forgotten. She just tossed her God damned collar. You are now my Interim Master. Fuck, this is a fucking nightmare."

Cheryl looked back at the collar. "I don't want this. Here you take it. Christ, the way Sheryl spoke it is like I would own you or some shit. That is insane. No one can own anyone. That is illegal, immoral and fucking messed up. Take this thing and leave. I don't even want to know what this shit is all about."

I started to hyperventilate. "You are not willing to take the collar? Oh fuck, oh fuck. I don't have another interim. God no, not now. My Master is gone. He can't do the job. Cheryl. Please take the collar. I can help you learn how to wield it. I can't hang in there without someone knowing what the fuck is going on that is not loony fucking toons. Sheryl must have chosen you for a reason."

Cheryl shook her head. "She told me that she picked me because if I did it then handed it back to her once she had punished you enough she would make me office manager again. That is what she said."

I felt the world spinning. "Oh shit. Sheryl didn't toss the collar she traded the fucking thing. Okay, so are you willing to take her deal? That would buy me a few weeks to find a replacement. I could find someone to take the collar off your hands…"

Cheryl raised her had interrupting me. "No, take this thing and leave. Sheryl is going to come back for this fucking thing. I know Sheryl. She is not going to keep her promise, Psycho. I could kiss her ass for a hundred years and that bitch will screw me anyway. I told her I wouldn't take the deal, but she left this anyway. I want you to get your whatever this bullshit thing is and get out of my sight. I not only don't like you, but I would also like to see you fired. In fact, the only good thing that came from this entire mess was the look of terror I got to see on your smug face. I am glad you are scared Psycho. I don't understand what this is all about, but I do know one thing, hearing you beg for my help made my fucking day. Now take it and get out now," she screamed at me.

### 18th /19thMaster (Refused the Collar)
### Cheryl-the useless
### Reign forfeited in February, 3 hours

I nodded realizing I had been defeated in this game. I walked over and took my collar from the desk and promptly left the building, parking lot and the city. I headed right for Darlin. It was time to bury the collar.

Until a new interim could be located, it was too dangerous to have laying around. I had managed to lose two Masters in less than thirty minutes. Sheryl and Cheryl were now history. Master Boyd now ruled supreme but he was too psychotic to even look after his own Bastard.

I cried most of the way to my beloved old cemetery home. If Master Boyd found out that Sheryl had traded off my collar, he would make me quit my job. He would also realize he had full control of me.

My unit trembled while I considered what would happen if he found out about this terrible fail. The idea of being forever bonded to my schizophrenic Master in both bondage and in marriage in a double collaring was my second worst nightmare come true. Schizophrenia itself is my first nightmare come true.

I knew I would be trapped in his service without a way out, nothing more than a glorified housemaid that he could fuck at his leisure. All that I had been fighting to earn, freedom, education, a life of worth (more than just a fucking prostitute), and societal respect would be lost. My intelligence would be ignored, and slowly my spirit would erode faster than my shattered mind ever thought to do. I just couldn't let that happen.

As I got out of the car and entered the old iron gate, I made a promise to the Gods I would keep Sheryl's betrayal a secret. I would not tell Master Boyd he was now my One and Only, ugh. I also would never allow Sheryl to call herself my Master again. I would treat her as my boss and nothing more. She was dead to me otherwise, the fool.

I buried the collar in my old hiding spot near the outhouse sighing as I realized I was not getting that desk job. I heard Cheryl loud and clear. Sheryl was a deal breaker born. I knew Cheryl was right. That was clear since I was in the cemetery digging a hole to hide my shame. She had already broken the one promise that really mattered the most.

I hurried back to Cumberland after depositing my circle of silver in the earthy embrace of Gaia. I realized I would also have to keep Sheryl's ascendancy to Area Manager out of my Master's sight. Whatever I had to do, I would do to keep my shitty job with DCFS. Sheryl has lost all rights to collar that she had traded away.

I needed the money from the job to afford graduate school. I had a plan. I was getting out of this mess. I just had to be patient. I knew that if I could get my Master's degree, I could get a better job, and then the damned normals would have to accept me. I was sure of it.

I arrived at the cottage much later than usual. Master Boyd was pacing and mumbling as I came inside. He turned to look at me appearing at first to not recognize me.

"Master? You doing okay." I asked cautiously as I put down my keys and purse.

He shook his head. "I don't know. Did you see your Aunt? How is she? I was worried her hip would break. That is a hell of a thing you know," he rambled.

I just nodded. "Yeah, she is doing fine. You feel like going dumpster diving? You are looking a bit thin Master. Are you hungry?"

Master Boyd looked at me stopping his endless walking back and forth. "Niemand? What day is it?"

I looked at the floor "I used to know but not anymore. Master, maybe we should get some help now? I am pretty sure we are sick but not sure with what."

He giggled. "The flu. The damned Boswell kids had it. We should have washed our hands. Get some rest baby. It will pass. I will make you some chicken noodle soup. Where did you put the pots and pans?"

I shrugged. "Thank you for Your mercy Master, but I am not hungry. Just very tired. Can we just go to bed? It was a long day."

Master Boyd nodded his head. "Yeah, I am really tired too. Let's just go to bed." He headed for the bedroom with me following.

He got onto the bed and I crawled in next to him. He grabbed my unit and pulled me into a spoon appearing to be smelling my hair as he breathed deeply while holding me tightly. I closed my eyes barely able to think from the fatigue. My beloved Sandman came quickly as I drifted into oblivion within moments.

I don't know how long I had been asleep when I was awakened by my unit being pulled across the bed. I opened my eyes groggy and frightened, unable to figure out what was happening. My Master had either never slept or had woken up desirous of my attendance to his needs.

He had managed to get me disrobed enough without waking me to take me from behind before I even got back to consciousness. My Master had grabbed me around the waist tightly holding me up while I tried to gain a bearing on my situation. His rough entry and harsh thrust startled me to full awareness immediately. I let out a surprised yell and began to try to get away out of sheer reflex behavior. This is not a nice way to wake up your partner. I totally would not suggest it.

Master Boyd usually was turned on when I behaved this way. My struggling or terror, whether feigned or real, was always his fetish. This time, it pissed him off. He grabbed my right arm and pulled it behind me as he paused his mount.

He leaned down still engaged. "Stop trying to get away. I am tired of you acting like I am a monster. I am your husband damn it. You are my One and Only. You are supposed to be thrilled to fuck me. Do you know how bad it makes me feel that you hate me so much? How would you like it?" He jerked my arm hard holding it far enough behind I thought my shoulder may break.

I screamed out in agony. "I am sorry Master. Please you just startled me. I swear it."

My Master then grabbed my other arm pulling it behind me just as brutally. "You hate me and I know you do. You hate my touch. You lie about loving me. You would run from me if you could. You plan to leave me. You are a liar." He held both my arms behind me painfully straining them in my sockets using them as reigns to hold me up while he took his privileges to a violent completion.

I did my best to endure the pain, but I was quite loudly begging him to forgive me for whatever I had done to anger him so badly. It was not uncommon for Master Boyd to be savage during lovemaking but there was something different about this ruthless engagement. He was not himself.

My Master was suddenly convinced I was faking my affection for him. Though that had been true in our turbulent history together, he and I had gotten past it. I did love him a great deal. Enough to risk everything to protect and defend him from Dennis and they. The Master Boyd I knew understood that. This guy wearing my Master's skin suit, well he was paranoid as hell.

I was terrified beyond words when even after he was spent, he continued to hold me in that excruciating position. Master Boyd was very slowly ripping my arms off and refusing to disengage while he yelled that I was a liar.

Nothing I screamed out, nor any amount of begging, was persuading him to desist his aggression against my unit. I was beginning to think he was considering tearing off my arms and legs so I couldn't ever leave him as he was claiming he knew I was planning to do.

"I should tie you up. How about that? Then you will never get away. You will learn to love me the way I love you. I will make you," he yelled manically increasing his pull a bit more.

"I love you. I love you, Master. Please stop this. You are hurting me. I love you like you love me," I yelled now blinded in unbearable suffering.

"Liar. I know you. You hate me. That is it. You infected me with your disease and now you are going to leave me like this. I see you're your plan." He let my arms go and I flew face first into the mattress with a yell of shock.

My Master grabbed my arm and dragged me off the bed. Then like a rag doll he hauled me kicking and fighting by my near useless arm to the living room. He dropped me to the floor and went into the kitchen returning with a knife in his hand. I saw the glint of the blade and backed in terror to the wall. He was blocking the door out of the cottage. I assumed I was finished. Master Boyd had finally blown his last gasket. I was going to be his completely because no one else would want a corpse.

I sat there with my screaming shoulders unable to get up trembling while he approached me. Insanity flowed through his blue eyes like a tempest of pure madness. I closed my own icy eyes hoping the death would be quick. I knew I was no match for my powerful Master. Struggling would only make my end more painful than need be. I said a quick prayer to the Goddess to look after my children and Seine after I was gone. I opened them back up to face the coming reaper.

Instead of attacking he sat down in front of me crossing his legs. He put the knife on the floor between us. Smiling he looked at me crazily.

"Now, where is my collar Niemand," he practically sang out.

I winced realizing he must have noticed the missing metal ring. That is what was causing all this. Shit.

"Your collar broke Master. I am sorry. There was fight the client broke it. I beg mercy. I just need you to give me another one. I will happily allow you to recollar with it," I lied hoping against all hope this would work.

My Master sucked in his breath then let it out slowly. "It broke huh? Then we will get another one." He smiled at me appearing in a daze.

I looked at the knife "Master please I apologize. I am happy to make it up to you however you wish but never accuse me of not loving you. I do love you. I always will."

He nodded. "Yeah? Do you? Well, you can prove it right now. I want you to kill me. Oh that is a directive." He pushed the knife toward me.

I looked up at him startled. "Pardon? Master? What? Why?" I could not understand this strange request.

Master Boyd chuckled. "Because you are going to leave me. God told me you will. I would rather be dead than lose you. I am tired of hearing him, and Bastard too. I am tired of the pain. You don't like me touching you. You don't want to really be with me either. I think you do love me, but you don't want to be with me. It is because I am sick like you are. Dennis says we can't be a match. God says you are my One and Only. I can't be with anyone else, and you agree with Dennis. So, the simple solution is you kill me. Show me mercy and end my pain. I don't want to spend my life hurting you to get you to stay. I will you know. I can't make it stop. Nothing works. I could kill myself, but I may hesitate. You my love, you have plenty of reasons to do it. I have been an awful husband to you. You deserve better. If you don't end my life I won't stop until you are mine. All mine even if that means tying you up and holding you hostage for the rest of your life." He pushed the knife right in front of me smiling in a full unblinking trance.

I took the knife and watched him close his eyes and brace for my strike. I must admit, I did consider doing it for a moment. Master Boyd was only being honest. I was aware his delusion was as strong as my own for Simon's Key. Nothing could keep me from following that key. Nothing would stop him from trying to possess his One and Only, that would be me.

Only death, or a cure for schizophrenia, could end our errored beliefs. We could logically understand what we do is insane but knowing it could not stop our insatiable need to fulfill our duties to these delusions.

I was aware I could cry all I liked at every collaring, but I will not be able to resist seeking the next Key holder.

Master Boyd could want to stop hurting me to get his way, but he would forever desire to hold me at his side as his true lover. His hard-wired assumption meant that he could never replace me with another. He understood losing me would result in his condemnation to a life of loneliness without a partner nor sexual thrill ever again. That would be not only scary but stressful for anyone to believe. For Master Boyd, it had become hell on earth.

I examined the knife briefly then put it on the floor out of his reach behind me. I looked at him sitting there with his eyes closed waiting patiently for me to send him to his peace at last. Pity for this tortured soul washed over me. Master Boyd didn't want to be a horrible person. He didn't truly enjoy hurting me at all. He was a fucking prisoner to the Mother of Madness, just like me. I got up and stood over him. I watched as he winced appearing to think I was about to stick him with the blade.

Instead I wrapped my aching arms around his neck and crawled into his lap. I put my head into his chest holding him tightly.

"I do love you Master. I don't want to lose you anymore than you want to lose me. I request punishment because I choose to disobey your directive. Better that you beat me to death than live my life without you in it," I said into his chest.

I felt his unit heave then his arms embrace me tightly as he put his face into my neck weeping loudly. I just held him while he let his pain go. I understood. It is so hard to be as messed up as we really are. Schizophrenia hurts more than you will ever want to know. No matter how tough you are it will break you sooner or later. That night, it had broken my Master. He was ready to give up.

We held each other a long while like that. He had several bouts of liquid despair. I spoke to him lovingly and promised to do my absolute best to make our relationship work despite all odds being against us. He promised he would love me in this life and beyond. I did the same without hesitation. I knew that I did and do love him. A very special kind of love in fact. We were and are of the same soul. We were and are violent psychotics in a world that misunderstands, fears and hates us. This kind of love is not a normal expression of that deep emotion.

Master Boyd and I are always lost. Even in our own heads. In our perpetual darkness, for a moment in time, we had joined as lovers to attempt what was never meant to be. I think that for the first time that night he began to realize that our unholy union was doomed to fail. That sudden clarity during the lowest point in his severe break from reality was simply more than he could bare. Together we battled his urge to end his life until finally we fell asleep in each other's arms. We didn't wake up till late afternoon the next day. Thankfully, it was Saturday and I was off work for a change.

We woke up still cuddled and tangled together. My Master took his privileges again, but this time he kindly asked for them rather than assailing me without respect. After our lovemaking he told me he thought maybe being cooped up inside all the time was getting to him.

I didn't argue that could be an issue. We decided to go to Well's and hang out on the streets for the afternoon just to get a change of scenery. It seemed to us the town was large enough it was unlikely anyone would recognize us or even notice our mentally ill asses.

Master Boyd drove. We parked at the Walmart then took off on foot. We raided several dumpsters for a quick meal before wandering the streets, sidewalks and alleys of that busy place. Sometimes people would stare at us, a few even crossed the street or went the other direction when they saw us coming their way. My Master and I just laughed at that while we held hands and enjoyed just being out. I amazingly didn't get a single page that day or night.

Though we were basically behaving like native schizophrenics (wandering, babbling, illogical, dumpster diving, odd looking, dirty and thin) we felt somehow, at peace. Trying to live by society rules when we could barely recall our own names or day of the week was just too much stress. Out on those streets none of that shit mattered. We were free and no one was telling us what to do. For a single afternoon and most of that night, Master Boyd and I were happy. As happy as one of our kind can ever get.

When my father the darkness cast his blanket over the land, my Master pulled me into an alley and once again demanded his rights. I did as he as ordered. I found a great deal of humor in his excitement at getting a blow job, then engaging in carnal congress in public (sort of, I mean we were hidden behind a dumpster).

In fact, nothing distracted him from his pleasures. We were right in the middle of coitus when a street person decided to wander into our territory. My Master had me face in the wall in a 'spread em' position so the fellow likely didn't realize we were, uhm, getting better acquainted. I gasped when I saw the bum and tried to break loose from our copulation for decency's sake. Uhm Niemand, you are in an alley in the open, behind a dumpster, really decency? Yeah, reality is just not my thing you know? My Master pushed me back into the wall refusing to end his aggressions.

Master Boyd turn and looked at the fellow then without missing a stroke said, "Get the fuck out of here man. This is my alley. Leave now or you are next."

I couldn't help giggling when the old man's eyes got wide. The poor guy hauled ass when he realized just exactly what 'next' meant. I watched as he ran away nearly busting his ass slipping and sliding on the slimy sidewalk. He didn't come back. Apparently, he was not interested in my Master's affections.

I however, noticed toward the end of our indiscretion I felt my orgasm mechanisms try to go off. My skin unit heated up but not quite enough to get there. Still it was better than the nothing that had numbed my sensations since our last vacation.

I smiled to myself as my Master found his climax loudly. I knew that soon; I would be joining him in the one of the only realities schizos can still appreciate. At last, I finally had something to look forward to.

As I re-dressed my lower unit, I informed my Master of the good news. He smiled then kissed me passionately. He took my hand and led me out of the alley. We walked slowly back to the car while he told me how desirous he was to experience the ecstasy of his wife's responses to his lust like she used to do.

The mood in the car was much more encouraging than it had been the night before. My Master seemed to have gotten his will to live back. We both had only shown some difficulty with memory slips and were a bit more logical in our speech. It was nice to kind of have some idea what was going on around us. It was something we both decided we would like a lot more of in the future. Master Boyd thought our getting out and just relaxing was the reason for our slow return from Mars that night.

Honestly, it was probably the lack of stress and no work demands on me, along with a bit of food and ample rest, that had calmed our more severe psychotic symptoms to a dull roar. Neither of us were right in the head by a long shot, but we both were functioning at bit higher than we had been since our massive breakdowns in December. We even discussed our hopes that our acute cycles were finally passing the fuck on to residual. Once again, I will remind everyone that Master Boyd and I are not familiar with Mister Reality.

We pulled into the driveway of the cottage around midnight. He and I necked in the front seat briefly while giggling like teenagers. My Master took out a half-eaten burger we had raided from a dumpster and began to eat it

275

while I unlocked the door and went inside. He followed mumbling about the foul food item having too much mustard. I flipped on the light to illuminate the dark room. Sitting on the couch silent but smiling was Dennis.

I let out a yelp as Master Boyd grabbed me and tried to pull us back out the door. However, Randell had already ambushed him from behind. I was knocked to the floor while the two struggled. This time, due to long term starvation, my Master was taken to the floor and cuffed with only some difficulty. Dennis had already pounced on my back before I could get off the floor cuffing my unit as well. The dirty law dogs had found us somehow and waited for just the right moment to sneak up and capture us without needing the entire police squad.

Randell lifted my Master to his feet while Dennis did the same to me. "Hello Niemand, Boyd, how the hell you two been? Boy you, and your girl here, have caused me enough trouble for two lifetimes. I suggest you come nice and quiet. Same goes for you sweetheart. This time if there is any funny business, I am ready to knock you both the fuck out," said Dennis appearing very angry.

"Dennis, you have no right. Let us go. I told you already I don't want your help damn it," said my Master with just a bit of fear in his voice.

I just looked at the floor. I knew that we were finished this time. Dennis was never going to stop hunting us until the hospital had made sure my Master and I were hooked up to ride the lightning. There was no longer any doubt in my mind that we would be able to plug electronics into our asses thanks to the volts that soon would be frying our eggs.

Dennis chuckled while shooting Randell a look. "Oh but I do Boyd. I believe you are psychotic as hell if you have forgotten just how much right I have. Look at you. You smell, you can't weigh more than one hundred and forty pounds and that forehead of yours, boy you won't have any brains left if you keep trying to bash them out on the walls."

My Master just winced at that and looked at the floor. "Let me go Dennis. I want to stay here with Niemand. I am not taking that fucking Thorazine anymore. You can haul me off, chain me up and even shock me if you want but when I get out I will just run off again. This time so far away you will never find us."

Dennis nodded. "Yep that is what I am figuring you will do. So, tell you what? I am taking your sweetie in with you this time. You two can stay in the same fucking room for all I care but you are going to get on medication. If not Thorazine some other kind. Then when you both pass your tests you can come home and shit will finally settle down. Boyd, I am really tired. I am sure both of you are too. Just let it go and do as you are told this time. Niemand will come with us if you can behave yourself."

My Master looked at me wild with terror. "Niemand?"

I shook my head. "He has us Boyd. Fuck it. Let's just go. He is right, I am tired. At least there I won't have to see any more kids beaten with barbed wire or molested by their daddy."

277

Randell snorted. "See Boyd, Niemand is willing to go peacefully. You can even ride in the back together this time if you can promise to behave yourself. No more window head banging. Do we have your word?"

Master Boyd was grinding his back teeth appearing quite agitated but even he could see we were boned. This was happening. He just nodded while refusing to utter another word to the old bulls. He and I were then roughly escorted to the back of the squad car they had cleverly hidden behind the cottage on the lawn. Dennis stuffed me in one side and Randell pushed my Master in the other door. We moved next to each other in the center of the seat while the old bulls got into the car.

I laid my head on my Master's shoulder. I could feel him trembling with fear. I felt pity again. He had not had ECT since he was just a teenager. He remembered the brutality of it. I too was not happy about the situation, but I was accustomed to my place as a prisoner of the normals' torture devices. This was not something my Master was going to endure well. I was grateful I would be at his side while he suffered this time. At least we would face the nightmarish treatments together.

I saw he was tearing up as the terror rose inside him. I kissed his neck watching him close his eyes as he leaned into me. "It's okay my love. I am here with you," I said softly to him.

He nodded appearing to trance slightly. "Yeah, as long as I have you, I can handle it. I know I can."

Randell tore off down the road hauling our D/s butts right to Well's Regional. The closer we got to that horrid place the more my Master's unit shook.

Master Boyd leaned down close to my ear, "if they use the strait jacket I am fucked. I never could get out of those damned things. If they strap, I can pick it. Meet me back here at the cabin?"

I nodded smiling bitterly. "Sure love. I will pick mine too and see you here. We can head out to the streets and forget the bullshit normals forever this time."

That seemed to calm him a bit. I was of course lying. I knew we both would be held tight this time. The Well's hospital would likely put us into the hole, jacketed and leashed for good measure. Or likely observation rubber room too. I just sighed; God do I hate psychiatric wards. Yuck!

We arrived at the ER admitting entrance in record time thanks to wicked speeds. Randell was a real demon behind the wheel, maybe worse than my Master. Dennis grabbed me jerking me out of my attempt to stay with Master Boyd. Randell did the same to my Master. The two of us were pulled into the waiting area while the admitting nurse ran to get help. The unlucky future patients and their loved ones in that room all got up and moved to the other side. They did their best to distance themselves from the two cuffed clearly mentally deranged prisoners. You'd have thought Master Boyd and I had the plague they all moved their asses so fast.

I giggled as Master Boyd shot me a smile at that silly behavior. Not like either of us were able to do shit to any of them. Nor would we want to. We just wanted to get the fuck out of there. We did not want to kill helpless emergency room patrons.

The nurse opened the door to the room and called us back rapidly. She was like everyone else. The hospital wanted to hide the loons out of sight before we upset the masses too much. We were taken to a private room and sat down together still cuffed while Dennis and Randell stood over us blocking the door. I rolled my eyes at my Master while he looked around the room. I was not sure, but I assumed he was searching for another exit.

The doctor came and shook Dennis's hand then looked at my Master. "I see you found our patient. Thank you very much. I have his room already prepped. We do appreciate the help."

Dennis nodded. "Yep, now you let me know when I can come visit him. He and I have a lot to discuss," he said while shooting a warning look at my Master.

The doctor nodded. "Oh I think after a few treatments he should be calmed down enough to receive visitors."

My Master began to tremble again. "What the fuck, Dennis. You said no ECT just to calm me down enough to bring me here. Fuck you. I demand to see a lawyer. You can't just do whatever the fuck you want to people, assholes." He tried to get up to flee but Randell grabbed him restraining him as the big male orderlies came into room taking my Master by his upper cuffed arms to drag him off to the third floor.

My Master looked back at me fighting with all he had. "Hey wait. Niemand, what about her? Dennis, you said she could come too. Niemand, help me, please help," he yelled now having a full-on panic attack as the big men pulled him along. I could hear him yelling down the halls very upset.

I got up to run after him, but Dennis easily held me still. "Sit down. Let him go. He needs help, damn it. Let them help him. You have done enough damage missy." He pushed me back to my seat.

The doctor had backed into the wall as my Master was taken from the exam room. He now walked back to stand in front of Dennis. "Well, we will be in touch. Don't worry about Mister Simmons. We will get him sedated and he will calm right down." The doctor nodded at me then left out the door.

I sat there dumbfounded looking at the floor while Randell returned. "Okay they got him on the elevator, Dennis. Nothing more we can do for him now. Let's head to the house. I am beat." He yawned.

Dennis nodded. "Sounds good to me. I am just glad he is safe. I will sleep well for the first time in weeks."

I cleared my throat. "Uhm, hate to break up this little meeting of the minds, but I am still here? Are they coming back for me too?" I looked at the door.

Dennis shook his head. "No Niemand, I only brought you along to keep Boyd calm. Randell and I will take you back were we found you. Oh, and you are not to visit him or come anywhere near this hospital till he is released. If you do, I will arrest your ass and keep you till you are drawing your social security check. I don't want him anymore disturbed than he already is. Hiding him out like that and lying to me had me ready to do that anyway. As it is, I am going to let you go for Boyd's sake. However, I suggest you stay out of my sight for a long while. I am not really thrilled with you gal. Do you hear me?"

I looked at the floor. "Yeah, I hear you loud and clear. You can explain to Boyd why I am not in his cell or visiting. I will keep my happy ass back in Cumberland." I growled feeling despair flow over me.

Dennis chuckled bitterly. "He is going to be so hopped up on sedatives he won't know if he is coming or going Niemand. Once they give him the ECT he may not even recall you and he were ever a thing. I hope he forgets anyway. It would be a blessing to all of us if that happened."

"You would know best now wouldn't you." I sniffed back my tears feeling my heart breaking.

"You are trouble, always have been and you know it. Boyd was fine until he started tooling around with you. Now look at him. Near starved to death, head scarred like a road map of Arizona. That is all your fault you know. I told you to leave him alone. You are too much for that boy. He can't even look out for himself. You are more than any one of my officers can handle. But Boyd, well he couldn't handle a fucking kitten. Then he goes and tries to tame a God damned lioness. You know God damned well you should have never trifled with that simple boy. This whole thing has nearly killed Carla with worry and aged me decades. You know what Niemand? Just keep your mouth shut and don't say another word to me. I am done talking to you. You never listen, so why am I bothering to waste my breath. Randell get her and let's get the fuck out of here." Dennis turned and stormed from the room.

Randell reached down and took me by my sore upper arm. "Look he is just worried about Boyd. We all are. He didn't mean half of what he said. Just let him cool down. This will all blow over. Boyd will get well and it will be back to normal."

I felt the first tears falling. "No Randell he meant it, all of it. It will never be normal. Not for Boyd and me anyway." I walked along with the old bull not offering to resist as I was escorted to the parking lot, uncuffed then put into the back of the squad car.

No one said a word in that police car as we raced back to the cottage. I sat in the corner of the rolling cage with my eyes closed recalling in detail my horrid first two days in Master Boyd's collar. It was the same seat and car my Master had brutalized my unit in.

I had hated him so much back then. I resisted his attempts to submit me to his will. Now almost two years since the deranged cop had consummated with me in the white cell, I felt I would die not being at his feet. I saw the world spinning while I silently wept. Nothing was recognizable in my life anymore. I had lost every single possible support system in less than forty-eight hours.

Everything was as shattered as my mind. Sheryl was gone. Cheryl refused my collar. Master Boyd was locked up and beyond my reach. Linda, Dennis and Randell were not speaking to me anymore. Jane had forbidden me access to the office during working hours. I could no longer see or hear Simon. I was never getting that desk job Sheryl had promised me. My job at the funeral home was long gone. I had not gotten enough money to enroll in grad school. Maiden Mary was stuck doing my fucking job as the mother of my children. I had not seen my fur buddy in so long I could barely remember his face. I had fucked up bad. Somehow, I had failed at life miserably.

The old bulls pulled up the driveway of the cottage. Dennis got out and opened my door. I got out and started heading for the door.

"Stay away from Boyd, I mean it," Dennis yelled after me.

I turned around and bowed to him. "As you wish my dearest lord." I unlocked the door and went inside slamming it behind me.

I went to the bedroom. I spent the rest of the night waffling between crying jags and head banging the wall till I was nearly unconscious. I had not been that depressed since the death of Matthew. I tried to ignore the images of them rolling Master Boyd strapped to a gurney to the ECT room. It kept me from sleeping. I knew what was going to happen to him. My need to protect and defend my Master from such assault was driving me, well, mad.

I considered burning down the hospital. I thought about running Dennis over with Julia's car. I considered driving back to Master Boyd's house, collecting his gun and ending my own pathetic life. In the end I did nothing but lay in that bed staring at the ceiling feeling broken and lost in the void and no longer caring that I was.

It was then I understood what I needed to do to fix everything. I jumped up smiling. It was all so simple. The short circuit was causing my troubles. I just needed to repair the unit. I ran to the car and sped off for the office. I knew where Psycho Tron had stashed our Robot repair items. A few wires, a little electrical tape and everything would be fine. I was sure of it.

I arrived at the office in the wee hours of Sunday and went right to Jane's office. I got a plastic bag full of coated wires, razor blades and electrical tape. I had learned that bear metal wires corroded inside the skin suit. This time I had splurged on the good stuff.

I spent the next several hours repairing the limbs of the machine. I wrapped all of it inside the electrical tape leaving only the neck, face and hands free of the rubbery, black covering. Uhm, yeah even the neither region was covered with a way to exit the calls to nature. Yikes, yeah I was gone. I was sure that I had not missed any possible area that could be malfunctioning.

I put all my nasty clothes back on to hide my custom job. I smiled feeling better already, while I cleaned up all the red oil that had leaked out during the inserting of the new wires. I found it difficult to bend my wrists due to stiffness of the thick wiring. I worked my hands harshly until I bent the wires beneath to a more comfortable position.

I then filled out all my paperwork and entered all my data from my work on Friday. My brother the sun was at his jump off point high in the sky when I finally left the building headed back to the cottage. I needed to pick up the cell phone and pager then check out. I no longer required a shelter.

Robots don't worry about roofs over their heads. They don't sleep, eat nor do they feel. I was damned grateful I recalled I was artificial intelligence. It would have been awful rough to be human with everyone around me treating me like I didn't matter.

Shit, I felt pity for fragile human beings. Unlike me, they would have probably been depressed or suicidal. Maybe they would even do something stupid, you know like insert wires under their skin and wrap them in electrical tape or worse. Nope, not Psycho Tron and The Chosen One. Those bitches were tough.

I smiled as I turned off the lights in that place for the last time. I didn't need a fucking collar, a Master or even a friend. Shit, I controlled the electrical grid. I was the most powerful being on earth. I looked up at the tapestry flowing and sticking to the world of the real. I reached out and borrowed some of its energy. Time to go and find those who deserved to be punished. I was ready to do what I had been programmed to do. Fight abusers and end evil.

My cell phone rang as I got into the car to head to wherever I was going. It was Sheryl.

"Howdy dowdy. What's up chicken little? What do you got for your momma, baby," I said in a sing song voice.

Sheryl sat there unsure what to say then finally., "Uhm did Cheryl call you Psycho?"

I laughed maniacally. "She did but that is okay. I corrected her. It was an error in the program. A true blue malfunction. Why did I call you? I forgot."

Sheryl snorted. "Cut the shit, Psycho. Look, I was just pissed the other day. I am sorry for giving your collar to Cheryl. I can come to town right now and recollar you. I am sure you learned your lesson and well, hell I miss you."

I made a raspberry sound. "Miss me. Miss me. Now you got to kiss me. We are sorry all our lines are currently busy. Our staff is assisting other customers. If you would stay on the line, we will take to your call in the order it was received. Hallo, kann ich Ihnen helfen? Weißt du was? Ich würde lieber sterben, als jemals wieder deinen Kragen zu tragen. Gehen Sie langsam und schmerzhaft an Krebs Arschloch sterben. Hahaha."

I hung up the phone singing an old rock song from the eighties while I pulled wildly out of the parking lot of the cottage for the very last time.

*German Translation: Hello, can I help you? You know what? I'd rather die than ever wear your collar again. Go slowly and painful from the cancer asshole.*

They held my Master for the next twenty-four days. He took six rides on the dreaded lightning. The doctors realized that he had stopped his medication due to undesired side effects. His psychiatrist understood if they didn't find an antipsychotic that both worked to mute his symptoms and didn't keep him from his favored past time of sexual conquest of his One and Only, he would just be right back in their bed in moments.

Master Boyd was put on heavy doses of Risperidone and Seroquel which appeared to be forcing him out of acute into residual rapidly. He was thrilled to find these new atypical drugs didn't affect him the same way the old school Thorazine had. My Master was still numbed by them, but the part that mattered to him the most was unaffected.

Master Boyd was released into Dennis and Carla's care by the second of March. To his credit, Dennis had told him the truth. Master Boyd was aware he had told me to go fuck off and die. I had taken the old bull seriously. My Master had not heard a word of my whereabouts or health for the entire inpatient treatment. He was eager to track me down, with an apology and to re-unit with his One and Only in every way. It was all he had been dreaming of for the near month of separation from me.

Dennis did his best to try to talk my Master out of trying to hunt me down to reclaim what belonged to him. My

Master was now back from Mars. Dennis was shit out of luck with his threats of inpatient treatment this time. Nothing was going to stop my Master in his quest to find his missing fiancé.

I was not missing at all. I had been working fast and furious the entire time. My case load was cleared with day and night attendance by the powerful duo of The Chosen One and Psycho Tron. Both shards refused to speak to Sheryl in any capacity other than to gain permission to take abused children into custody. Their unheard-of clearing of calls and seeming to be everywhere at once caught the attention of the powers that be. The pair was granted a special letter of recognition for excellent service and a pay grade raise of a whole one thousand dollars more a year. Woo hoo, douche bags.

Sheryl would have liked to fire me, but with the State big dogs in love with their DCFS investigator (they had never met me in person by the way except Harold and he was happy to tell anyone who listened how awesome I was), she was stuck dealing with me. She begged almost every day for my reconsideration of allowing her to re-collar. Sheryl even tried to say her mind had been clouded by her medication and she should not be held accountable for her poor decisions the day she traded me off.

Her star investigator would just hang up when she started her whining. The shards knew she was a liar. Sheryl intended to punish us, but she had punished herself. She would not receive another chance to betray us and that was final.

We shucked the morning visits with Julia, daring Sheryl to say a damned word. We were happy to call Harold and make her life a living hell if she insisted on making ours one by ordering us to visit that shady bitch. The coffee talks were effectively ended the second the Taurus was returned the day after Dennis ambushed us in the cottage.

Even when Julia whined to Sheryl that she wanted us to return to her kitchen table, we stood our ground. Sheryl's power over us was broken by our vicious threats and hard-core resolve to stand up to our slave driving boss lady no matter what it took.

We were barely sleeping, eating and lived in our repaired Taurus full time. Showers were unheard of. We would simply go buy a new outfit ever so often and toss the old one when anyone complained about our smell. Our mind was unraveled, and often our speech was circular, rhyming or spoken in a sing song fashion. By the time our Master was out of his white padded cell, we were even having difficulty interviewing client, testifying in court and showing up at the right addresses when working a case. Yet still no one had bothered to send us for a psychiatric evaluation.

Instead, when a complaint or concern was called into Sheryl, she would call me and take me off work for twenty-four hours demanding I get some rest. Her tiny band aid of mental health days off was not even soaking up a smidgen of our gushing psychosis that flowed like a river out of the cracks in our head.

Master Boyd had called my cell phone the day he was released from the hospital. I had answered it appearing disorganized, confused and didn't appear to recall my relationship to him.

"Hey baby. It is you Master Boyd. I am back, time to come home. I have missed you so much. Did you miss me," said the man on the phone said as I stood on the side of an old county road watching the transmissions from they trying to overtake the hapless horses that lived in the field in front of me.

I felt my neck and found no collar. "Sorry I don't have a Master anymore. They got him. It was very sad. Did you send flowers to his family? I was going to, but I didn't know the address," I mumbled out while secretly hoping the roan horse would see they soon and run away before they got to him.

"Niemand? Honey, what did you just say? You are not making any sense," he said sounding alarmed.

"How dare you call me up and accuse me of counterfeiting nickels. Jerk. I happen to know the ink was in your shed when they found it. Now buzz off and let me be with my caseload. God damned nutball. Crank calls are illegal you know." I hung up feeling irritated that some people got their rocks off by taking nonsense to strangers on the phone.

I got back into the Taurus reading over my faxed list of reported cases of abuse. I giggled a bit while realizing that if I hurried, I could get to everyone on that list by Armageddon for sure. I noticed a note I had left to myself that I had court testimony the next morning in Jessieville.

I had taken a seven-year-old girl into custody over serious physical abuse, but she had spouted to me privately details of sexual abuse in the home too. The judge had subpoenaed me to court to discuss what she had told me that day the week before her 'stepdaddy's pony rides. Yay. This sounded like a bunch of fun, not.

The phone rang again. I looked at the number now pissed that this crank caller simply had no respect at all.

"Look mister, I am working. Why do you keep calling me," I yelled out into the phone.

"Niemand, I need to know where you are baby. I think you may be very sick right now. Please honey tell me and I will come and pick you up," Master Boyd pleaded into the phone.

I chuckled while dropping the phone into the seat and taking off towards Cumberland. I had already forgotten that someone was on the other end of the line.

Our mind was like a rubber band that was full of dry rot.

## Chapter 81: A Little Child Shall Lead Them
## Master Boyd & Submissive Neimand

Well, plenty of chapters chalked full of weirdness, loss, tragedy and what the fuck. Are you ready for more? This chapter will mark the transition between who we were and who we became. It is the half-way to hell, errrr, the present day. Yeppers, we are just almost to our destination. So, reach back and give yourselves a pat on the back. It has been one fucking crazy ride, but you have done so great. We are damned proud of you. It is not easy to see through the eyes of another person and that is just talking about a normal person. You have elected to take a journey inside the head of a schizophrenic. You deserve a fucking medal for that.

Speaking of metal, someone seems to have lost hers. The circle of silver rests like buried treasure in the submissive's home. On and on she wanders, lost within the vortex of her madness. No one noticed the rising threat when it was only the psychotic at risk. As the insanity gains momentum everyone is a target, and the Psycho is the sniper. The loss of a useless psychotic was of little interest. When that victim of mental illness lashes out at productive citizens, a posse of normals will have to hunt down the mad dog before she makes them all believers in the power of vengeance.

Master Boyd is feeling better these days. He has ridden the lightning and heard the voice of God. The Dominant has returned to Earth much wiser and more empathetic to the true nightmare of his submissive. Master Boyd knows just how dark the night can really get. He has met the shadows that devour the souls of the touched. He sees the tapestry webs have collared what belong to him. The Master will seek out aid but finds hypocrisy instead.

Ah will you look at that? The hour is late; in fact, it is almost the darkest. For this chapter, you will want to open your minds, loosen your cannons, and pull out your suitcase of emotions. Sometimes there is no happy ending. The pot at the end of the rainbow is not full of gold. It is full of blood.

*"Don't be scared. I am not going to hurt you. I know you don't remember but you have always been my best friend. Don't bother to try to recall me, just accept what I am telling you. What once was will never be again, so it doesn't matter what happened. It only matters what will. The psychiatrists have really fucked this up. Recovery is going to be a bitch."*
**--Simon introducing himself to Niemand, Harbor View Mental Hospital, November 1999**

I sat there staring at the blank computer screen while fax spit out his gossip in the back. The office had closed only an hour before. Jane told me to never show up while the other staff were on duty. I could barely wait to get in to enter my data but now I couldn't, for the life of me, remember what was so damned important that I needed to get it into the CHRIS program.

I sighed then began to look through my files. I must have written it down somewhere. That was how I kept up with anything these days. If I didn't write it down, I would forget it quickly. Something was just in the back of my mind. I knew it was imperative that it was done, but what was it?

The phone rang nearly scaring me out of my skin suit with the sudden racket. "Yeah, oh I mean DCFS speaking, errr, can I help you," I sputtered out while still thumbing through my mountains of notes.

"Niemand? Honey, it is Master Boyd. Baby, I am on my way to see you. Stay at the office please. I have been trying to track you down all day. Do you know who I am," Master Boyd said sounding upset.

I smiled. "Ah, Master, how are you doing? Is it Sunday already? Shit. Well let me get my data entered and I will get ready to head to dinner at Dennis and Carla's home. Thank you have a nice day." I hung up the phone no longer recalling the discussion as I found the notes I was looking for at last.

I began to mumble about forms and legal rules to Fax who complained back that I was boring.

"There is a time and place for gossip Fax. You need to get serious about your job. If you keep fucking off then they will fire you like they did PC you know. Around here if you become obsolete, they toss you in a dumpster. Hey, did you bring anything for lunch," I called out to Fax.

Fax reported he didn't think to bring anything to eat either.

I chuckled. "You see that is what happens when you spend all your time at the water cooler, you fool."

I noticed my electrical tape was starting to bunch up on my left wrist. It was time for new repairs, but I just never seemed to have the time anymore. I got up headed to the supply closet for paperclips to stuff under the black gooey mess on my arms. I had become magnetized and watching the metal stick to me made me laugh. I could use some entertainment.

"Did you remember to cut deep," said Dude through the walls.

I nodded. "Yep, sure did Dude. Hey, how are the wife and kids man? Did you drown them or set the house on fire? I love it when you tell that story." I giggled while grabbing the box of paperclips.

"You are going to die. Die, die, die loser," Dude growled out.

I smiled at that. "Promises, promises. Ah, look, do you hear that Dude? The sound of thunder. It is a storm, you know. It is coming. Simon went to try to build a dam, but we know he is too late. Hey, is PC with you? I can't find him anywhere."

Wicked laughter shook the walls. I laughed with it, though I had no idea what was so funny. Truth is I was very confused these days. Not much made any sense anymore. That was okay. I never really knew where I was going, what I was doing, or how I even got there most of the time anyway. I had a lifetime of experience at being lost. This was just another walk through the nightmare that I could never wake up from.

I heard the thunder rock the office again. I smiled that the Gods were so angry. Good, I never was favored by them. Why should I even care?

I returned to my desk and took out the paperclips. One by one I pulled them straight and stuck them under the electrical tape around my wrists. It seemed to help me focus on the real. It is better to have my wires repaired. I had to admit it wasn't working as well as it had in the beginning. Lately, I was unable to see the real head on.

Only glimpses of their world like a flip book would make it through the delusional tapestry. I assumed that very soon I would be completely through the shattered looking glass. Then I would not see the strange world of the normals at all. Maybe never again. Oh well, I never understood those odd creatures. My passing away from their sight was probably a good thing. Not like any of them cared anyway.

There it was again. Thunder, damn this was going to be a really nasty storm no doubt.

"Niemand? Niemand, open this door," yelled out a voice in the distance.

I chuckled to myself while entering my notes into the computer. "Shut up, Simon. You stay out there and get wet." I was not going to let that Judas come in from the rain.

I was pissed at him for giving me the silent treatment for the last several weeks. He had no right. What did I ever do to him? Seemed that he could just stay out there and get soaked. That would teach his bitter, old, drunk ass a lesson.

The phone rang again.

I picked it up now feeling irritated at all these distractions. "DCFS office. What the holy fuck do you want? I am busy, God damn it," I yelled into the phone.

"Uhm okay Niemand. Open the door. It is your Master. I am here. Open the door and let me in, damn it," said Master Boyd sounding mildly irritated.

I looked at the office door "Master? You are here? Where?" I was very confused since I could not see Master Boyd, but he was telling me he was here somewhere.

"I am at the front door. Come open it please," growled my Master.

I dropped the phone and walked out to the waiting area and saw my Master standing there still holding the phone to his ear looking in through the glass at me. He pointed to the knob indicated I needed to let him in.

I walked over and unlocked the entry. He grabbed the door, rapidly came inside and relocked it.

He looked much better than when last I had seen him. His hair had been cut; he was clean shaven and though still very thin he had put some of his weight back on. Master Boyd's color was back to normal. He was more handsome than ever. I smiled while he looked me over with his piercing blue eyes. I noticed his black t-shirt and jeans were clean for a change. Well for the first time since December.

He took a breath. "Niemand, I have missed you so much. You have no idea. Baby, I am so sorry about what Dennis did and said to you. He shouldn't have, but that is on him. I thought I would die not getting to see or hold you all this time. I hope you didn't think I share Dennis's beliefs about us. I feared you would think I didn't want you anymore. Baby, that is the farthest thing from the truth. You are all I ever wanted. Please come here to me. I want to hold you." He reached out.

I looked at his hands. "Where have you been Master? I couldn't find you. I thought you left me like Simon did. Everyone left me. Did you come back?" I was confused by his sudden appearance after his being gone for a month.

Master Boyd frowned. "Baby, they put me in the hospital. You remember right? You were there. Dennis took me to Well's Regional. Honey, are you okay?"

I shook my head. "No, I remember stabbing you. I killed you at the cabin. I must be hallucinating again. Damn, I guess I need more sleep. For what it is worth, I apologize for killing you Master. You were a great Master. I really did love you. I had to follow your directive. Besides, I know you wanted the pain to end. It is okay. I will be there with you soon. Then we can dance all you want." I turned around and headed back for my office feeling very sad that I had killed Master Boyd.

My murdering him at his directive had bothered me a lot. I never betray my collar, but he told me to do it. I had to follow his orders. I wish he had not asked me too. I had been very lonely with him gone. I had wanted to go to his grave and talk to him, but I couldn't recall where I had buried his unit.

Master Boyd followed me to the office. I saw him but assumed he was a ghost or figment of my imagination. Then he reached out and grabbed me hugging me tightly. I struggled to get free as the shock filled me to unbearable levels. He used his strength to keep me from breaking free.

"Oh God, baby, you are sick. I am so sorry. I failed you. Thank God you are still here. It is going to be okay. We will go get some help. Dennis shouldn't have let you leave that night. Damn it, you were there for me all those weeks and no one was there for you," he said sounding full of remorse.

"Let me go. What are you doing? I have work to do, Master. Special services have to wait until I am done. I can get fired you know," I growled still trying to pull out of his hug.

My Master let me go. I pulled away glaring at him angrily as I sat down to finish my task. He stood there appearing befuddled. I ignored him while he got Jane's chair and pulled it next to me never taking his eyes off my unit.

Master Boyd pulled his cell back out of his pocket and dialed a number. "Hey, Sheryl. It is Boyd. I am here at your office with Niemand. She is off her beam, completely off. What the fuck have you been doing to her? How did everyone miss this? Jesus woman, have you seen her? I can smell her from a mile away. That is not all, she is not making sense. She is skinny and wearing electrical tape again. I am taking her in. Fuck you. Yeah, well do it then. Do you think I give a damn? This is bullshit. You are the biggest asshole on the planet. You just mark her down as on vacation bitch. Sure, and same to you sideways." He hung up the phone with a strange look in his eyes.

"Come on baby. We are going for a ride." He stood up and offered his hand.

I looked at his hand briefly then went back to entering my data ignoring him.

He sighed then knelt next to me. "Niemand, come on baby, we are leaving now. You are to follow me, that is a directive," he said softly.

I jerked my head up from my keyboard. "Huh? Master, you are not dead? But I thought I killed you. I remember doing it." I suddenly realized this really was my Master and not a ghost.

He looked at the floor shaking his head. "No Niemand, you didn't kill me. You saved me from dying baby. Now, take my hand. We are going to get you some help. You are not well honey." He reached out for my hand again.

I shook my head. "I don't need help Master. Sheila is my secretary and Fax takes care of the lists. We managed despite PC being fired. I am very happy that I didn't kill you." I hugged him around his neck ignoring the shock feeling relief that I was not the murderer I thought I was.

He hugged me back allowing me to kiss his mouth as I began to feel my raw sexual drives begin to roar. I had stopped the Thorazine over a month before. My deep psychosis allowed for an exaggeration of sexual aggressiveness. I had been quite frustrated having to deal with my random urges solo. Okay, if you missed that I was masturbating. There I said it, deal with it. Nurse, nurse, meds, and bring the jacket.

My Master began to pant as our kissing got more furious. He had missed me too apparently. My Master moaned as he reached out to grope my unit. He was swept away for a moment by the eagerness of my interest in his carnal affections. I got out of my seat and began to undo my pants while still kissing him, but he suddenly backed up. Master Boyd gasped for air demanding I leave my clothing on.

I stood there more confused than ever. "Uhm, you cannot have sex with clothing on can you? You don't want your privileges? I am happy to grant them Master. I want to grant them."

He groaned while adjusting himself. "You have no idea how bad I want to have you just now, but that will have to wait. You are not well. Come on baby, button your pants and come with me. There is time for this when you feel better." He motioned for me to follow him.

I looked at the floor. "I feel fine Master. You can feel for yourself." I smiled at my sexual invite.

He shook his hand then grabbed my upper arm dragging me with him to his car. "I am sorry to be so rough, but you are not listening. We are going to get help right now. This has gone far enough. Be still and do what I tell you, that is a directive," he said as he pushed me into his black car.

I sat there more confused than ever as he got into the vehicle speeding off for Well's Regional. He was acting crazy again. I feared saying a word in case it set him off. Psychotics can be temperamental and even violent when pushed. He sat there in silence at first. Then he began to speak to me very calmly.

"I want to tell you that when God told me you were my One and Only, I was pleased to have such a beautiful wife. Then finally after all those years of yearning to be with you as you husband it happened. It was beyond what I had always dreamed it would be. I know at first it was hard for you to accept, but that is because of the disease we have. There were a lot of misunderstandings, but we worked it out. When I got so sick you were there for me. I was beyond scared. I never knew it could be so bad. I watched you suffer all these years, but I never understood just how much. I have seen what you go through myself now. I understand the terror, the confusion, the pain. Baby, I am sorry that I didn't know sooner. What you and I have is a curse worse than hell. I finally know the truth." He stole a glance to see if I was listening to him.

He smiled then took my left hand. "I will spend my life doing all I can to make you as comfortable. I will love you, protect you and make your life as easy as possible despite the challenges. They gave me ECT in the hospital you know. It was horrible. I could hardly remember my name. The smell, oh God it was just awful. Anyway, the only thing that kept me going was knowing when I was out you would be there waiting for me. I want to do that for you too. Give you that reason to fight. Forgive me for taking you to these assholes who will put the numbing medication into you and maybe run that electricity through your head. But baby, no matter what hell it is to be treated, it is better than letting you rot in that psychotic nightmare you are in right now. When you are well again, we can be together the right way. Not violent and messed up. Rather like a real husband and wife should be. I hope you can understand." He pulled my hands to his lips and kissed his engagement ring.

I just smiled at this insane Master. I had no fucking clue about what he was talking. I was fine. Nothing was wrong with me. I had never felt better in my life. Shit, I controlled the electrical grid. I had special powers over the elements and could ride the vortex. This bullshit about me being diseased was apparently some delusion the nut was trying to pull me into. I decided to be peaceful and not stir him up. I heard once that if you upset a schizophrenic, they can get violent. I was in no mood to set off the bats in his belfry. Hell, he just told me he was so crazy they gave him shock treatment. Wow, he was gone.

We arrived at Well's Regional and my Master hauled my unit behind him refusing to let go of my wrist. He winced when he felt the electrical tape under my sleeves but didn't say anything. I knew he didn't approve of my methods but to his credit he decided not to interfere.

It would only have pissed me off anyway. I could care for myself. Unlike him I neither needed a guardian nor had I been hospitalized. Shit, this nut ball had already been in the psych ward twice in three months. I, however, had only been for pneumonia. Who was the screwball here? Not me.

We sat quietly in the waiting area until they called out my name. We were taken to a small exam room. My Master had me sit on the patient bed while he took a seat in a chair watching me. I just hummed to myself while listening to the thoughts of the other people in the hospital. At least that kept me from getting bored. I listened to them moan and groan over various pains while others worried about how they would pay their medical bill.

Finally, a doctor came in. I listened to my Master tell the middle-aged fellow in the white jacket that I had schizophrenia and was dangerously psychotic. The doctor was stealing looks at me while he took notes. I just smiled at him thinking this whole situation was pretty silly and a total waste of my time.

The doctor asked my Master to step into the hallway while the he and a large nurse spoke to me in private. Master Boyd shot me a nervous look but agreed to leave for a bit. I watched my Master go out the door leaving me alone with the doctor and his nurse Rachet.

"Okay Missus Voss, your fiancé is concerned that you may be a danger to yourself or others. Are you having thoughts of hurting yourself or anyone else," the doctor asked.

I chuckled. "Of course not., sir. I am a DCFS investigator. The last thing on Earth I want to do is hurt anyone. It is my job to protect those who can't protect themselves. You don't have to believe me. Call my boss Sheryl Fressmen."

The doctor shot his nurse a look of surprise. "Are you currently working at that job Missus Voss?"

I laughed hard at that. "Uhm, no. I am currently sitting here in your ER silly. But yes, I have court in the morning. I am testifying in a child abuse case out in Jessieville. Again, call Sheryl. You can check on my credentials."

The doctor sighed. "Your fiancé seems to think you are psychotic and confused Missus Voss. It is not likely that if you are those things you could be working or testifying tomorrow in court."

I nodded. "Duh. Look, just fucking call Sheryl. I don't want to be ugly about this but my fiancé just got out of your fine establishment. He was a guest on your third-floor man. This is his delusion, not mine. It is not his fault. He has schizophrenia, poor guy."

The doctor looked up surprised. "Wait, he said you have schizophrenia, Missus Voss."

I smiled while winking. "Sure he did. Check your records boss. Look under Boyd Simmons. You will see he is the one who has schizophrenia, not me. This is his weird ass hallucination. Let me give you Sheryl's number. I need to wrap this mess up. I don't mind humoring my fiancé a bit, but I do have court at ten. I need to get some rest. Do what I told you and you will find my story checks out. Boyd is your boy-o. I belong to the state office of DCFS. Check, I dare you. I double dog dare you." I rattled out Sheryl's phone number for the doctor.

The doctor nodded. "Okay, I will. You stay here Missus Voss. I will let Mister Simmons come back in. I will return shortly."

"You bet sport. Say hey to the wife and kids for me. Thank you have a nice day." I smiled knowingly.

He chuckled. "You are funny. I wish more of my patients had a sense of humor." He left with the nurse while Master Boyd came back into the room appearing concerned.

"Where are they going," he asked me.

"To hell if they keep trying to play the part of God. The sin of man is always in the hearts of those who think they are powerful," I replied tangentially.

My Master shook his head. "Wow, to think I was sounding like that just a few weeks ago. Baby, this is one nasty disease we have. Not something to be taken lightly, that is for sure."

"Take the tour of the hospital's allure. If you're lucky they will give you the cure," I said still smiling at him.

He sighed while crossing his arms settling in to wait for the doctor to return. Within twenty minutes the nurse came into the room with a discharge slip. She handed it to my Master indicating I was free to go. The sheet said the attending physician had diagnosed me with mild work-related stress disorder. I was given a prescription of Xanax and released to the streets once more. I was dubbed sane. Damn I am good.

Master Boyd looked at the diagnosis in disbelief. He glared at the nurse then started demanding the doctor return to the room immediately to speak with him.

"Mister Simmons, Doctor Hawks is a very busy man. Missus Voss is free to go. Fill out the prescription and follow up with her regular doctor as soon as possible. Have a nice night." The nurse started to leave the room.

My Master got up and angrily held the door so she could not get out. "I said go get that fucking moron you call a doctor. This is bullshit. Niemand needs help. She needs to be in the hospital. You cannot just let her go with a fucking prescription of anti-anxiety pills. This is not nerves, lady. She is going to kill herself or someone if something is not done, damn it. She is wearing fucking electrical tape on every inch of her skin. Did you even bother to check?"

The nurse looked back at me appearing terrified. I smiled at her kindly. "Honey, let the lady go, will you? She is supposed to be getting me a cup of coffee. I really could use a cup of coffee. Oh, and a donut too if you don't mind Ma'am. Thank you so much, have a nice day."

My Master looked at me angrily. "Do you fucking see what I mean. Get that rate bastard back in here. I mean it." My master let the door go and the nurse scrambled out running for the front desk.

I giggled. "She should be a football player, Master. She would really kick ass I am sure."

My Master stood at the door with his arms crossed with a look of irritation on his face. "Yeah baby, I am sure she would. Honey, when the doctor comes back in, show him your arms. That is a directive." He sighed.

I looked at the floor frowning. "Okay but you will not like it when his pens get stuck to my magnet. That could be ugly."

Master Boyd chuckled. "I will get over it. Just do what I told you."

The doctor sent two big orderlies to deal with us rather than returning himself. The nurse came with them. The three came into the room. The nurse looked at me then at my Master.

"Mister Simmons, the doctor has requested an emergency hold on you for observation. He is concerned about your resurgence of aggression and delusional thinking about your fiancé. He is contacting your guardian to inform him of this situation. Missus Voss, can you please leave now? Mister Simmon's will be okay, we promise. We appreciate your compliance and hope you understand. Mister Simmons just needs a few more days of rest is all. He will be discharged in no time." The nurse looked at me then to the orderlies who started to grab my Master.

He looked at them with complete confusion. "What the fuck are you all doing? I am not delusional. Let me go, you assholes. Niemand, call Dennis. Fuck, this is not happening. My fiancée is sick, not me. Niemand, call for help. Shit!" The big orderlies dragged my Master off down the hall to be readmitted to the third-floor psych unit.

I sat there on the exam table also stunned. I had no idea what had just happened there. The nurse again asked me to leave while shoving my discharge papers at me. I got up and wandered shocked into stupidity to the exit of the emergency room. Somehow, instead of me getting sent to the third floor, they got my Master? Wow, that was unexpected.

I walked to the sidewalk and used a pay phone to call a cab. My shattered mind whirled in circles while I awaited my ride back to Cumberland. The world of the real was certainly a strange and scary place to be. I swore I could hear my Master yelling for me from the third story windows of the hospital behind me. I kept looking back but I didn't actually see him. I decided this shit was so fucked up I had to be hallucinating it. The cab showed up and I got inside, leaving Well's Regional and my imaginary Master in my dust.

**NOTE:** *This was no delusion folks. It happened. Now if that doesn't make you say holy shit nothing ever will. Master Boyd had just been released after being inpatient as a violent and difficult patient for almost a month. I on the other hand was calm. Sheryl had told the doctor I was indeed due to testify the very next morning. We would have both gotten out of there without trouble but my Master's sudden aggression and pushy demands to be heard got his ass a second helping of white cell hospitality. Oh well,* *sucks to be a schizophrenic trying to point the finger at another schizophrenic.*

The next day I appeared at the Jessieville courthouse to testify in the "Morgan Steeps" case of alleged sexual and physical child abuse. I was so foul smelling when I sat down the Guardian ad litem, the lawyer representing the child in this case, got up and moved further down the bench.

The old grouchy Honorable Judge Straight entered the room and we were all asked to rise, then be seated. I was called to the stand fourth after the Judge heard the testimony of the child's therapist, caseworker and foster mother. I was sworn in and asked to sit down for questioning.

It went well at first. The DCFS lawyer asked me to repeat what Morgan had told me that day while I was transporting her to foster care. I had taken good notes, so I just read them mostly. Piece of cake.

Morgan had confessed to me privately that her stepfather was taking her on special pony rides that included penetration and oral sex on his unit. The child had told me of this horrid situation but then promptly clammed up refusing to tell anyone else. This raised alarm. Though it shouldn't have, I had just saved her from a terrible beating and shown her much kindness and empathy during her darkest hours. She felt safe confiding her secret to me.

The therapist, caseworker and foster parent were cold, too busy to bother with rapport and left the child frightened. Morgan was already a beat down, scared little kid. A little honey goes a long way with a hurt child. No one knows how to be sweet in the face of pain like I do. I was a trained professional before I lost all my baby teeth.

Too bad in the world of the normals they seem to think that being nice is something reserved only for fictional stories and philosophical discussions. They all talk about what should be but then never do it.

After the DCFS side got their chance to speak to me, it was time for cross examination by the offender's attorney.

"So, Missus Voss, your job was to interview Morgan with the aid of the Steep family's caseworker and then transport the child to the home of the Mason's, right?"

I nodded. "Yeppers, Captain Howdy."

The lawyer looked up from his notes startled by my response. He shot a look at the Judge.

"Missus Voss, just answer the question without the humor please," warned Judge Straight.

The attorney cleared his throat. "Why do you think Morgan would tell you about this so-called sexual abuse in the car but not in front of her caseworker Missus Gray?"

I shrugged. "Look pal, I just listen. I didn't bother to read her mind. It would have been rude. Besides, she is just a kid. No one should sneak into the thoughts of a child."

The lawyer gasped. "Uhm, thoughts of a child? Missus Voss, did you or did you not hear Morgan say her stepfather William is sexually abusing her? Or did you just, as you say, assumed it?"

I chuckled. "Old Willy Nilly, he knows how to pick a dilly. I assume nothing, sir. Ask King Arthur, he didn't trust his sister either. She was a witch and hated Merlin." I smiled completely off my nut.

The entire courtroom began to mumble. The attorney looked at the Judge shrugging. The DCFS attorney raised his hand and asked the Judge if he may approach the bench. He was granted permission while my testimony was put on hold.

I sat there smiling blankly at the befuddled lawyer while my own lawyer whispered something to the old Judge.

Judge Straight listened for a moment then looked at me appearing startled. "Bailiff remove Missus Voss from my courtroom, and make sure she leaves the courthouse. Missus Voss you will call your superior immediately. I recommend you receive psychiatric clearance. He threw a look at the DCFS lawyer. I suggest you make sure that happens before you ever bring Missus Voss back to testify in front of me. We are taking an hour lunch recess." He banged his gavel while Bailiff Health showed my loony ass the door.

I was skipping across the parking lot toward my car when the DCFS lawyer yelled for me to hold on to speak with him. "Missus Voss, I need you to go make an appointment with Doctor Holcomb. You are effectively relieved of duty until he deems you mentally healthy enough to return to your office. Sheryl has already been notified. Look, you have done a great job, but this job would get to anyone. Go get some rest. See the doctor and I will see you in a few weeks." He handed me Doctor Holcomb's card.

I glanced at the card. "Whatever you say Dad. Hey, mom says don't forget to bring home milk." I got into my car and left the shocked lawyer standing there scratching his head in disbelief.

I drove right to Doctor Holcomb's office. I knew him from the many abused children I had referred to his tender care over the past year. He was only six years older than me. The good Doctor was not a psychiatrist or MD doctor but rather had a Ph.D. in Sociology. His Master's was in Developmental Psychology which qualified him to teach in a school of higher learning, but he could not prescribe medications like a psychiatrist can.

Doctor Holcomb was a great therapist for abused, neglected and damaged children. He was not experienced nor had he ever worked with the organic mentally ill (natural mental illness) or psychotic disorders. His only background that even dealt vaguely with such disease was a good Abnormal Psychology class as an undergraduate.

I walked into his office and went immediately to his secretary Kayla, "Hey lady. Is the doc in? I have a problem I need him to fix." I chirped out happily to the pudgy gal with short black hair sitting behind the glass.

"Ah Niemand, honey, where have you been? It seems like an age since we last saw you." Kayla smiled appearing genuinely happy to see me.

I narrowed my eyes. "Oh, Kayla it was awful. They came and hauled my ass off to a vacation. I spent weeks in prison, bread and water shit you know," I whispered.

Kayla laughed out loud. "My God have I missed you. You are always good for a few laughs. Yeah, James is in. Let me see if he has time to chat. Don't you leave without giving me a hug girl," said Kayla while she dialed Doctor Holcomb's number.

I smiled wickedly. "Kayla if you will meet me after work, I can give you a hug you will not soon forget gorgeous. I could rock your world while I change your religion you know."

The secretary blushed. "Niemand, is here. Oh okay. I will send her right back. Okay he says come in, the doors open. Oh, if I don't get a date soon, I may take you up on that offer." She chuckled while playing with her nails nervously.

I frowned. "What. No dates? Well that is a crime. A beautiful woman like you should be running for her life daily."

Kayla's face grew stormy. "Well if I would run daily maybe I could get a date. I am just a bit of a big girl. Guys don't like that."

I rolled my eyes. "If you were my girl, I would show you why fluffy is finger licking good, Kayla. Come see me sometime and I will show you how I worship a Goddess gal." I winked as her jaw dropped nearly to the floor.

I left the now stammering Kayla and rushed through the back door to visit my old friend James Holcomb Ph.D.

"Niemand, have a seat. What can I do you for? Are you here to check on Tawny, Bridget, or Bradley," the young doctor said smiling brightly.

I sat down feeling a bit tranced. James was about six feet with mousey brown hair cut a bit long. He was rail thin with a goatee and well kempt moustache that appeared slightly redder than his hair. His eyes were a pale watery blue and set under heavy brows. He kind of reminded me of a humanized version of a devil with his sharp face and sunken cheekbones. His facial hair only made that demonic look worse.

"Nope, doc. I am here over some bullshit in court a bit ago. Judge Straight and Tommy told me I have to see you and get clearance to go back to work," I said while rolling my eyes.

James frowned. "Oh? Why would they need my clearance? What happened exactly?"

I chuckled. "Well I was being my old rude self you know. No tact. My momma never taught me proper manners I suppose. Too busy having me learn German you know. Anyway, I pissed off the opposing attorney is all." I smiled feeling very unreal and dreamy.

James looked at his desk. "I guess they want me to write a note saying you are of sound mind? Sometimes when the caseworkers are having stress out fits from the case load, divorce, you know life in general, they send them to me to get approved as, you know, sane."

I looked up startled. "When you claim they are sane does everyone respect that?"

Doctor Holcomb nodded. "Of course they do. I am a psychologist. If I say the worker is good to go they are."

I smiled feeling I had just won the lottery. "Okay I need you to get out a pen and paper. Write me one of those letters claiming I am sane and sign it please." I could hardly contain my excitement.

He chuckled. "I likely will be doing just that Niemand. Before I do that, is there some reason, they thought you were having a problem? A recent break up maybe?" He smiled at me.

I shook my head. "That is the point I am not having a break Doctor Holcomb. Now if you could just write that letter for me, I would be most grateful." I was now starting to sweat and wring my hands afraid I would not get the letter I had waited a lifetime to have. One that told all the normals I was sane.

James shook his head. "Not that kind of break? I mean are you getting a divorce, broke up with a boyfriend, or having any recent relationship problems?"

I looked at him puzzled. "Uhm no? What does this have to do with me getting that letter, Doc. Look I need to get back to work. If you would just write a letter. I need that letter."

The doctor leaned closer. "Okay sure I will write it for you. Calm down. I have always admired your love for the kids. Especially how good you are with the one's no one

317

wants to deal with. You are really and truly an angel on earth, Niemand." He began writing the letter of my dreams.

I snorted. "Oh is that so? Well, now that I have this, I can be just that. Shit, you don't even know how glad I am they sent me here today. Doctor Holcomb, you just made my millennium." I watched him finishing his letter and signing it. I was wringing my hands and nearly coming out of my seat with thrill.

He laughed. "Call me James, I have never had anyone say that before. Most people don't want to be in a psychologist's office, you know. Someone told me you have a degree in psychology yourself. Cum Laude I heard, impressive. What are you doing in DCFS? You should be in the Ph.D. program getting your Clinical." He handed me the letter that my greedy eyes practically eye humped while reading.

I couldn't believe it. At last, I had a statement saying I was competent. Finally, no more bullshit about my being Psycho. Uhm, fucktard, yeah you Niemand. Did you just see reality run by here? No you didn't, you Helen Keller motherfucker. Get a grip.

"Thank you so much uhm, James. You have no idea what this means to me. You are a prince among men. I owe you one." I stood up ready to go pay Kayla for my unexpected treasure.

James stood too. "Hey, wait, uhm, I would like to call in that favor if you would be so inclined." He blushed.

I could hardly look away from the paper barely paying attention to the Doctor. "Yeah?"

He cleared his throat. "Go to dinner with me this weekend? Uhm, just a friendly dinner. Nothing creepy I swear." He looked at his desk.

I looked up stunned. "Huh? Dinner? Seriously? you think I am going to sleep with you for a fucking letter that says the truth about me."

James looked up shocked. "Oh lord no. I am so sorry Niemand. No I mean I would like to get to know you better. I didn't mean, I mean, I didn't expect. I mean if a relationship developed, I would be happy. But just dinner, no other obligations. I swear my interests are honest."

I snorted. "Ah, okay gotcha. You think just because they say I am schizophrenic you can force me to fuck you to get this letter. Well, for your information, I am sane. I will not suck your cock to pay for what is mine by right."

His eyes went wide. "Schizophrenia? What? Who said that? You are not anymore schizophrenic than I am. I am so sorry to have even brought any of this up Niemand. I just, well, you are a beautiful and intelligent woman. I wanted to get to know you better and hoped something would develop between us. I was out of line to overstep my bounds. Forgive me. But I can tell you schizophrenia is a misdiagnosis. No psychotic could do the job you do, have the education you have and function so well. If you change your mind that is my home number on the form."

I glared at him suspiciously. "I already know it was a fucking misdiagnosis. Thanks for the letter, James. Don't hold your breath. I will not call your number. Damn dog, you are all a pack of fucking dogs. You aren't even worthy to be in my sight. I am the ruler of all electricity. You are just a mortal pig. I could destroy you with a thought. Thank you and have a nice day." I stormed from his office angered beyond words but quickly forgetting why.

When I got to the car the cell phone was ringing off the hook. I picked it up groaning as I realized it was the Queen Bitch Sheryl herself.

"Yeah, yeah, what do you want momma," I moaned out.

"What the fuck, Psycho. Tommy called me from the courthouse and you went retarded on the stand. What are you doing."

I looked around the parking lot. "Uhm leaving Doctor Holcomb's parking lot. I have the clearance letter that says I am competent. You should see it. Amazing," I practically sang out.

"Oh, you do. Well I happen to wonder how you managed that. Did you fuck James too? Your marbles are out of the bag, Psycho. Everyone is calling me bitching about your weird speech and behaviors. That is it. You are grounded to the office until May. You will enter case files and stay out of the field until your scrambled eggs cool off. You are causing too much trouble out there. You march your ass back into Holcomb's office and make an appointment. You are going to counseling until I say you are done. I want your medication checked too. Enough of this crazy shit, God damn you," she yelled so loud it made the phone echo.

I rolled my eyes. "No Sheryl I didn't fuck James. He wants to fuck me. You want me to go back in there and give him what I gave Harold? Is that what you are saying? Well you don't hold my collar anymore so tough shit. Not going to happen. You can't take me out of the field. I have a sanity letter now. I am not going to see the dumbass for counseling either."

There was a pause. "You are right Psycho. I don't hold your fucking collar, yet. I will, you wait and see. As for not being able to take you out of the field or forcing counseling I do believe I am still your boss. So, you want to fuck with me? I can fire your ass. Go ahead, tell me no again."

I sighed "Are all you Masters the same? Did you all attend the same fucking school or something? This whole don't tell me nothing? I won't tell you no. I will go make the appointment and you know what? I don't want to be in the fucking field anyway. So fine by me. I do have a sanity letter so now I can get a good job, a real home and respect. So there is no collar, Sheryl. I am so done with that stupid shit. See you around at church. Don't forget Saturday is the punch bowel dance for little Billie's pet goat."

Sheryl groaned. "Exactly, there is the fucking Psycho everyone keeps calling about. Go make the appointment and then go home. Be at the office for data entry tomorrow. You are grounded honey until May. Enjoy your fucking vacation, loon bird." She hung up.

I went back into the office and made the appointment. Doctor Holcomb's first opening was for June 10th. I smiled as Kayla handed me the appointment card. Shit, I planned to be long gone from this shitty job by then, and how right I was. I walked back to my car and headed home to Master Boyd's house. Sheryl told me to go home. His place was the last home I could recall. So that is where I went.

*Now for the next two months my memory is very foggy and well mostly non-existent. I will be unable to tell you anything other than what few things I recall and what Master Boyd told me happened over a year later. So, forgive the scattering. I was severely psychotic by this point. My next vivid memories are for May 5th, but we are getting there. For now, I will focus on the events I can verify to keep the story accurate.*

Master Boyd was able to gain his release within twenty-four hours of his emergency hold. Since he was not psychotic the hospital was left with a bit of egg on their face for overreacting to him. They didn't realize they had left the real threat out and incarcerated the wrong psychotic. They would soon discover this sad fact, but again we are getting ahead of ourselves.

He had just barely beaten me to the house when my Taurus came spinning into his driveway sideways. My Master was standing on the porch angrily speaking with Dennis about his recent indignity when the Queen Bitch of Madness decided to finally come playhouse like he had always wanted me to.

Dennis shook his head as I got out of the car and took off dancing across the yard giggling, "Looks like your fiancé just blew into town and left her sanity wherever she just came from."

Master Boyd just growled, "You owe Niemand an apology. Dennis, do you see this shit? You and Randell let that go that night. I just got my ass pumped full of sedatives trying to get them to listen. What is wrong with everyone? The girl needs help."

Dennis shrugged. "Call her fucking Guardian, Boyd. This is Mary's problem. Only a Guardian can fix this kind of hard-core shit. That is why Niemand wore that collar thingy for so long. I noticed she tossed that for good this time. I bet she thinks you and she no longer need the help. Well I have news for you Boyd, she needs someone to take care of her. You ain't it. You can't even stay out of the damned psych ward. All you had to do was leave when the docs ignored you. You don't act the fool. That anger of yours will get you in hot water, worse than it already has."

"Dennis arrest her and take a hold. They will listen to you," said my Master while he watched me twirling and dancing around the yard wildly.

Dennis snorted. "If that is what you want Boyd. Just know they will send her ass right to the Snake Pit if I do it. I don't think she will forgive you for that."

Master Boyd groaned. "Shit. If only Harbor View had that opening. She needs help Dennis, but no one will listen."

Dennis patted Master Boyd on the back. "You may have to face sending her up state to the Pit. Otherwise you must keep her tied up tight or locked in a room. That girl is driving around. If I catch her in my county, well I will do what I must do. See you tomorrow morning. I am headed home for some shut eye. You stay out of trouble, will you? Damn Boyd, I will be glad when shit gets back to normal around here." He waved at me as he got in his squad car and left.

My Master decided two things after that discussion. Number one, I was going on a medical leave. He called Sheryl and the two of them agreed to leave me off work until May 1st. My Master only agreed to the return date because he secretly assumed Harbor View would come through right after that effectively ending my job. I will have used up my leave allowance by May 1st in case you are wondering.

The second thing he decided was to take Dennis's advice. He ran me down in the yard, knocked me to my face and restrained me with rope. I was dragged into his home where I would spend the next two months, tied up, locked in or handcuffed. My Master was determined to keep me alive until the promised assessment and possible inpatient treatment opening became available sometime in May.

Most of this time I was so far gone, I cannot recall anything. For all I know he was hanging me by the rafters and beating me daily. Though I believe I would have some memory of that. I do recall the constant bondage, the forced baths, medication, feedings and his taking of his special services rights whenever he felt like it, which with him was constantly.

**QUICK NOTE:** *That last part may seem a bit harsh but let's face it, he was definitely earning his privileges. Attending to a fully grown psychotic who is pissing her pants and drooling most of the time is a real labor of love. If all he asked was a fucking when he felt amorous, hell, let the man have his way. Shit it's not like I was complaining. I was pissed about the baths and forced meds but sleeping with my Master, no problem.*

*You see that is what the collar does. One male or female that has an interest in exclusive right to sexual conquest is assuring my safety till I can get back from Mars versus helplessness on the streets where God knows I would likely be gang raped and probably murdered by strangers.*

*Just think on that a moment. That is why I call the collar and key delusion controlled exploitation. Like it or not I am helpless a lot. That makes me an easy target for victimization. The Key offered me a chance to control the number of violent acts and gave me a choice on who is committing them.*

I was always leashed, tied up, or pinned in some way. I was not allowed to leave or even go to the bathroom alone. He feared I would harm myself. He had reason to fear it. He had discovered the wires under my tape. My Master took me to Wheatly Regional where the wires were removed and wounds treated.

As usual, no beds on the third floor were available. Master Boyd was forced to take me home and deal on his own with his septic psychotic ward. Welcome to hell Master.

While this may all sound savage and cruel the truth is I would have gotten much of the same treatment, likely worse, had he sent me to the Pit. I am sure a dog has more consciousness of his surroundings than I did at that time.

Master Boyd told me I was vile, crude, hateful, violent, feral, tangential, illogical and mad as a hatter. Yeah sounds about right. If I had not been his One and Only, I seriously doubt he would have tolerated me for long. I got lucky this time despite how bad all that sounds.

Master Boyd was the second-best Master I would ever know. He managed to keep my crazy ass alive, clean and healthy all the way through to May first. He even managed to calm down the very worst of my symptoms by constant medication vigilance.

In fact, by Beltane I was starting to show signs that my acute cycle was finally starting to pass. I have memory for the very last week of April and first week of May. I can recall Master Boyd starting to untie me occasionally. I do remember talking to him and even eating without his fighting me the entire time.

When my medical leave was up, I can recall even taking a bath when he told me to without argument. Things were starting to look up. Master Boyd was thrilled to see his collar recognizing him as Master and making minor improvements almost every day.

I told my Master during the last week of April I was ready to return to work, honestly believing the worst of my psychosis had now passed. He was not happy to let me go, but he had to honor his promise to allow me to work for Sheryl until her death. He still didn't know she had tossed my collar but he did find out she was Area Manager.

We argued about it mildly but again; he assumed Harbor View would call any day and then he would just have me put inpatient. He believed that would end Sheryl. Of course, he did not share this plan with me. Clever bastard. I totally would have done the same to him if the shoe were on the other foot.

**QUICK NOTE:** I *have often wondered what my life would have been like had I just quit that fucking job right there. Maybe I could have avoided the horrendous nightmare that was just about to begin. I didn't know it but the day I took off to return for my first day back to work, I was headed right into a disaster of epic proportions. It would be another year before I would see my home with Master Boyd. It would be another four before I would even recall that I had once been a cemetery kid called Psycho. I have wished a thousand times that I had just listened to my Master and left the hideous Sheryl to rot. I guess in the end Dennis was right. I am fucking hardheaded. I never did listen to anyone. This time, I fucked up beyond royal.*

I returned to the Cumberland office on May 3rd. That Monday Jane was initially unhappy to see me, but she quickly realized I was back to just disturbed. Not the seriously psychotic I had been the last time she had met me back in March. I was still a long way from okay but this clean, somewhat coherent Psycho she could tolerate. My ban from the office during working hours was finally lifted.

The first two days were hectic, but not too uncommon for the job. I was getting back into my stride and already had five court testimony dates coming up the next week. It seemed there would always be job security in a career with the funerary business and as a child abuse investigator. Sad but true.

Wednesday's schedule included a check on a schizophrenic mother and her two children. I have already told you the funny story of the Norman Rockwell case so I will not repeat it here.

I sent that poor mentally ill mom right to Well's Regional by squad car taxi. She kicked screamed and told me it was all a misunderstanding.

I nodded as they carted her off thinking. "Yeah you misunderstood that you are a fucking screw ball."

I got into the Taurus marking off the name of this deranged mother and almost fainted when I saw the next case name: Jenny, Dirk and Karrie from the stand-off that had started this entire psychotic episode back in December. The child had been taken hostage by Dirk and Randell and his boys barely saved the five-year-old little girl from being murdered by the scum bag. I had put her in the Fairbanks Foster home. How the fuck did she get back into Jenny's custody with Dirk there.

In absolute horror I read the report from the hospital that Karrie had been in the ER that morning with half her ear missing. The idiot doctor had let the mother take the child home without seizing an emergency hold even though the ear looked as if it had been bitten off.

I admit I grabbed my chest almost emitting a scream when I read the address. It was the rock house I had rented from Sheryl when the kids and I had first arrived in Cumberland trying to outrun Master Boyd. The stars were aligning in a prophetic fashion on this nightmare. I should have run away, quit the job, killed myself, anything but what I did do. I raced off to the rock house. To save Karrie and put Jenny and Dirk back in jail where they fucking belonged.

I called Charlie the big man cop, and the one Sheryl had read the riot act to during the infamous fake ticket set up the year before. I told him I needed local Cumberland officers on the scene. I was already aware this was going to be ugly. Dirk was known for his violence toward authority figures and if Karrie's ears were literally being chewed on I would need a cell for two by nightfall.

I arrived before Charlie and his boys. I dared not wait for them. I could hear Karrie screaming inside the house from the driveway. It made my blood go cold. I ran for the front door and began banging on it, hoping if nothing else it would stop Jenny and Dirk from harming the precious little girl.

The door suddenly popped open, but no one was there. I stepped inside to the horrid sounds of heavy desperate groans of pain in a child's voice. I walked into the living room. There was no furniture in the place except for a huge TV.

On an overturned bucket sat Dirk playing a video game up close to TV screen. He didn't even look at me because he was so engrossed in the task. Next to him sat a broken beer bottle. A pool of clotting blood was under it becoming tacky in the warm air.

I heard a noise and I looked to my right. Leaning in a corner legs outstretched was Jenny. She had a tourniquet on her arm and a syringe laid next to her bare feet on the hard wood floor. She groaned, her eyelids heavy from the heroine coursing through her veins. She smiled at me weakly.

"Hey Psycho, what are you doing, chick." She groaned again as her head leaned to the left.

I looked around wildly for Karrie. "Where is the baby Jenny. Where is she." The child's cries were beyond wailing at this point.

Jenny moaned. "Her bedroom Psycho. Go see her new dre..." She passed out midsentence.

I took off down the hallway kicking open every door unable to tell where the cries were coming from. Then the last door on the right I kicked it open. In the center of the floor was Karrie. She was on her back in a pretty pink and white dress. She was wailing. Between her legs blood was pouring onto the floor outlining the child in black, maroon, and red.

She heard me kick open the door and turned her head wailing. "Momma, momma. Ah, momma," the little girl screamed.

I ran to the child looking around desperate for something to stop the bleeding. So much blood for a little unit, so much blood. There was nothing in the room but Karrie. I had to get the bleeding to stop. I picked the baby up and her ear fell off into the floor. It had been bitten and was barely hanging. The child shrieked into my ears. The sound looped around my head as all my audience's voices screamed with her.

Blood poured out of the child down my legs, stomach and arms. Dirk had raped the baby with the broken bottle. Her tiny vagina was hemorrhaging. It was too late to call 911. I had to get her help. I had to stop the bleeding. I stopped in the hallway noticing her screams weakening fast.

I laid her down gently and tore off my own shirt. I packed it between her tiny cubby legs praying aloud while the walls shook with thunder and lightning light up the sky. I then picked her back up and held her in my arms rocking and cradling her trying to keep pressure on the gushing wounds.

Karrie had stopped screaming, tears poured down her rosy cheeks. She looked at me with her big hazel eyes gasping for air. I could see the lights in them were dimming fast.

"Momma. Momma. I want my momma. Mommy. Mommy. It hurts. Mommy. Miss Alex get momma," she cried out quieter each time never taking her sight off me as she put her little hands around my wrist clinging with terror, shaking all over.

"I know baby. I know. Don't Karrie, stay with me," I screamed trembling as my own tears poured down my cheeks.

Karrie let out a gasp. Her unit seized up. Then she shuddered and went limp. Her little soul portals closed halfway. I screamed out as I realized her sun had just set for all time. I was gutturally wailing as Charlie and the boys broke into the front door. I fell over the dead child screaming with pain tearing my heart apart. I begged for death to take me instead as the world spun and the sounds of a thousand cicada rose from hell to plague the world.

The police came into the hallway and found me beyond consolation. Charlie looked down at the now late Karrie.

*"Karrie was a little girl of five who looked just like a porcelain doll. Her hair was brown, her eyes were hazel and her chubby cheeks rosy. She must have been the model for every dolly ever created and sat on a store shelf. This little dolly was broken and could never be fixed again."*

"Christ sakes, she's just a baby. God damn it. John, call 911. We have a situation here," he yelled back to the other officers as they cuffed the murderers.

"Psycho honey, she is gone. There is nothing else you can do for her. Look, let me go to the car and get a couple blankets. One to cover her up and one for you." He pointed at my near topless unit.

I just nodded still crying now silently staring at the poor little lost girl. He left and I took my shirt from the child's unit. I put it back on no longer aware that it was drenched in her blood. In fact, I was covered head to toe in the sanguine liquid. I trembled and sobbed while my shattered mind completely broke apart. I picked Karrie up into my arms rocking her a moment telling her it was going to be okay. She just needed to sleep. I would get her help.

I stood up carrying her with me right out into the front yard. Charlie saw me holding the dead baby. He ran up appearing to realize I had blown a fucking gasket.

"Psycho honey, give me the baby. I got her from here. You need to just go relax a minute. The ambulance is on the way. Here give me the child." He reached out and took Karrie from my arms laying her on the grass.

I saw Jenny looking at her daughter and me from the back of the squad car. I walked by it headed for the Taurus. I had work to do. This case was now finished. Next!

As I walked past the caged couple Jenny yelled out, "Hey, did I handle that okay? I mean I didn't even give you any trouble."

I walked back staring at her through the window while she looked at me. I reared back and punched. The window prevented me from hitting Jenny, but the sound made her cower to the floor. I had nearly broken my hand I hit that window so hard. The sound alerted the police officers who had been examining Karrie's unit and cursing the monsters who did this.

"Psycho, Psycho, you cannot do that. Hey, I need you to stay put. I need to make a report on what you saw. Where are you going? Psycho, come back. Damn it. Shit, John, we have another situation here I think," yelled Charlie as I got into my car and sped off down the road to attend to my next case, me.

I pulled off onto a dirt road and took my stash of electrical tape. I needed to stop the short circuit that was making me hear everyone's thoughts, the radio waves, and the dead. I just need it all to shut up. Please make it shut up.

This is another event in my life I have never talked about in detail. It was horrible to helplessly hold that dying child calling for her mother. I knew Karrie, she was one of my foster babies. She knew me too. She even called my name as she died. If that kind of thing could hurt a normal's heart imagine what it did to a schizophrenic just barely clinging to her sanity. Well, next chapter, we are going to find out. You will not have to guess.

I am taking it easy on this one. This story still hurts even twenty years later. Karrie would have been twenty-five this June. Instead she lays in an unmarked grave, forgotten, and unsung. I visited her often when I lived in those horrid places but now even I am gone.

I am grateful that I have a chance to pass her short life story on here, but that is never enough. I will tell you what happened to her killers in the next chapter but for now I would like to just move on. Just understand, in this brutal world there are so many Karrie's throughout the ages. I had removed the child to a safe home that December. It was May and the courts had already returned her to die like that on alone on a hardwood floor. I am thankful that she did have the mercy of being held as she passed on even though it cost me all I had left to grant her that small kindness. She deserved better.

No matter what I have been through, no matter how bad it got, I can still see her eyes and I realize how lucky I really have been.

**To be continued in Book Eleven of the
"27 Masters" series entitled
"A Harbor with a View"**

## About the Author: Alexandria May Ausman

Alexandria May Ausman in her 16th year was diagnosed with Schizophrenia. She was quickly abandoned by her foster parents. While still only a teen, she was forced to battle this devastating illness alone.

Alexandria has struggled with lack of a support system, numerous psychotic episodes, exploitation, homelessness, and an uncaring mental health system.

Alexandria raised two healthy children. After obtaining her bachelor's degree in psychology she worked as a child abuse investigator and became a diagnostic psychologist while acquiring her Master's in psychology. Alexandria never forgot the experience of 'slipping through the cracks.' Her life's goal is to help people suffering abuse and/or mental illness have access to necessary services. By accident, she became a model of 'gothic attire' and the World Goth Queen.

She began writing a fictionalized account of her life experiences after a catastrophic return of psychotic symptoms. Today, Alexandria is retired, and homebound due to crippling symptoms of schizophrenia. She currently lives in Tallahassee, Florida, with her loving husband and loyal support dogs.